To my three children, A, N, and V. To my loving husband, C, who has stood by me through everything. You are my Josh. To my sisters E and B, who put up with rewrite after rewrite.

I also wants to dedicate this to all those who have struggled with something in their lives. You are not alone. The sun will always rise, even after the darkest, coldest night.

Chapter 1

Abbi

"So let me get this straight." I close my locker and turn to Cienna. She's glaring down at her English essay like it personally betrayed her. The bold red B+ bleeds across the page. "You really think Mr. Brians has a twisted vendetta against you?"

"Why is that so hard to believe?" She glances up at me, one eyebrow raised, her piercing golden brown siren eyes full of fire. I try not to laugh, but she's unraveling in true Cienna fashion. It's kind of beautiful.

"All because he never gives you an A?"

"I've never received anything lower than an A- on *anything* in my life. Mr. Brians has it in for me. I swear." She shoves her essay in her bright yellow sunflower backpack and runs a hand through her thick black curls.

"Maybe he's just jealous that you're smarter than he is." I'm only half joking. Lucienna Jacobs–'Cienna'–is the smartest person I know. She demanded our teacher give her extra credit in *Kindergarten*.

She smacks me lightly on the arm and we both burst into giggles.

"What are my two favorite girls talking about?" James' arm wraps around my waist, pulling me against him. I bite the inside of my cheek to push down the blush trying to form on my cheeks.

"Ugh, James," Cienna sighs. "Do you have to interrupt everything?"

"Love you too, sis." James brushes a hand through his rich dark chocolate curls. He truly is quite handsome. My heart flutters and I pop up on my toes, stealing a quick kiss to his cheek. He turns his gaze to me, his golden eyes seeping into my soul. I almost forget what we're talking about. Almost.

"We were just discussing Cienna's tragic English streak with Mr. Brians." I manage to spit out before total loss of brain function.

James laughs and releases his hold on me. He grabs Cienna in one arm and ruffles her hair with the other. "You're supposed to be more careful with that stress. You don't want those frown lines to get any deeper."

Cienna pushes him off and gives him a not so gentle punch to the shoulder. I step back out of their range while they playfully shove one another.

"You two leave me out of this," I laugh as I fix my dark green satchel, my blonde hair trying to tuck itself firmly under the strap.

"James, we still on for today?" My head snaps up to see Josh standing there, as casual as ever. His muss of dark copper hair falls over his forehead in waves. His grey eyes are looking directly into mine and he smiles. I smile in return, a slight flutter in my stomach.

"You know I wouldn't miss it." James leans down and kisses the top of my head again before they both make their way towards the parking lot.

When they reach the doors, James immediately pushes it open and walks out into the afternoon sun. Josh touches the door but turns and says something to his younger brother Quint, whose locker is next to the door. Josh's eyes flash towards us while he speaks with a wide smile. I can't help but smile and wave shyly. He waves back and hurries out to catch up with James.

"Should I be worried?" Cienna's eyes narrow, part teasing, part worried. Her usual polished mask flickers.

"What are you talking about?"

"Oh, come on."

"What?" I say defensively.

"You ready to go?" Jared hurries up behind Cienna and wraps his arms around her. Cienna's frown shifts to a radiant smile—the kind reserved for him and very few others.

Just in time.

Jared Gutierrez has short brown stubble sprouting around his mouth and jawline. Cienna rises up on her toes and kisses him before stroking his face. "The beard is growing on me."

"Really?" He lights up like he just got candy store privileges with no budget. The corner of my mouth curls up in a smirk. Six years and they are still the gold standard. Still the kind of love that walks without checking its step.

9

"Text me later, okay?" Cienna hugs me quickly. I nod and watch them stroll away hand in hand. They're swinging their arms back and forth as they walk. Jared's eyes never leave Cienna's face as they walk out into the afternoon. It's like watching gravity work.

Guess that's my cue.

On my way out, I pass Quint who is attempting to throw a big wad of paper into the trash bin across to the other side of the hall. Quint and Josh could pass as twins. They have the same grey eyes, full lips, and straight nose. The only real difference is Quint's short brown hair. Josh also beats him in the height department by a couple of inches, something Quint regularly complains about.

"Are you coming tomorrow?" I ask Quint.

"It's not like we go to the mall every Saturday." Quint's sarcasm knows no bounds. "What makes you think I'll miss this one?" He laughs and takes the shot. Once it goes in, he cheers loudly. A few girls walking by give him weird looks, then giggle their way through the door.

"I don't know," I snicker. "There was that one day you were *pretty sick –*"

"Hey, no! Sick days don't count you dork!" He throws another wad in my direction and I turn just in time to avoid getting pegged in the face. I throw a playful punch his way, hitting him right in the gut before laughing and rolling my eyes.

My friends really have it in for me. No mercy. Ever.

"Did Kasey leave early today? I thought I saw her this morning."

His smile falters slightly before he shrugs and turns back to his locker. "She had an appointment."

10

"I'll see you tomorrow then." That looks tells me all I need to know.

Drop it.

"Leave the punches at home maybe?" He shoots one last paper wad across the hall, but this one falls just short.

"Only for you." I flash a bright smile and flutter my eyelashes playfully.

He covers his chest with his hand and grins. "I feel so loved."

I step out into the sun, the warmth beating down on my face. It's a perfect May day. One of the last before school ends next week. Walking down the sidewalk towards my car, I hear my name being called.

Looking around, I spot James jogging over in my direction from Josh's truck. Josh is leaning back against the side of his pale blue truck, one leg braced, arms crossed.

"Hey!" James is a little breathless from the jog. His hands grab my sides, pulling me close.

"Hey. I thought you were shopping for your tux with Josh." I shade my eyes from the sun while trying to look up at him. He moves just enough to block the sun's path, and I drop my hands smiling. All I can see is him.

"I couldn't leave without giving you another kiss." He cups my face in his hands and gently lowers his lips to mine. I loop my fingers through his belt loops and pull him closer. He wraps an arm around me, and I melt into him. I love how he always tastes like peppermint.

When we finally part, my head is spinning. "I love you," he presses his forehead to mine. A small shiver runs through me.

"Love you too." Now it's my turn to be breathless. That's the first time I've said it.

With that, James steps back and races over to Josh who's already climbing into the truck with Quint.

Once I start my car, I relax against the seat. Two months together and everything seems more intense, like a countdown. It's thrilling, maybe even dizzying, but I'm not ready for that next step. Just thinking about it leaves my stomach in knots. James was my first kiss. Just because I'm eighteen doesn't mean I'm ready for *that* step yet.

How do I tell him that?

I remember the day he asked me to be his girlfriend. We'd gone on several dates before that day, every one of them simple and sweet, but on this particular date he was nervous. James has nervous tells. He either has his hands in his pockets and you can see him opening and closing his fists in them, or if he's sitting, he is rubbing his hands on his thighs. That day, we were seated on the park bench across from my house:

"What did you want to talk to me about?" I ask. The cold March air seeps through my thin jacket and I shiver.

James notices and removes his dark blue zip up hoodie and wraps it around my shoulders. He's wearing a dark red V-neck underneath and I can see his arms covered in goosebumps. I'm grateful for the warmth of his jacket, but I feel guilty for taking his warmth away. He's always done this—given things he won't ask for back. He notices my concern. "I'm fine. It's not terribly cold today."

I scoot closer to him, hoping the closeness helps fend off at least some of the cold from him. He's got a brave face, and I know he'll refuse the jacket back, but I want to help.

James clears his throat, his hands rubbing up and down his pant legs. "So we've been on a few days.. uh, dates."

12

"A fair few." I smile.

"I like you." His eyes are studying my face. I can see it in the way his eyes move.

"I like you too." I feel my cheeks warming.

"Do you think you like me enough to be my girlfriend?" I had been waiting for him to ask. His golden eyes are open and longing. They're searching my face. My heart beats louder in my ears.

"I think so." I smile.

His face breaks into the widest smile I'd ever seen on him. I've known him since we were babies, and not once did I ever see such a smile before.

"Can I kiss you?" My heart skips at his question. I've never been kissed. I've never had a boyfriend either. Once, I thought Josh would be the one. But James asked. And that changed everything.

I tilt my head in confirmation.

He cups my face gently and leans his face close to mine. I lean in and the feeling of our lips touching is new and... nice. He tastes like peppermint, spicy yet sweet. He smiles against my lips and kisses me again.

Kissing is all we do now, but it's not like he hasn't tried to go further. I just turn him down. He never pushes though when I say no. I love that about him.

Pulling into the neighborhood, I spot Dad in the yard winding the cord of the edge trimmer. Work must have been smooth sailing today if he's already home. It's still early though. Pros and cons of running your own business.

Once in the driveway I collect my bag from the passenger seat and allow myself one final deep breath before exiting my car. Dad has already put the trimmer away and is sweeping the clippings back into the grass. I drop my bag by the garage and grab a second broom to help.

"How was school, Kiddo?" Dad asks once I walk down to the sidewalk.

"It was alright. Cienna got another B in Mr. Brians' class."

"Ooh, she must be furious."

I snort. "Oh you have no idea."

"I'm starting to think that English teacher just doesn't like her. He was always a sourpuss, even when we were in school together."

Sometimes it was easy to forget just how small of a town this really was. Everyone knows everyone else. Secrets were hard to keep. There are definitely smaller towns, but ours was just right. We have a mall, a hospital, even a few big businesses. But with only fifty kids in our graduating class this year, it's still rather small.

"Of course," he continues. "It could also be because her dad was a piece of work back in the day."

Cienna and James' dad, Ryan, had been somewhat of a bully in high school. That was, until Ryan tried to pick a fight with Dad. They never told us why. Just that Ryan broke Dad's nose, yet Dad was the one standing in the end. Lily, their mom, worked some real magic on Ryan in the end. Over the last twenty years, all the parents of our friend group seemed to put their disdain for each other aside. Ryan and Dad even go out for drinks every once in a while.

"How was work?" I decide a change in subject is necessary.

"I'm just waiting for the other shoe to drop before the night's over."

"Such an optimist," I snort.

14

"You know me. I'm a ray of everlasting sunshine every day. Besides, Alec is there right now. I'll be trading him out in a few hours. I think he said something about Josh and James working on something together today."

"Yeah, they're going to get their tuxes."

We put away the brooms, and I grab my satchel before we make our way into the house through the front door. Once we're inside, I drop my keys on the dresser in front of the door and then lay my bookbag on the dark blue backless couch that sits in front of the bay window on the right.

Above the bay window is a stained-glass window Cienna's mom made for mine when they built the house – A red fox surrounded by white flowers and greenery. Foxes were Mom's favorite animal. She always felt they were misunderstood creatures. She believed everyone deserves a second chance. I tend to agree. The whole section is framed in by sheer blue curtains that match the couch, loveseat, and backless couch.

I walk into the kitchen and pull out my water bottle from the fridge. I take a long drink, allowing the shock of cold to wash over me, my tension disappearing instantly.

"I'm off to my room. Love you." I grab my backpack and head up the weaving stairs. When I reach the first landing, I stop in front of our family portrait.

Mom sits to the right on a stool in a dark amethyst-purple summer dress with embroidery beaded purple butterflies on the bodice. Her naturally straight golden blonde hair falls past her low back. Her soft ivory skin is sun kissed with freckles. Her green-blue eyes shining up towards Dad.

Dad is standing next to Mom with his hand on her shoulder. His milk chocolate hair is brushed back and his bright blue eyes are gazing lovingly down at Mom. He's wearing a dark navy blue suit. It was Mom's favorite on him. I remember her fussing about it, telling Dad he better wear it. In the middle sitting between then, there I am at fourteen. My hair is naturally straight like Mom's, but not quite as long. Everyone says I look like her, but I don't see it. I'm wearing an emerald-green summer dress identical to the one Mom's wearing.

"I miss you, Mom." I press my finger to my lips and brush my fingers over the canvas of the picture. It's been three years since she was killed by a drunk driver. Three years is a long time not to hear her laugh. The days soften—but some moments still cut sharp.

When I reach the final landing, I walk into my room directly across from the stairs. The walls are painted a light lilac, and the slanted ceiling is a stereotypical white. Mom painted it when I was little, and I've never bothered to change it, even though purple isn't my favorite color. It reminds me of her now. It helps me keep her close.

I cross the white carpet and drop my bookbag next to my desk which is still covered with old study notes I have to go through. I open my bag and place a pile of new papers on top of the notes. The papers contain sweet letters from James that he loved to slip into my locker between classes.

My small amethyst swivel office chair is covered by clothes for me to put away. I set my water on my built in nightstand connected to my white bed frame with gold dusted floral carvings and lift the pile of clothes onto my matching purple comforter. I hang up my shirts and pants in the closet behind me and fold my intimates into the matching white dresser beside my bed.

Grabbing my tan towel and matching hand towel, I take them into the bathroom between my closet and desk. It's painted a sage green with gold floral bordering along the top of the walls. I'm lucky to have my own bathroom. Having a dad in construction definitely has its perks.

I gaze around my room, my eyes trailing along my built in book shelves surrounding my window. They are full and beginning to overflow onto the ground.
A brand new book sits on my amethyst reading chair. A reminder of my loss of reading time these past few months. Today was the day for that to change. It isn't a very thick book, but it's about faeries. Anything with faeries in it, I have to read at least once.

After the laundry is done, I curl up on my window seat with a crocheted green blanket. I love how green makes me feel surrounded by trees and moss.

I successfully engross myself into the faerie realm until the sun goes down and I'm forced to close my curtains and turn on my lamp.

Just when I get comfortable in my reading chair, there's a grumble from my stomach.

I close my book with a sigh.

The Fae will have to wait.

I leave my book on my chair and find no sign of Dad in the kitchen aside from a neon pink sticky note on the fridge. He must have left already.

Chicken salad in the fridge. Love you kiddo.

I make myself a plate and sit at the counter enjoying every last bite. The clock on the stove reads 8:30p.m.

Knowing the weather outside is nice and cool, I decide to go sit outside on the porch to finish reading by porch light. I grab

James' blue hoodie from the closet and slip it on. In the last two months it's taken on more of my smell, but there are still hints of James in it, even after washing.

When I step out the door, I hear voices from the right of me. I peak around the house. Josh and Quint are playing a one on one game of basketball.

I set my book on the swing and head over to their yard. "Hey!" I call over. Quint wraps me in a sweaty hug.

"Hey, wanna play? This one," he points to Josh over his shoulder, "seems to have lost any and all sports abilities. It just isn't a competition anymore." I giggle and Josh shakes his head with a smirk. "Maybe he's taking the "getting too old" too seriously."

"You're only winning because I'm letting you," Josh snorts.

"Shall we test that theory?" I steal the ball from Quint, and we begin the game.

I'm a terrible shot. Everyone knows it. It's never stopped me from playing though.

I can't tell if Josh is taking pity on me, or if he's having an off day. He misses quite a few baskets.

"I think you're right," I pant. "I think I see a grey hair," I joke, reaching up to Josh's hair.

"Oh, I don't think so!" Josh grabs my waist and starts tickling me. I try to squirm free, but he manages to pull me to the ground. He knows I can't compete with his weight. I laugh loudly, trying harder to wriggle from his grasp.

"Okay, okay! I give! You're not old!" I squeal. His face is so close to mine. His breath warm on my face. His jaw tenses and our eyes meet. My breath hitches in my throat. His eyes flick to my lips, just for a second before returning to my eyes. I manage to keep my voice level, "You just suck."

"Oh, do I?" He grins. Before I can break free he's tickling me again. No matter how much I twist and wiggle, I'm stuck.

"I take it back! Mercy!"

"I thought we were playing a game here. Do I need to leave?" Quint throws the basketball, and it hits Josh on the butt. With that, Josh is up and tackling his brother. I take a few deep breaths to reground myself, feeling slightly cold in the breeze now that Josh's warmth is gone. After a good five minutes, their wrestling match ends with Quint crying, "UNCLE!"

They finally collapse in a heap. Both of them are covered with bits of gravel and grass. I'm leaning against the edge of the garage, my arms crossed, trying to look unimpressed.

"You done?" I ask. "Or should I call animal control?"

Josh flicks a pebble at my shoe, still lying on his back. His shirt is pushed up and I can see the lines of his abs as he tries to catch his breath. I quickly look away, my cheeks burning. "Only if they take Quint first."

I'm underage," Quint mutters. "Technically I get released back into the wild."

Josh chuckles and I risk another glance in his direction. His eyes are closed.

"Hey," I say nudging his shoe with mine. "You okay? Or has your ancient spine finally given out?"

He opens one eye and gives me a lazy smirk. "Just catching my breath. Old people need recovery time, you know."

"Alright, *Grandpa*," I say offering him a hand up. "Get up before we have to ice your hip."

He takes it, his fingers warm and solid around mine. He squeezes slightly, a charge shooting through me. Something stirs deep in my chest.

"I've got to call Kasey. I'll catch you tomorrow." Quint hugs me right before pulling out his phone and racing up the front steps and through the door.

"I'll see you guys tomorrow," Josh's arms encircle me. There's a strange, still moment. Like I've found something I didn't know I was missing. I let go quickly, afraid he'll notice the way my fingers hesitated.

I mutter a quick, "goodnight," and head home, my heart thudding too loudly in my chest.

Back in my room, I attempt to get lost in the last few pages of my book. It's a complete waste of time. All I seem to be able to focus on is the feeling of Josh's arms around me.

That's not good.

Chapter 2

Josh

I watch Abbi hurry back to her house, my stomach in knots. I still feel the warmth of her hand in mine, the sensation lingering like a ghost. The way her face was so close to mine. Her blue-green eyes staring at mine. I have each gold fleck in her eyes memorized.

I lean against the railing, my heart racing even as she disappears through her front door. The night is quiet, but my thoughts are anything but. She laughed with me tonight. Let me hold her. But she's still his. And I'm... still the guy who waited too long.

I made a mistake letting James beat me to the punch with her. I did try a few times to ask her, but each time I chickened out. Now I'm stuck. She's with James and there's nothing I can do. James rubbed it in earlier when we were looking for tuxes for the end of year dance:

James steps out of the dressing room in an all-black ensemble. "If this tux does the trick, I am getting lucky. She has been so stubborn lately." He adjusts the collar on his shirt as I try to fix the fit of the sleeves around my wrists.

Quint glances between us, "You're calling the shots early."

James smirks. "I'm just saying," he tugs at the black cuffs, "If I show up looking like this, maybe she'll finally stop overthinking."

I'm adjusting my navy blue tie, my eyes trained on the mirror and not on James' face. "Maybe she just hasn't decided yet."

James doesn't flinch. "When she sees this," he gestures to the suit, "no more holding back."

I nod, desperate to change the subject. "How's Kasey doing?" I turn to Quint who is skimming over the different ties. He's not picking his tux yet. He's waiting for Kasey to pick her dress.

"I don't know. She's been better, I know that. We're just taking things one day at a time right now."

James, suddenly sober, lets his grin fade halfway. "She talk to you about it?"

Quint shrugs. "Bits and pieces. I'm just trying to make sure she knows I'm here."

I press the line of my navy jacket flat. "You're doing what you can."

Quint glances at both of us. "I'm just trying not to screw it up by noticing too much. I'm letting her lead."

James reaches for a black pocket square. "Sometimes noticing is the only thing that doesn't screw it up."

I don't respond, even though deep down I want to. James, you only notice what you want.

I turn back to the rack and run my thumb along another blue jacket edge.

A sudden gust of wind rustles the leaves, bringing me back to the present. I shiver and pull my jacket tighter around me, the cool air a stark contrast to the warmth of Abbi's touch. I glance around, realizing how late it's gotten. The streetlights cast long shadows, and the distant sound of a car engine reminds me that life goes on, even if my heart feels stuck.

Chapter 3
Abbi

"This is it! This is the dress!" Cienna steps out of the dressing room in a gorgeous floor length gold dress. It's simple and sleek. A single, wide strap curves from her left shoulder across her collarbone and disappears across her back, leaving the rest of the back daringly open. The fabric pools just barely at her feet. It's bold without trying to be loud. Simple and elegant. Just like Cienna. She's already grabbing for the gold heels she bought from the previous store.

Next Friday is the end of year school dance, and try as we might, we hadn't found a single contender for a dress in just over a month. This is the last school dance we will ever attend, and we want it perfect.

"You always find the best dresses," Kasey notes. She's holding a sleek silver knee length dress, but I see the hesitation as she's second guessing her choice.

"Try it on, Kay. I think it'll be perfect. It'll match the pink in your hair." Kasey's buttery blonde hair is dipped in a bright pink, the most recent color choice of hers, and by far her favorite.

I'm still looking at three different dresses, trying to decide which one to try on first. There's a blue floor length mermaid gown with silver beading on the bodice which Cienna wants me to try on. Kasey picked out a purple bubble dress with matching rhinestones around the waist. It reminded me a bit of my mom.

Then there's the dress I grabbed from the rack. A sage green halter floor length dress with a gold belt. The soft tulle shimmers gold and sage as it moves. I take the hanger and go into the changing stall. The fabric is soft against my skin and once it's zipped up on the side, and the halter is fastened, I enjoy how weightless the dress feels.

When I step out, Kasey, who is now in her silver gown, turns slowly in front of the mirror. Her hands smoothing the silver fabric like she's waiting for it to betray her with one single pulled thread. The dress fits perfectly. The soft shimmer as she moves, the sweetheart neckline all compliment her. Nothing is out of place. But her eyes stay locked on her reflection, like she's searching for something only she can see.

"You look stunning, Kay."

She glances at me over her shoulder, and smiles. It's the kind of smile that ends too soon. It doesn't reach her eyes. It doesn't even try. I've seen this version of her more than once lately, and every time it leaves something unsettled in my chest.

"That dress is perfect on you," she compliments back. I walk over to the mirror and surprise myself. It really does shimmer. Turning side to side, the gold underskirt peeks out.

"I think we finally did it guys!" Cienna joins us in front of the mirror with her phone. She holds it up and we all squeeze together, making funny faces while she snaps a few pictures.

The glass door swings open with a swoosh of cold mall air and distant food court smells and sounds. I look back just as Jared and James walk in. Jared bright eyed and casual as always, while James is a little slower. He's taking in the racks of glitter and satin like he's afraid they might bite him if he gets too close. That makes me smirk.

Cienna turns slightly in the mirror, the gold of her dress catching in the light. Jared abruptly stops, his face plastered with surprise.

"You good?" Cienna asks, pretending she isn't the reason for Jared looking dumbfounded.

Jared huffs a half-laugh and shakes his head grinning. "Yeah. Just...wow."

Meanwhile, James' attention slides past them and lands squarely on me. Suddenly something under my skin buzzes in response. It's not entirely uncomfortable. His gaze moves slowly, almost reverently, from the floor-length hem to the curve of the halter neckline.

"You've been busy," he smiles slow and crooked.

"It's called shopping," I reply, crossing my arms. Not defensively exactly, just... *aware.*

My eyes are up here.

"You look…" he trails off, jaw tightening just a little, like he's biting back something. He pulls me close, goosebumps flowing up my arms at his touch. "God, Abbi."

Cienna coughs dramatically. "You aren't alone you know." My cheeks redden and I hurry into the stall to change into my plain black t-shirt and jeans. I don't even know if I'm blushing because of what he said or because of how I felt hearing it.

That was… wow.

Once we change and purchase our dresses, we stroll over to the food court for lunch. The smells cause my stomach to grumble. James takes my hand, an electric sensation runs through our hands.

This is foreign territory.

The twins, Don and Rees, are already at our regular table, smack center of the food court. Their bright red hair make them easy to spot. Don is dipping his fries in a tall chocolate shake listening to Rees who is talking in between bites of pepperoni pizza.

"Do you want a smoothie?" James squeezes my hand.

"Maybe some fries, too?" I squeeze back. He leans in for a quick kiss and then strolls over to the line in front of the smoothie counter. Jared has made his way over to the new Chinese restaurant after Cienna made puppy eyes and kissed him.

Those two are the definition of love.

"Can we just take a moment and talk about James' expression? He looked like a golden retriever who spotted bacon." Cienna laughs, but it sounded a bit strained. She coughs and places her bags on the chair next to our table set up. Kasey and I follow suit.

"Don't get me wrong. He's an idiot most of the time, but I know he means well. He just..." she scrunches her face like she's searching for the right thing to say. "He forgets how to handle a wow-moment without turning into a cartoon character." A slight smirk forms at picturing James like a cartoon character with bulging eyes, jaw on the floor, and tongue rolled out like a red carpet.

Kasey, quiet since we left the store, suddenly bolts ahead of me. I glance up just in time to see her leap into Quint's arms. He catches her without effort and spins her once, both of them laughing, wide smiles lighting up their faces.

When he sets her down, her lips start moving. She's probably got some sassy remark ready, but he cuts her off with a kiss. When he pulls back, there's a smirk waiting for her, like he knew exactly what she was about to say.

She blushes, but it doesn't slow her. They head towards the burger stand, Kasey animated now, hands flying as she talks. I can't hear her, but I don't have to. I know her well enough to guess she's walking Quint through every stitch and shimmer of her dress.

Only Quint gets that version of her. That full, unfiltered excitement. She's not holding anything back, guarding her tone, or calculating her expression. She's completely at ease.

For a second, I just watch - and then, I smile. Not at what they have, but at how easy and right it is for them.

Cienna sees it too. She doesn't say anything though. She doesn't call it out or nudge me with an elbow the way she usually would. She just looks at me, her expression softer. The corner of her mouth pulls into a smile that says it all.

It says, *you see it too, right?*

28

I incline my head slightly without meaning to. It's not a big gesture, but just enough. She'll talk to us when she's ready. Until then though, we just watch, quiet and ready.

"You two alright over there, or are we preparing for a telepathic intervention?" Don holds up two fries like a cross.

I blink, caught between concern and a laugh.

Cienna doesn't skip a beat. "If you've got snacks and a psychic link to the other side, we're listening."

"But we're prioritizing the snack," I add, stealing a fry from Don's tray.

Rees leans towards Don and whispers, "We trained them too well," and all I can do is smile.

I hear James laugh. I turn, and there they are. Josh and James, walking side by side, each carrying a smoothie. James also has the tray of fries I requested. James is saying something, probably finishing whatever joke made him laugh too loudly.

Josh isn't saying anything at all. His expression is unreadable. There's no expression or signal. He's just there. And yet somehow, I still feel it. It's like gravity. I bite the inside of my cheek to stifle the red making it way to my cheeks.

Quint, Kasey, and Jared all arrive right behind James and Josh. James sits down next to me and holds out the green smoothie, and a plate of fries. I take a sip and scrunch my nose, setting it down. Green apple.

Gross.

He knows I don't like green apple. They are way too sour, especially for a smoothie. I look over at James who seems oblivious to his mistake, so I focus on my fries.

29

Josh, however, wasn't oblivious. Sitting directly across from me, he pushes his smoothie over in my direction and then proceeds to grab mine and starts drinking it, all while trying to be as inconspicuous to the group as he can.

I give him a quick smile, mouthed, *thank you*, and take a sip. Papaya, delicious.

Now that's better.

Cienna twirls her noodles, still mid-rant about how "this place is *actually* seasoning things," when Kasey leans forward and snatches one of Cienna's spring rolls from her tray.

"Alright," she announces. "Bucket list. Summer. We're doing more than just camping this year. Something wild. Something possibly illegal," She points at Quint with the spring roll, "but like, vaguely."

James perks up instantly. "Jet skis."

Jared arches a brown. "Do any of us even own jet skis?"

"No," James laughs. "Which makes the idea even better."

"Put that on the list," Kasey grins. Cienna produced a small notebook and pen from her purse and jots it down.

That girl is always prepared.

"Wedding crashing," Cienna chimes in. "I've always wanted to lie about being from the bride's side."

"I thought you hated strangers," I muse.

"I do. That's what makes it a challenge."

Quint nodded solemnly. "No summer is complete without emotional warfare."

The list grows fast. Inside jokes, grand plans, and slightly illegal schemes are all written down in a pink glitter pen.

"Josh, what do you want to do?" All eyes turn to Josh. He's staring at his phone with such an intense focus, that it took

Jared nudging him for him to snap out of it. Josh's eyes shift from person to person.

"What?" It's apparent he hasn't heard what we're talking about. His cheeks go from his perfect tan complexion to a dark shade of pink.

Is he blushing?

"What's her name?" I ask before my brain catches up to my mouth. Now it's my turn to go pink. I take another sip of the smoothie trying to remove the heat from my face. Josh looks over at me, his mouth in a straight line. His eyes are indecipherable. He just shrugs and sits back in his chair.

Quint is the one to break the silence. "We should do the campout next Saturday. Dad said he and John are taking the weekend off. It'll be perfect. We leave Saturday, get back Monday."

By the time we run out of food and ideas, the group is ready to unravel. Don and Rees leave to check out the new game store down the road. Quint and Jared are now on the hunt for corsages after Cienna scolded them for not getting them ordered sooner.

"We'll see you at the house." Cienna grabs her shopping bags and leaves through the giant glass doors, Kasey's right behind her. James agreed to drive me back to the house. Plus, it gives us some alone time.

"You ready?" James picks up my shopping bags and holds out a hand to me. I take it and squeeze. His palm is warm and familiar.

I let him lead me through the bright spill of late afternoon light, past the crowded escalators, to the other side of the mall.

Outside, the spring air is warm. James pops the trunk, drops my bags in, and is reaching for the driver side door when his phone buzzes. He glances at his screen and blinks. His shoulders square, but he slides into the driver seat, stuffing his phone into the cup holder.

"Everything okay?"

"Yeah, I can handle it later." He switches the car on then turns to face me. "You know you looked absolutely radiant in that dress. I can't wait to see it on you again." His hand strokes my leg, the gentle scratch barely felt through my jeans, but it sends a shiver through me.

"Oh yeah?" I quirk a small smile.

He leans over, his lips gently brushing mine. My heart flutters. His lips crush mine, and I breathe him in. His hand slowly slides up my arm, sending a tingling through each spot he touches. When I think he's going to wrap his hand in my hair, he instead lowers his hand across my collarbone to my chest, where his fingers graze the fabric of my shirt. Something stirs deep inside me. Once his fingers reach the bottom hem of my shirt, I still. He lifts the material and his hand, cold but gentle, strokes my stomach.

Taking his hand, I pull back. "Not here. We're in public."

His phone starts buzzing again, and he snatches it up before I can look at the screen. "Damn. That... I can't ignore this." His fingers fly across the screen. "Something's come up and I need to take care of it now. It's kind of an emergency."

"Is everything okay?"

"Oh yeah," He starts rubbing his hands on his legs. *He's nervous.*

"I guess I can find another ride."

"I'll make it up to you. I promise."

He allows me to grab my things before he speeds out of the parking lot, leaving me not completely sure of what just happened.

I go back inside, the mall doors *whoosh* behind me. I'm halfway through pulling up my contacts when I bump into someone, causing my phone to drop along with all my bags.

"Sorry," I mumble self-consciously, reaching down and grabbing my bags first.

Josh crouches at the same time, grabs my phone, and holds it out.

"Thanks."

He gives me a quick smile. His eyes flick from my duffle, then to me. "Everything okay?"

"James had an emergency."

"Oh. Is he okay?" His browns furrow in concern.

"I don't know." But he was in a hurry." I shrug.

"You need a ride?" He holds his hand out and takes everything before I can protest.

"Thanks. James was supposed to take me to his place."

Yeah... That didn't come out right.

Josh chuckles. "You've had these sleepovers since we were six. That's why James is at my house every last Saturday of the month." I honestly had no clue it was Josh's house he'd stay at those nights.

Josh hauls my bags to his truck like they weight nothing. I watch him for a moment and think. *I could really use those arms.* An image of me walking around with his biceps causes me to snort.

Josh glances over, one eye brow raised. "What's so funny?" He opens the passenger side of the truck and sets my things on the middle seat of the cab.

"Just imagining what I'd look like with your arms." I giggle some more.

He stares, but slowly his lip turns upward into a smirk. He shakes his head, his shoulders shaking with silent laughter while he walks around to the other side of the truck. "Okay, weird. But not your worst idea."

I laugh. "Thanks I think."

"Anytime." He says pulling open his door. "Glad to be of service."

It's been a few months since I've sat in his truck. It's old, but Alec had given it to Josh to fix up when he turned sixteen. He loves this truck. The smell of cypress and leather is comforting. There's a pang in my chest.

I've missed spending time with just Josh. He always pushed me to try new things, no matter what the outcome. I think back on the time he talked me into climbing the biggest tree in the woods behind our house when we were eleven.

"Don't be a chicken!" Josh jokes. I stick my tongue out in response.

"I'm not a chicken," I protest folding my arms in a small pout.

"Prove it," he taunts. I look up at the tree and my stomach flips. I'm not a chicken. I'll show him. I reach up and grasp at the bark, finding the right spot to place my fingers before I get my foot to the perfect spot. Slowly, I climb up to where Josh had just been moments before. He's even higher now.

"You're going to get stuck up there," I warn. He laughs and continues higher. Feeling braver, I follow suit. My heart races with excitement. When I look down and see how far up I am, I lose my grip and fall back.

34

My left foot goes under me before I land, and I hear a snap. Everything in my leg screams. I can't tell if I stopped breathing or if I'd just forgotten how.

"Abbi!" Josh is scrambling to get down as fast as he can manage, but his foot gets stuck between two branches, and he hits the ground hard. He landed on his arm, but without stopping, he leaps up and runs to get help. My dad comes and carries me to the truck and we all drive together to the hospital.

I ended up with a broken ankle, and Josh ended up with a broken wrist which he tried to say didn't hurt much, but only when he thought someone was watching.

It's never just one of you, is it?" Louis, Jared's dad, and our doctor, joked when he saw the two of us.

That wasn't the first time we ended up in the ER together. When we were seven we had been in a similar situation. Josh fractured his foot, and I sprained my wrist after we were jumping on his trampoline. Alec, Josh's dad, tore the trampoline down that same day.

We still had so much fun without it. Truth be told, we could have played with a box and still have had the best time. It wasn't until I started dating James that things seemed to shift.

I glance over at Josh without meaning to. He's got one hand on the wheel, the other resting loosely in his lap. His jaw is tense, and another flurry deep in my stomach appears. His brows are drawn in the way he gets when he's focused.

The truck rumbles softly beneath us, I turn and watch the street signs, trees, and buildings blur past, too aware of the silence, but somehow not wanting to break it.

The ride is too short, and an ache grows deep in my chest as we wind through the neighborhood to Cienna's.

"I miss this," I whisper, unable to help myself.

I don't think he heard me, but he responds, "me too." He reaches over and rests his hand on mine. My hand tingles at his touch. My face grows warm, but I peek back in his direction.

Even though he isn't looking at me, I see the change in him. His features softened, and I can see his Adams apple move as he swallows. Turning back to the road, we're at Cienna's.

Couldn't this last just a bit longer?

"Thanks, Josh." I unbuckle my seat and turn to him. His eyes are back to the unreadable they had been earlier. "I'll talk to you later?" I grab my things and rush inside before he can see my face go crimson again. I can still feel where his hand had touched mine, and I shiver. It isn't the nervous shiver I get with James, but excited. Like I want it to happen again.

What's wrong with me?

"I thought James was bringing you home." Cienna's inquiry snaps me back to reality as I come through the front door. A box of snacks and a case of soda in her arms.

Cienna blends with the chaos of the room. Her front room is painted teal, like cool water in summer. Bright, but soft, just like Lily, her Mom. The couches sit where they always have. Amethyst velvet. They're a little worn around the edges from years of use, but a memory for Mom. Sunflower yellow pillows are stacked along the couches, bright and soft, scattered like sunlight. Lily's artwork adorns the walls. Her creativity never slows. Her free spirit is like the pillows, a light in the dark.

After dropping my shopping bags by the front door, and draping my dress over the closest couch, I face Cienna who's still waiting on a reply. "He said he had an emergency," I shrug.

"So Josh brought you?"

I nod and try to walk past her up the stairs like that's the end of it.

"Uh-huh," she says behind me. "You're blushing by the way."

"I am *not*."

"Okay," she muses. "But you might want to check a mirror before you try that lie again."

Kasey is busy setting up the sleeping bags. She already unzipped the three and were fluffing them like she's prepping a guest-suite instead of your average sleepover.

"Okay, Abbi," she calls over her shoulder, not bothering to look at us. "You get the side closest to the closet. You always end up rolling that way anyways."

I drop my duffle by Cienna's desk across from her bed which is draped in a big yellow sunflower duvet. "Wow, thanks. Good to know my sleeping habits are being studied."

Cienna snorts, tossing a pillow at me. "She's not wrong."

"I prefer *graceful night swimmer* actually."

Kasey sits back on her heels, brushing her hair from her face. "Whatever helps you sleep. Just no stealing my blanket this time."

"No promises."

She points a perfectly pink manicured finger at me. "I *will* tape it to my body."

"No, you won't."

"You're right, I won't. But I'm not opposed to letting you go for a swim. I know where Ryan keeps the buckets."

"You're bluffing," Wide-eyed, I glance at Cienna. She holds her hands up as if to say, *"I'm out."*

Kasey doesn't say a word. She just leans, slow and deliberate, over her sleeping bag, eyes locked on mine. Her hand finds the edge of a pillow.

I narrow my eyes. "Don't–"

Too late.

In one fluid motion she yanks it up and swings. It catches me right in the shoulder with a satisfying *whump*.

"Okay, okay. I get it. Don't touch your blanket." I scramble for my own pillow, laughing.

I launch a counterstrike. Cienna screams with glee, diving to the other side of the bed, grabbing for a backup pillow stashed in the corner under her bean bag.

"Oh no," Kasey said straight-faced. "Not the *emergency pillow*."

"Desperate times," Cienna declares, yanking a fluorescent pink and purple monstrosity from its hiding place. It's absurdly lumpy and covered in synthetic fur.

I barely have time to duck before she swings it, giving me a face full of fluff.

Eventually, we collapse into a heap, heads resting on half-deflated pillows, hair sticking to our foreheads, and still trying to laugh between heaving breaths.

"Okay, Abbi."

I groan and roll over. "What now?"

"Go pick out a game for us while I reorganize the snacks, and Kasey finishes..." Cienna gestures towards the sleeping bags, now a jumbled mess, Kasey's handywork destroyed, "whatever this is."

I groan louder but I'm already rolling onto my feet. "Fine. But if I come back with *Apples to Apples,* it's on you."

"Then don't come back at all," Kasey mutters, already straightening the sleeping bags into their designated spots.

The basement smells like old wood and dryer sheets. The dryer thumps steadily in the corner, the washer gurgles like it's just kicked on. I peek around the corner of the shelf and spot Lily scooping a basket of laundry from the floor and popping it onto her hip.

I smile. "Need any help?"

She jumps at the sound and drops the basket with a slight yelp. Clothes tumble onto the orange rug, but luckily most of them stayed within the basket.

"Oops, sorry." I rush over to help, but she holds up her hand.

"It's okay, hon, I got it." She collects the few dropped pieces and stands up with a sigh and a smile. "No harm done. What are you up to?"

"I've been charged with game duty."

Lily shifts the basket higher on her hip, her smile widening. "Ooh, serious responsibility."

I glance at the shelves. "One wrong choice and it's, '*why did you bring that*' for the next six hours."

She laughs, moving towards the stairs. "Just make sure you don't pick one with half the pieces missing. That's how war starts."

I grin and turn back to the wall of games while listening to the sound of her feet steadily thumping against each step on her way up the stairs.

I crouch in front of the wall, reading the faded spines. *Sorry, Life, Twister, Apples to Apples.* Then I spot it.

Monopoly is wedged between *Yahtzee* and *Clue*. Opening it, I see the pieces all seem to be there. "Let the chaos begin."

On my way back up the stairs, I run straight into James. The game box drops, and pieces scatter everywhere.

Crap.

I stoop down on my hands and knees to clean up.

"I'm sorry. Here, let me help." James sets a bouquet of vibrant red roses on the kitchen counter and leans down to help collect the pieces. I pretend not to notice the flowers while we gather up each piece. After searching under chairs, and in rugs, we don't find any more, so I close the box. That's when James starts speaking.

"I'm sorry I ditched you earlier." He holds up the bouquet towards me, and I force a smile. Roses are so overrated. I know they're the symbol of love and all, but peonies are fuller and more beautiful. They can't decide whether to keep blooming or to explode.

"I had a job interview," I take the bouquet and breathe in their scent. I may not like their look as much, but the smell is amazing. "They wanted to meet with me again before making their decision. You are looking at the newest member of The Smith's Auto. I start next weekend." He's beaming.

"That's amazing!" I hug him. There's a hint of vanilla on his shirt. It must be from The Smith's. "Congratulations!"

"I didn't want to say anything in case I didn't get the job." He squeezes me tight, the smell of vanilla making my nose wrinkle.

"I'm happy for you." I smile against his shoulder, but the scent lingers. Too strong. Too...floral.

Definitely not engine grease.

"Thanks," he sighs, pulling back just enough to look at me. His eyes are bright.

I clutch the roses a little tighter than I mean to, a missed thorn digging into my palm.

"Big weekend for you then," I manage. That's when I remember. "Wait. Didn't we just plan the camping trip for next weekend? Does that mean you aren't coming?" Relief makes an appearance in my chest before I can stop it. Frustration rushes in right behind.

James runs a hand through his hair. "I completely forgot."

His eyes drop to the floor, then flick up again. "I mean, I didn't think I'd actually get the job, so I didn't put it together. But maybe... Maybe I can talk to them. Push the start date?"

I watch him. Watch the way his brow knits like he's annoyed with himself. That's another of his tells. When he's honest he looks frustrated that he got it wrong.

I believe him. Of course I do. My stomach untwists a little. The relief is so quick it feels guilty.

I give him a small smile, "It's okay. We'll figure it out."

He pulls me into another hug, and I let myself fall into it. The vanilla is still there. He pulls back, and I don't realize it, but my nose is wrinkled again.

"Something smell weird?" He asks.

I shake my head. "I think the auto shop needs a different smell than vanilla."

Probably, he laughs. He tilts my chin up and kisses me softly. I melt into his kiss without a second thought. My fingers curl slightly against his jacket, and for a second, everything goes quiet. The mall, the vanilla, the job. None of it mattered. Just the way he held me like he hadn't slipped away a short while ago.

"Don't you have a sleepover to attend?" A smile pulls at the corner of his mouth. My brain is still somewhere in the kiss - soft, slow, and warm. The words take a second longer to land.

He takes the bouquet. "I'll take these to your house on my way to Josh's."

My chest tightened, just a flicker. I nod, still trying to pull myself back to reality. "Okay, thanks." I give him one last kiss before heading back to Cienna's room.

"What on Earth took you so long? I thought a wormhole opened and sucked you in." Cienna's love for exaggerating causes a small chuckle in both me and Kasey.

"Sorry, I dropped the game. It took me a minute to clean it up." I set the game on the bed and walk over to Cienna's desk. I sit in her yellow swivel chair and face the others. Kasey has taken over the giant yellow bean bag between Cienna's bed and dark brown dresser where the TV glows, ready for us to pick a movie from Cienna's DVD collection.

Cienna's room is covered in sunflowers. Curtains, drawer knobs, bedspread, rugs. She doesn't have closet doors but instead has embroidered sunflower curtains. Those same curtains frame her bay window surrounding her desk.

Kasey is munching on a big bowl of chips. She is the only girl I know that can eat all she wants without gaining a single pound. She could almost out eat the guys. Almost.

"Truth or Dare?" Cienna sets down the DVD cases in defeat and gives us her undivided attention.

"I did grab *Monopoly* you know." I try to cover my disdain for the game with laughter.

"Truth or Dare, Kay?" Kasey just laughs in surrender, knowing there's no way around it.

"Dare."

"I dare you to let us see the last conversation with Quint you had." Kasey turns bright red, but she pulls out her phone and hands it over. Cienna scrolls through to her texts and opens her conversation with Quint.

We burst into giggles. The last conversation is from today. It's just pictures. Pictures of Kasey and pictures of Quint, both of them using different filters. The best one was Quint with a baby face that made him look constipated.

"That was more PG than I expected," Cienna tosses the phone back to Kasey.

"Well, not all of us have been with our boyfriends for six years." Kasey rolls her eyes. "Your turn Ci. Truth or Dare?"

"Dare, obviously."

Oh, obviously.

"I dare you to call Jared and sing to him."

"Easy." She whips out her phone, and it's ringing within seconds. Before he answers, she puts it on speaker.

"*Hey sexy thang.*" Kasey covers her mouth to stifle the laughter. I bite the inside of my cheek to keep quiet.

She starts singing *Twinkle, Twinkle, Little Star*. Before she can get the first verse out, Jared is singing along.

It's no use. Kasey and I roll over in laughter.

"You must be playing Truth or Dare, huh?"

"Can't talk, love you!" Cienna hangs up and turns to me. My laughing abruptly stops, the feeling of dread washing over me.

Please no.

"Truth or Dare?"

"Truth." I say with a straight face. She knows I don't want to play.

Does that stop her though? Nope.

"Boo, you're no fun." She blows raspberries at me. "Okay fine. What is your biggest secret fear?"

My heart jumps. Just a little. Not that she'd know. Not that either of them would see how fast that one hit.

Quick, say something.

I smile. "Lice."

Kasey snorts, "Seriously?"

"They spread fast, and they bite." I say faking my best horror-movie shudder. "Plus, the shampoo smells like chemicals and broken dreams."

Cienna laughs, tossing a gummy worm at my head. "I agree. Lice is terrifying." She scratches her head, catches herself, and then runs to look in the mirror hanging on the back of her bedroom door. "Great. Just thinking about it makes me itch."

Kasey is still watching me. Her head is tilted slightly, like she knows there's more.

The last thing I want to tell them is that I'm afraid of losing myself for the person I love.

Chapter 4

Abbi

"I heard you got a ride from Josh," Kasey keeps her eyes on the road, hands steady on the wheel.

The memory of yesterday causes my heart to skip a beat. I glance out the window. "Yeah."

"Cienna told me."

"I figured."

This is not a conversation for first thing in the morning.

Kasey parks the car in front of my house. "She also mentioned you turned the color of a tomato when she brought him up."

I groan, burying my face in my hands. "Of course she did."

"She tried to make it a joke, but..." I sit up and Kasey's gnawing on her cheek. "I don't know. She seemed kind of off when she said it."

My blood runs cold. "Like mad?"

Kasey shakes her head. "Not mad. Just…" she purses her lips, looking for the right word. "Like she was trying not to seem like she cared."

I don't know what to say to that.

"She's protective." After a short pause, she continues. "I think sometimes she gets stuck between being your friend and being his sister."

I hadn't thought of it that way before. I look down and notice I'm picking at the skin around my nails, so I ball my hands into fists trying to stop.

Kasey gives me a small smile and takes my hand. "I just want you to know, you're allowed to feel however you feel. Even if it's messy. Even if it's not what people expect. It isn't what he says, it's how he makes you feel." The air catches in my throat, a nervous giggle wanting to escape. "How does James make you feel?"

Well that's not fair.

I bite my lip trying to think of what to say.

Warm. Frustrated. Nervous. I never know how serious he's going to be, and it stresses me out.

"How does Josh make you feel?"

"That's…well… I mean…" My face is hot, and the embarrassment is openly plain on my face. Kasey's smirking now. I bite my cheek and look down.

"Just think about it, kay?" She wraps me in a hug before I slip out, unsure if the heaviness I feel is from my bags or something else.

I watch her car roll next door where Quint jogs out and climbs in the passenger seat without missing a beat.

I notice James' grey Subaru isn't there. Josh and James *both* said he was spending the night. I check the time. 9:32a.m.

I guess he could have left already.

I haul my things into the house. And there's a sizzling coming from the kitchen. The smell of bacon overwhelms my nose, and my stomach grumbles.

After dropping my bags by the couch, I step into the kitchen. Dad is in one of his faded college shirts, flipping something in a cast iron pan. He glances up, his brow furrowed in concern.

"You look like you barely slept."

"Isn't that what sleepovers are for?" I yawn, rubbing my eyes.

"Perfect conditions for a rescue breakfast."

"You made this for me?"

"Who else has a post-sleepover hangover around here?"

I hurry to the sink to wash my hands. The smell is overwhelming. Real food after a night of chips, gummy worms, and chaos.

A steaming pile of scrambled eggs, bacon, and assorted fruit decorate the table. I peek inside a dish with a towel draped over it and smile. Homemade bagels.

"Eat first," he says. "You can tell me about your night once you're more conscious."

After smothering my bagel in cream cheese, I take a huge bite. My taste buds take in the flavor and all my stress from the conversation with Kasey disappears. "This is the best bagel I've ever had," I say with my mouth full.

Dad chuckles. "I think you're just hungry." He passes me some eggs, and I happily pile them on my plate.

"No, you're just a really good cook."

"I learned from the best." He takes a sip of orange juice.

Mom had been the cook, but she insisted we all learn how.

"She really was the best." I reach over and give Dad's hand a squeeze.

"So," he says after a moment. "What did you find yesterday?"

I perk up instantly. "Oh – hang on."

I dart into the front room, nearly tripping over the glass coffee table in the process. After a quick dig through the bags, I pull the dress out carefully and return to the kitchen, holding it up excitedly.

Dad sets his glass down and gives it an appraising look. "That's beautiful. It brings out the gold in your eyes." He smiles and takes a bite of bacon.

"I haven't gotten shoes yet, but I still have time."

"Are you still going with James?"

My heart stutters.

"What does that mean? Of course we are." I know I sound defensive, but the conversation with Kasey creeps back in my mind.

Dad raises an eyebrow, as cool as a cucumber. "It's just a question, kiddo."

I cross my arms. "It sounded like a *loaded* question."

He takes a bit of bagel, chews, and swallows like there's no rush. "You know I like James."

Not helpful.

"But..."

"But," he echoes deliberately. "I also like the way you are when you're with people who make you feel like yourself."

That sits heavy on my chest. "He does." Even I hear the edge in my voice this time.

Dad doesn't call it out. He just tilts his head. "Okay."

That's it. There's no lecture, no warning, just, *okay*.

Kasey's words echo louder now. *It isn't what he says. It's how he makes you feel.*

I pick at my breakfast, suddenly not as hungry.

"Is he going to wear green or gold?" Dad begins clearing the table.

"I honestly hadn't thought about it. I just figured he could wear whatever he wants." I join him in carrying the dishes to the sink.

"What time is he coming over tonight?"

I completely forgot. *How could I forget?*

Sunday was the day he always comes over for dinner with us.

I haven't even done the shopping yet.

"I don't know. Let me check." I pull out my phone and see a missed call and text. When I open the text, my stomach knots.

Hey. Can't make it today. I promised I'll make it up to you.

The sigh slips out—half relief, half frustration.

"Is everything okay?"

I clear my throat, slipping my phone into my back pocket. "Looks like it's just us tonight," I sigh.

"Oh?" I roll my eyes.

Smooth Dad. Real smooth.

"Well, in that case, I'm going to go invite Alec and them over for a barbecue. It's been a while since I've cooked for a full crew."

Out of the frying pan and into the fire.

"You can try, but Quint just left with Kasey. I don't know when they'll be back."

"I'll head over and see what their plans are today. Would you finish the dishes?" He wipes his hands on the towel and passes it to me before going out the front door. If I didn't know better, I'd say he was almost skipping.

Taking a deep breath, I turn on some music from my phone, connect it to the speaker on the counter, and carry the rest of the dishes over to the sink. Today is going to be extremely awkward if I can't keep it together.

You just need to breathe. No hasty decisions.

The memory of Josh's hand on mine causes my breathing to hitch in my throat, my vision blurring.

What are you doing?

I shake my head, clearing the image away.

Josh is your friend, just like he's always been.

"They said they can make it." Dad breaks me from my thoughts, and I drop a glass causing it to shatter all over the kitchen floor, a large piece bouncing up and cutting my leg.

That's what I get for wearing shorts.

"Gosh dang it!" I jump back and rush to the pantry to get a broom. My leg stings, but not bad.

"I'll take care of it. Go clean up that leg. He takes the broom from me. "Watch your step."

I hustle up to my bathroom before I can bleed on the ground. When I examine it, I'm relieved to see just a scratch on the outer part of my leg, near my ankle. I grab a bandage from under the sink.

I balance on one foot, the other on the counter. Once I manage to stretch the bandage across the scratch, my elbow knocks into my hairspray canister. It lands with a loud clink.

With a huff, I lean over and pick it up, making sure the lid is secure before leaving the bathroom.

I hate messes.

I spot them on my vanity while leaving the bathroom. A full bouquet of red roses.

I bite my cheek again.

It's the thought that counts.

I make the descent back to the kitchen. Dad has already taken out the vacuum and is going over the floor several times.

"All good?" He asks after turning the vacuum off.

"Just a scratch," I assure him.

"I had a thought."

"A new hobby?" I jest.

"Hardy har, har. Why don't you take Josh to the store to pick up stuff for dinner?"

Not obvious at all.

I'm half-way through tying my hair up in a messy knot and don't pause before answering. "Sure."

"He's outside," Dad adds, far too casually. He's acting like he *didn't* just detonate my morning.

I freeze mid-twist." Like, *right* now?"

He nods, way too casually.

My stomach does a weird flip, and I glance down at myself. Black tank top, sleepover-wrinkled pink shorts, no makeup.

I try to smooth down the edges of the knot in my hair, already regretting putting it up. It made my face look rounder.

"You could have warned me, you know," I mutter grumpily.

Dad shrugs, clearly not sorry. "You look fine."

Such a dad answer.

"Besides, it's just Josh. He's seen you like this a million times."

He's right.

I grab my purse from the couch just before Dad practically shoves me out the door.

"Pick out something good. Love you." He shuts the door, and I can hear him turn the lock.

Wow.

Josh is in the driveway, leaning against his truck like he's been waiting a while. He's wearing a loose fitting white V-neck with dark blue jeans.

I take a steady breath.

It's just a grocery run. Not a date. Nothing more.

Still, I tug my tank top a little straighter before walking down the steps. It doesn't matter. But it does.

"Hey, stranger," he walks towards me with that easy lopsided smile that shouldn't make my knees weak.

Without hesitation, he rounds the truck and pulls open the passenger door like it's second nature.

"Thanks."

He shrugs one shoulder, that smile still tugging at his mouth. "Figured I'd try to be a gentleman for once."

"You say that like you're usually a menace."

I climb in, doing my best not to overthink the distance between us. The soft thunk of the door when he closes it, or that the only space is between us is the one small seat.

He jogs around to the driver's side and hops in, smiling over at me as the engine roars to life. "Where to, Milady?"

"I figure we have the best options at the store on Main Street. I mean, it's the only grocery store in town open on Sundays."

"Can we make a quick detour first?"

"Uh, sure." I glance over at Josh whose eyes are focused on the road now. He makes a left turn instead of a right towards the grocery store.

The cemetery's this way.

He makes one final right, and my assumption is spot on. We *are* going to the cemetery. My stomach tightens. The tires crunch along the gravel path until he eases it to a stop next to the tall headstone with worn edges and a little vase of dying purple daisies.

Mom's grave.

Josh puts the truck in park and climbs out. I quietly follow, feeling a tug at my heart. It's been over a month since I've visited, and the guilt hurts.

Josh produces a pot of flowers stashed in the bed of his truck. More purple daisies.

He walks over to the headstone, picks up the dying bouquet and replaces it with new flowers just left of her photo.

"Do you come here often?" I ask taking in the nicely trimmed grass around the headstone. I hadn't really paid attention before, but thinking back, the grass was always perfectly trimmed. This was one of those minimal maintenance cemeteries. You can plant flowers or leave things, but so long as you care for it.

Some of the headstones are over-grown and neglected while others have beautifully intricate decorations.

Sure, Dad could have trimmed it, just not when we're together.

You're overthinking this.

"I try to come every few weeks." He shrugs like it's nothing. "More if it's been a rough week."

My throat tightens. I blink up at the stone, then over at him. He's watching it like it means something to *him,* too.

Something in my chest cracks open. I wrap my arms around him without thinking, holding on tight.

"Your dad said you haven't come in a while so I thought we could come together. I was already planning to come today anyway."

He really is perfect.

"Thank you," my voice is barely a whisper. He squeezes tightly, and I don't want him to let go.

"I'll give you a few minutes." When he releases me, he heads back to the truck and hops in. I turn and kneel next to Mom.

"Hey, Mom." I stroke the marble picture. "I'm sorry it's been a while. It's not that I didn't want to come, it's just... everything has been a lot lately. School. People. Me."

With Josh safely in the truck playing music just loud enough I can hear the bass thrumming, I feel more comfortable saying some of this out loud.

"I think I made a mistake, and I don't know how to fix it." I'm subconsciously picking at my nails again. "James is a great guy. I like him. I really do. But I don't think that's enough."

I look back at the truck and Josh is tapping on the steering wheel to the music looking in the opposite direction.

"How did you know Dad was the right one?" I trace the curve of her name with my pinky. "I really wish you could tell me what to do."

The breeze stirs just a little. Just enough to ruffle my hair.

Eventually I know it's time to go. I stand up and brush the grass from my legs. "I love you, Mom."

Back in the truck, Josh turns on my favorite country song. I smile, knowing he's trying to cheer me up. I slide to the middle seat and rest my head on his shoulder – no fear, no embarrassment or worry – Just peace.

"Thank you."

He wraps his arm around my shoulder in response.

By the time we pull into the parking lot, the knot in my chest has loosened just a little.

"How does steak sound?" Josh asks when we grab a cart and walk into the store.

"Steak sounds *amazing*." I know I just ate, but the thought of steak has me drooling. "What about sauteed mushrooms?"

"Ooh, yes!" He takes a container of mushrooms and plops them in the cart. "Potatoes or corn?"

"Corn," we say in unison and laugh.

Grilled corn it is.

Josh steps over to the corn display and starts peeling back the husks to check each ear.

"Look at you, all produce-savvy," I grin.

"I know what I'm doing," he says with mock pride. "Corn's a serious business."

I leave him to it and veer off towards the fruit. I load the cart with everything bright and fresh. Strawberries, blackberries, oranges, grapes, bananas, pineapple, and apples. Not green – never green.

When we meet back up, Josh gives an approving nod at my haul. "Going for rainbow vibes?"

"It's for the salad," I smile. "You're welcome."

Once we are content with what we grabbed in produce, we stroll to the back and pick out our steaks.

"I feel sorry for people who hate steak." I quip.

"Me too."

"I say I could be a vegetarian, but then I remember steak. Honestly, how do people say no to it?"

Josh places four Ribeye in the cart and shrugs. "They haven't tasted your cooking." His comment makes me blush.

"I'll be right back."

"Okay. I'm off to desserts."

"I'll find you there."

With that, we part ways. I pull a pack of lemonade and soda from the shelf before getting lost in the bakery.

A freshly made French silk pie calls to me like a beacon. *Josh's favorite.*

After getting it from the center of the display case, they package it for me in a white box, sealing the contents inside with their scanning label.

After rearranging a few things, I manage to set it gently in the cart.

Something white and soft appears in front of me.

Not just something. Flowers.

I blink down at the bouquet. White peonies. They're full, ruffled, and impossibly fresh.

Josh stands behind me, one arm extended, a crooked smile tugging at his mouth.

"They're beautiful," I take them and hold them to my face enjoying their rich fragrance.

"You deserve beautiful things." My whole body tingles and my heart aches to break through my chest.

The air feels impossibly still, like the world is holding its breath right along with me. His smile softens. Those ridiculous, unreadable grey eyes are locked on mine like they can see every thought flickering across my face.

I grip the bouquet tighter, like it's the only thing anchoring me to the floor.

I can feel myself longing to step forward. My heart yearns to close the space between us.

Don't do it.

I clear my throat and look away. The petals rustle in my hands, the only sound I can trust.

That was too close.

Once our items are bagged and loaded into the bed of the truck, we check the time. It's barely one. The sun's still high, and warm against my skin as I slam the tailgate shut with more force than I mean to. He doesn't flinch. He just smiles like he knows me too well.

Josh peeks over at me, squinting against the light. "Wanna grab lunch on the way back? My treat."

I tilt my head, my brow lifting just enough, with a quirk to my lips. "You sure you're not just trying to bribe me into unloading everything?"

"Maybe," he grins. "But mostly, I'm hungry, and I figure you might be too."

"Yeah. That sounds perfect."

We pull into the drive-thru a few minutes later, windows down, the truck humming beneath us.

When it's our turn, he leans out the window. "Can I get a three piece chicken tender with extra crispy sweet potato fries, and a peach lemonade?"

"Is that it?" A bored sounding girl echoes from the speaker.

"A deluxe chicken sandwich with extra sauce, waffle fries, and a coke please."

"Is that everything?" The girl somehow manages to sound even more bored than before.

"That'll be all. Thank you."

I blink. "How did you–"

He shrugs like it's obvious. "You always get the same thing."

"And you never ask?"

He glances at me as we pull forward, smirking. "Did I get it wrong?"

I shake my head, equal parts annoyed and impressed. "No. You got it *exactly* right."

We enjoy our food on the way back to the house. The chicken is moist, the fries are the perfect mix of crispy and soft. Josh has one hand on the wheel, the other holding his sandwich.

"Want a fry?" I pick up one of his waffle fries.

"Yes please." He doesn't take his eyes off the road but holds his mouth open so I can feed it to him. "Thanks," he says after swallowing. "Best co-pilot ever."

"I should get a badge or something," I say, brushing salt off my fingers.

He hums in agreement.

That's how we finish the rest of the drive. Music plays softly from the stereo while we enjoy our food.

Back home, the house is empty. Dad and Alec must have already gone to work. We take the bags into the kitchen and together put the food away. I find an empty vase and place the flowers in the center of the kitchen table. I think about what he said at the store.

"You deserve beautiful things."

The words make me smile.

Can we also talk about how he remembered my order?

I don't want to name this feeling yet. But it's soft, steady... and getting harder to ignore.

"Dad just texted and said they'll be back around four. That leaves us a few hours. So, what do we want to do in the meantime?" He stuffs his phone in his pocket and leans against the counter. He folds his arms and his muscles expand. My knees buckle slightly, but I manage to play it off by leaning against the counter next to him.

"Honestly? I need a shower. I haven't since the sleepover, and I feel absolutely feral."

He laughs. "You say that like it's a crime."

"It is," I say already heading for the stairs. "Against my skin, and possibly public health."

"Take your time," he calls after me. "I'll find something to do that doesn't involve burning the house down."

I pause on the stairs. "Please don't rearrange my bookshelves again."

"No promises."

Chapter 5

Josh

I hadn't meant to end up in her room.

I was just wandering. Her room is cracked open. The only sound coming from her bathroom is the gentle patter of water from her shower.

I step inside, slow and curious. Her space feels like her. The scent of flowers hits me quick and hard. Like lilacs and something faintly citrus. The smell is warm and soft. A smell that clings to pillow and old sweaters. Of course she smells like flowers. She practically is one—vivid, intoxicating, and made to bloom in her own season.

Her room is awash in soft lilac and white. Sunlight spills across the dark purple window seat and bed.

Books climb the walls on either side of the window. Her shelves are packed tight with stories. A green blanket is draped over her purple lounge chair, clearly her reading spot.

A vase full of bright red roses sits next to her bed.

James doesn't know her at all.

Her CDs are lined up on her dresser near the bed, some with jewel cases, others with homemade scribbled titles. I run a finger along one – *'Playlist for Rainy Days'*, her handwriting is uneven, even slanted. I don't intend to open it. Just to feel the presence of all this. All *her*.

Then I see her dress. It's hanging on the hook of her closet door, long and lovely. Completely still.

I stop breathing for half a second.

Floor-length sage green satin, with layers of soft gold tulle catch the light in quiet, deliberate shimmers.

I exhale slowly, my chest tightening in the stupid, embarrassing way that only happens when you get ambushed by feelings you didn't see coming.

I can already see her in it.

The sage green pulling warm against her skin, the fabric swaying when she turns. Her shoulders are bare, her hair pinned up just enough to make me forget how words work. That quiet smile she gets when she doesn't know anyone is looking playing on her lips.

I tear my eyes away, more flustered than I have any right to be.

Escaping to the opposite end of the room, I let my fingers drift over the books like they can reground me. But the truth is, I'm already gone.

I'm ruined by a dress she hasn't even worn yet.

The bathroom door clicks open behind me. I turn without really thinking, expecting her in pajama pants or something oversized. I'm caught off guard.

Instead, Abbi steps out in cut-off shorts and a sage green tank top, her damp hair braided over one shoulder.

She's barefoot, her skin still warm and pink from the shower. The braid slips forward as she adjusts the tank top strap at her shoulder, not even realizing she has my full attention.

It's not the dress that gets me this time. It's *this*. It's the casual version of her that shouldn't short-circuit my brain.

But it does.

She looks at me and smiles. "You still lurking in my room?"

I quirk a smile, grateful for the cover. "I got distracted by your CD's. Might have judged you a little for owning the soundtrack to *Twilight*."

"I stand by my taste," she says walking past me to her dresser. "That album is iconic."

And I'm standing there like an idiot, pretending I'm not completely undone by damp hair, jean shorts, and a green tank top.

Chapter 6

Abbi

"Aww, you bought me flowers," Alec jokes when he spots the peonies on the table. Josh and I were curled up on the couch in the den watching *How to Lose a Guy in 10 Days*.

"Hardy har," Josh sighs, untangling his arm from around my shoulder and standing. "I'll be right back," he whispers.

"Okay," I say softly, sitting up and watching him walk into the kitchen. I catch him leaning towards Alec, whispering something I can't quite make out. Alec snorts. Dad's mouth twitches, fighting a smirk behind the rim of his mug. I narrow my eyes and shake my head.

Traitors, both of them.

I guess I can see how it looks. His arm was around me, and I was snuggled up against him. It wasn't intentional. We didn't start the movie like that. It was somewhere in the middle.

Probably not the best choice, but it was comfortable and calming.

Checking my phone for the first time since being home, I'm surprised to see not a single text or call from James. He's usually bombarding me with messages by now. Little jokes, emojis, sometimes poems. But today–nothing. Absolute silence.

I lock my screen and slide my phone face-down on the light grey ottoman in front of me.

"Let's start dinner." I shake off the worry and walk into the kitchen.

Twisting the faucet on, I run my hands under the warm stream, watching the suds swirl down the drain. I'm actually relieved for the radio silence.

That's not a good sign, is it?

"What are we having?" Alec finds the blackberries and plops one into his mouth. The streaks of silver in his dark hair catches the overhead light, tousled like he ran a hand through it on the way home and called it good.

That's definitely where Josh gets it from.

"Do *you* want to cook?" I snatch the berries back and take them over to the sink so I can rinse them.

"Nah, I'm good," he chuckles.

"Didn't think so. Shoo."

"Okay, we get the message loud and clear." He backs off, but not without another longing glance at the fruit. Of course he's the kind of menace who pretends to retreat and then steals one more on the way out.

"Don't do it, Dad." Josh warns, already holding a paring knife and cutting board.

"I'll behave," Alec surrenders. Dad steers Alec through the den to the backyard, leaving Josh and me in the kitchen.

"You can join them," I tell Josh.

"Are you kidding? This is where the party is."

He takes out his phone and fills the kitchen with music.

"I thought you said *Twilight* music sucks."

"You're right. The album is iconic."

We dance while we work.

Bad dancing seems to run in the family. I giggle as he tries to moonwalk across the floor and ends up hitting the pantry door.

I can't help but think about what it would be like to do this every day. Just the two of us.

Wouldn't that be something?

Chapter 7

Abbi

The sun is bright, the metal from the bleachers warm against my back as I lie there. This is the one place people don't tend to go around during lunch. Not sure why. It's a pretty great spot.

Each moment from yesterday plays behind my eyelids: The way Josh made me laugh. How his arms felt—warm and protective. The fact that he visits Mom. Not even James does that.

It's easy and comfortable with Josh. The idea of being anything more than friends has been nagging at my mind consistently since last Friday, but the thoughts have come and gone for several years.

What about James?

James spoke up and asked me. Josh never did.

James has been a great boyfriend aside from Saturday and Sunday. Life happens, I get that. I can't be mad at him for having a few bad days. He has a job now. Graduation is this Friday. Everything is changing, and it's not going to slow down.

"Hey, beautiful."

A shadow darkens the light behind my eyelids. I squint. James is standing above me looking down with a mischievous smile.

"Laying like that could give someone the wrong idea." He places his hand on my knee.

I smirk. "Wouldn't want that. Don't want to be the reason some poor soul loses its way."

James bends down, his hand slowly edging up my leg. "Too late."

I let out a small involuntary gasp, shivers rolling through my body.

When he reaches the inside of my thigh, I freeze.

Not here.

I grab his hand and squeeze it. "We're at school," I remind him.

"No one's here," he says this confidently, but then proceeds to glance around us.

He leans close and kisses me sweetly. My hand instinctively twists into his curls. His other hand leaves mine and starts skimming the bottom hem of my shirt. When it lands on the button of my shorts, he easily undoes it with one hand without missing a beat in our kiss.

I don't stop him.

Instead, I pull him closer, enjoying his kiss and the feel of his hand.

67

His hand slides into my shorts and reality catches up.

I push him back, my head spinning, my breathing heavy. "Not here."

"So it's not a *no*?" He's grinning again.

"It's a *not here*." I reemphasize, buttoning up my shorts.

"I'll take it."

He laces his fingers through mine and we enjoy the silence around us before the bell signals the end of peace.

The rest of the school day is a blur of students chatting in their classes while the teachers hide behind their desks daydreaming about summer vacation.

James catches me off guard as I'm trying to unlock my car. He wraps his arms tightly and swings me off my feet.

"I missed you," he whispers in my ear once he sets me down.

"It's only been two hours." I retort.

"Two hours too long." He strokes my arm. "I'm still thinking about you on the bleachers."

My cheeks redden and I try to cover my blush with turning towards my car again. The red paint is starting to peel near the door frame.

"Maybe we can continue where we left off?" He traces the curve of my sides with his fingers. My breath catches.

"Actually, I have to go shopping for my shoes today. Still haven't found any to go with my dress."

He kisses my nose. "Well, whatever you pick, it will be beautiful."

I swallow. He knew just what to say.

I rise up to my toes and kiss him. He doesn't linger this time. He pulls back with a smile and retrieves his own car keys.

"Text me a picture when you find the right pair."

"Okay," I smile softly.

He turns and saunters towards his own car. He doesn't look back, but I watch him go anyway. Just in case.

Chapter 8

Kasey

The store is bustling with girls shopping last minute for their shoes. The dance is four days away. Judging by this chaos, half of us waited until now. There are about a hundred girls at our school, and I'm pretty sure half of them are here. Cienna was the lucky one of us. She managed to find shoes even before she found a dress.

I ignore the girls around me hollering at one another like I'm not even there. I haven't really thought about what shoes I want, but I do know that I want something simple.

I need more simple in my life. My therapist says I need to allow myself to enjoy simple while also learning that simple doesn't mean I need to disappear.

"You don't have to sparkle to belong."

His words ring out in my mind while I try to ignore the girls shoving one another for the shiniest and most extravagant shoes.

Simple doesn't mean invisible. That's what he said. But sometimes simple feels like fading. I just want quiet without vanishing.

It's been three days since I started my new medication. I'm not sure if it's working yet. He told me it could take several weeks, but I do feel a bit different. Maybe it's just hope that things might get better. Or maybe it's the chaos around me that's making it hard to tell. The last four medications didn't help. In fact, one of them was so bad, my family told everyone Mom and I went on a trip for a few weeks until we could get another medication.

"Kasey?" Someone taps my shoulder and I jump, my fist tightening around a pair of black peep toe stilettoes.

I whirl around and come face to face with a wide eyed Abbi. She holds her hands up and steps back a little further.

"Sorry. Didn't mean to startle you." She tries to laugh, but it comes out as a weird breath.

"Sorry. This is chaos." I gaze around at the insane amount of girls. "I wish I picked a quieter store." I grumble.

"You and me both," Abbi's face is a serious scowl while scanning the different shelves emptying before our very eyes.

"Guess we can't just stand here," I shrug.

"I suppose," Abbi sighs. The crowd has thinned some since I arrived, but not by much.

Abbi pushes her way through towards the edge of the aisle, where there are less people, and more options. I am still gripping the stilettoes, one in each hand, and that's when I realize they aren't even my size. I set them down and we both start grabbing boxes, checking sizes, and colors. I'm looking for black, and Abbi hopes for green or gold.

"How about these?" Abbi holds up a pair of black pumps. "They're your size."

I take them from her and slide them onto my feet. They're simple and yet elegant. "Perfect." Slipping my sandals back on, I place my new shoes in their box and hold them tightly under my arm.

"Now all that's left is shoes for me?" Abbi sighs while shifting around the boxes. The sounds of the girls around us are starting to quiet as each girl finds their pair, pays, and leaves. It's not as stifling now, but it's still too much.

I really don't like being around people.

That's why I'm grateful I made friends when I was little. It doesn't take effort to socialize with them. It's easy and simple.

As we look around the emptying store, I notice a pair of sage green lace peep toe stilettoes with a gold heel tucked away behind a stack of boxes. I quickly grab them and hold them out for her.

"What about these?" I ask, hoping they're her size.

Abbi's eyes light up as she takes the shoes from me. "These are perfect! Thank you Kay!"

I smile, feeling a small sense of accomplishment amidst the chaos. Maybe things are starting to look up after all. Or maybe, I'm finally looking up on my own.

Chapter 9
Abbi

"I can't believe we are officially done with high school!" Cienna spins, a vision of pink. "Tell me I don't look like a cupcake in the best way." She wears a pink sundress with silver flats.

"You're a glittery cupcake." Kasey nudges Cienna and smooths the skirt of her own dress. A blue corset halter that hugs tight through the waist, showing off how truly tiny she is, before it flares out in soft folds. Tiny silver star sequins scatter across the fabric like constellations. She's paired the whole thing with black flats. 'Plain' is not in her vocabulary. "Now sit down so I can finish your hair."

She takes Cienna's arm and leads her back to Cienna's desk chair. Cienna surprisingly sits still long enough for Kasey to twist her hair up and clip it with silver butterfly pins she brought over for Cienna to wear.

I add the finishing touch of black to my eyeliner and face them both. I chose an emerald tie dress that makes me feel like I'm part of a fairytale. I pair it with black flats. It's practical, considering how long we'll be on our feet today, it feels like the perfect balance of grace and comfort.

Kasey adjusts her halter dress, her usual edge softened by glitter. She catches me looking. "Too much?"

"Not possible," I reply honestly.

"Look at us," Cienna pulls us into a hug. "We look like an overly dramatic flower arrangement."

"Emphasis on dramatic," Kasey mutters, but she takes the compliment. "Abbi, your turn." She pats the bright yellow chair, and I obediently sit.

"Don't let me forget my tassel," Cienna says, digging through a drawer, her clothes strewn over every surface.

"It's on the doorknob," Kasey mumbles around a bobby pin. Closing my eyes, I let her pull and twist my hair as she sees fit. No one does hair quite like Kasey.

It doesn't take long before she shouts, "Finished!"

Opening my eyes, Kasey is holding up a mirror for me. She's braided my hair into a half up half down jeweled rosette.

"What do you think?" Worry is thick in her voice.

"It's beautiful, Kay. Thank you." I stand up, hugging her close.

I wish you could see what we see.

James honks his car horn to signal it's time to go. Cienna reaches for her black gown. Kasey is holding all three of our purses. I sling my gown over my arm, my cap tight in my hand, my tassel sways as we rush down the stairs. Behind us, the bedroom looks like a glittery tornado ripped through it.

"Watch, he's gonna be all business about the pictures and pretend he isn't secretly sentimental." Kasey jokes before the front door opens.

We laugh, but I hesitate for just a breath. I straighten the waist of my dress and smooth the bodice before stepping outside.

I haven't seen him all week. Monday he didn't text me back after I sent him a picture of my shoes. I waited until almost midnight for the response, my phone on the pillow next to me, fully charged. Just when I shut my light off and gave up, a text comes through.

Sorry. Long day. Talk tomorrow.

Tuesday we were supposed to grab a bite from the local diner. I waited by my locker for an hour before I gave in and just went home. His car was nowhere in the parking lot when I got to my car.

Wednesday, he was a no show at lunch. There was no explanation. When I passed the senior hallway, I thought I saw him talking to a few people he never mentioned before. I didn't ask. It must have been important because when he *did* finally text it was just another excuse.

Got held up. Sorry.

Thursday he canceled our regular movie night. I even wore the hoodie he gave me months ago just so it might feel familiar. His excuse that night was that he was too stressed to sit for a movie because work starts Saturday. I offered for us to do something else, but he said no.

When I got to their house this morning, he wasn't home. I resorted to leaving his hoodie on his bed. I don't leave a note or explanation – I'm just done.

Now James stands before me all smiles, but it's directed at his phone. He's in a red button up and black slacks with his black gown slung over his arm similar to mine, but he's tucked that hand into his pocket. Together, we weirdly look like Christmas. Luckily, it will be hidden under the robes.

"Let me get a few pictures," Lily and Ryan stop us all before we can get into the car. Lily holds up a camera and we all huddle together. I stand between Kasey and Cienna while James stands on the other side of Cienna. We shift through a few poses—cheesy, dramatic, one half-serious.

"Okay, okay, let them go. They're going to be late." Ryan takes the camera out of Lily's hands and shoos us off. "We'll see you guys in a bit. Now get going."

Cienna wraps her parents in a tight hug before climbing into the back of James' car. Kasey slides into the other back seat.

James hugs his mom and only nods to his dad, phone still in hand. His dad leans over and whispers something to him. James puts his phone in his pocket and steps around to the passenger side, reaching for the handle before I do.

"Hey," he says, voice softer than I expected. He opens the door for me and holds it there.

I blink, caught off guard. "Hi."

His eyes skim over me, not hurried or dismissive. For once this week, I can actually feel him taking it in – the dress, the braid – the fact that I *tried*.

"You look beautiful."

76

Even though something between us still feels like it's been left out in the cold too long, I nod, slide into the seat, and let the warmth of those words settle against the ache deep in my heart.

The ride is silent. The energy thrumming between everyone.

When we arrive at the school, Josh, Quint, and Jared are standing by Josh's truck. Cienna practically leaps from the car and into Jared's arms. He whispers something in her ear, and she rises up and kisses him.

Quint is at the door before Kasey can get out.

I swallow hard when I look at Josh. He doesn't have his robe zipped up yet, and you can see he is in simple black slacks with a dark blue button up shirt. He smiles and waves in our direction, and I sheepishly wave back.

James doesn't bother to help me out of the car, so when I climb out, I'm the last to join our group.

Let's just get through this.

Don and Rees pull in on our other side, cap and gowns ready. The reality starts sinking in.

"We ready to get this over with or what?" Don hollers. The other students around us all cheer. I glance around at our fellow classmates. A mix of excitement and nervousness runs through everyone.

"Let's do this," Jared sighs. Cienna, Kasey, and I link arms, and we go in laughing and talking.

Today is going to be a great day, and nothing is going to ruin it for me.

Chapter 10

Abbi

"Where did I put those earrings?" I ask myself aloud. I open and close every drawer in my vanity and don't see them.

Knowing me, I probably put them someplace '*safe*', which means they are only going to show up *after* the dance.

"Whatever," I huff and finish getting myself ready. The bad mood from this morning has slowly simmered into my whole day.

My hair is in loose curls, half up with gold jewel flowers woven into it. My makeup is done with rose gold eyeshadow and my go-to cat eyeliner.

Slipping on my dress, I stand in front of my full-length mirror on my closet door. I admire how the dress shimmers in the light, the fabric soft against my skin.

Checking the time, I grab the shoes I stored under my bed and step into them. They're a beautiful sage green to match my dress with a peep toe and a gold heel.

The doorbell rings to signal time to go.

I reach for my gold wristlet hiding in the top of my closet and when I transfer my license into it, I find my earrings tucked neatly inside the pouch.

Of course I did that.

I hold them in my hands admiring them. They're golden elf ear-shaped cuffs with rhinestone flowers along them. They had been Mom's.

Maybe she'll give me strength tonight.

After putting them on, I give myself one last look in the mirror before heading down to meet James.

"Wow," Dad is at the base of the stairs, camera in hand. James is right behind him.

He looks handsome in his all black suit. His chocolate brown hair is brushed back from his face and his chestnut brown eyes are bright like his smile. I reach the bottom of the stairs and Dad wraps me in a hug.

"You look just like your mother," he whispers and then lets me go. He brushes my hair away from my ear and gazes at the earrings. Tears trickle down his cheeks. I reach up and brush them away before giving him another hug.

"You do look amazing," James holds an ivory rose corsage towards me.

Again with the roses.

"You didn't have to do that."

No, you really didn't.

"I couldn't come empty handed though." He slides the band around my wrist, and I gaze down at it.

We've known each other our whole lives, and yet he still buys me roses.

Glancing over at the kitchen table, I spot the bright white peonies that are still going strong in their vase. A floral explosion that sends a pang to my chest.

"Thank you," I kiss his cheek.

Just get through tonight.

"Will you two let me take your picture now?" Dad holds up the camera. James places his left arm around my waist and I lean into him. Even with five inch heels, I wasn't as tall as him.

Once Dad felt there were enough pictures, he hugs us both and shoves us out the door.

"Your chariot awaits, Milady," James bows and extends his arm towards his car. I shake my head, forcing a small laugh. My thoughts trail back to Josh last week calling me the same thing. I bite the inside of my cheek.

"Thank you," I take his arm, and we walk around to the passenger side. He lets go of my arm and pulls me to him, his lips crushing mine. The taste of peppermint–sharp, almost bitter on my lips. I return his kiss, but when we break apart, my stomach sinks.

Please stop. You won't be looking at me like this after tonight.

"I love you," he smiles. The words are too thick on my tongue. I will not lie to him. I lean back in for one last kiss in response.

He opens my door, and I climb into my seat. His car was never extremely messy, but it looked as though he had his car detailed since this morning. There was a new smell in the car–something piney, with hints of vanilla or maybe floral.

We drive in silence to the school. His free hand holds mine. Occasionally he gives it a squeeze, and I return it while watching out the window at the lights of the town passing by.

The parking lot is already packed when we arrive, so it's hard to tell if anyone from our group has arrived yet. James opens the door and holds his hand out for me to take. As we make our way through to the gym, there's a scream from behind us.

Cienna is running towards me, Jared hurrying close behind carrying her matching gold clutch. Cienna's hair is done up like mine, but instead of flowers, she has painted gold glitter throughout her dark hair. She looks stunning with the gold all over, very ethereal.

"You look amazing," we say–almost in sync, hugging each other.

"You just told me we were going to stick together you dork," Jared comes up behind Cienna and wraps his arms around her in a tight hug. She lifts her hands to his arms and leans back, giving him a small kiss. She's persuaded Jared to wear a dusty rose pink suit with a white shirt. It's rather fitting on him.

James takes my hand, and we continue to the gym.

The party is already in full swing with music blasting from every corner of the gym. Light strands hang from one side of the gym to the other with white and red lanterns evenly distributed along each strand. Red and black tinsel curtains cover each side of the gym.

Well, no one can say they skimped on school spirit.

After finding an empty white table, Don and Rees arrive. Don is in beige suit pants, white shirt, and an identical beige vest. Rees is wearing light blue suit pants, a white shirt with rolled sleeves, and a matching blue suit coat slung over his shoulder. Rees spots us and waves, heading over to our table, Don on his heels.

"Remind me who was in charge of decoration," Rees shouts over the music.

"That would be Lisa Smith," James answers, pointing us to a tall brunette in a red strapless mermaid dress with black lace flowers along the bodice. Lisa Smith, head cheerleader, and on every committee possible.

She looks over in our direction and waves with a big toothy smile. We wave back much less enthusiastically.

The song that had been playing ends and the next song to start happens to be my favorite Usher song. I look over at James who raises his hands in defense, "I have two left feet remember." I really want to dance, but James sits down at the table and leans back in his chair perfectly content.

"Shall we dance?" Rees holds out his hand and I happily take it. I didn't come to the dance to just stare at everyone. He spins me onto the dance floor and Cienna and Jared follow. I let the music take control. It's nice to be able to just let go sometimes. I glance over at our tables and find James is no longer there. I'm too busy enjoying myself to let it affect me though.

We all dance together for several songs, laughing and having a blast dancing with everyone in our vicinity.

When it's time for a slow dance, James is still missing. Annoyance starts to build inside me.

Don't invite me to a dance if you don't intend to dance with me.

Rees managed to pair up with a cute black haired girl named Laicee. I decide to head back to our table defeated.

"Would you like to dance?" I hadn't made it three steps before Josh's voice cut through the noise. I spin around and my breath catches in my throat.

Josh is in a navy blue suit that compliments his copper hair. He has a smile that makes my stomach flutter, and my knees shake.

I take his outstretched hand, and he pulls me to him. He wraps his left hand around my back, his right hand holding mine out to the side in the standard ballroom style we learned in sixth grade.

"Where's James?" His grey eyes are focused on my face as we sway to the music. I could happily gaze into those eyes for hours, but then I remember he asked me a question.

"I have no clue," I let out a frustrated breath and begin scanning the crowd again.

"His loss," Josh shrugs and spins me around making me laugh. When he pulls me back to him again, I close the space and rest my head on his chest. As we sway, I close my eyes and enjoy the moment. Being here on the dance floor with Josh at *this* very moment has to be the best part of my night. The world seems so small right now, and I wouldn't want it any other way.

"Thank you," I say.

"What are you thanking me for?"

"For just being here," I gaze up at him and see a glisten to his eyes that makes my heart stop. I feel myself rising ever so slowly up on the balls of my feet, closing the distance between us.

Josh pulls back and clears his throat. The music is back to the upbeat pop it had been before.

What did I almost do?

The cool air hits my face, and my body relaxes a little while my mind still spins.

I almost kissed Josh.

My heart flutters again at the memory until I remember why it's a bad thing.

Not cool Abbi.

I shuffle a rock around the sidewalk that had been moved from the garden bed.

What would James do if he had seen that?

The thought of hurting him made me sick.

Snap out of it! He pulled away. He wouldn't pull away if he likes you.

I huff in frustration and a small group of girls raise their eyebrows at me as they walk into the dance.

Quit making a scene.

I take a few seconds to collect myself and head back inside.

Before going into the gym, I decided I need to freshen up a bit. I pass a classroom that has its door slightly ajar, and there are voices coming from inside. I quietly take a peek.

The couple is at the far end of the room. They are definitely in an embrace. It's dark, but thanks to the emergency light, I can just make out who they are. The girl is wearing a red mermaid dress. She's moaning, and I feel my face grow hot. I know I should turn away, but I really want to know who the guy is.

They pull apart and she drops down to her knees in front of him and starts undoing his pants. I bite back bile when I see who the guy is.

James.

Before they see me, I hurry into the bathroom further down the hall and shut myself into one of the stalls.

James is cheating on me.

I want to scream, to cry, to punch something. Instead, I stand against the door, my hands on the walls to steady myself.

He cheated.

Now everything starts to make sense – why he left me at the mall, the plans that kept falling through, his distance.

I swallow.

The vanilla.

It's her perfume.

I take a few more deep breaths, in through the nose, out through the mouth, the tears threatening to spill out.

Think Abbi. What's next?

I could make a scene.

But what good would that do? I'd be the crazy ex-girlfriend. They'd all know it's my fault. If I hadn't refused him, we wouldn't be here now.

Every thought is swirling through my head, the stall tilting slightly in the haze.

After a few more deep breaths, I exit the stall and go over to the sink where I wash my hands. I take a paper towel and some cold water and pat my face with it.

You can do this.

In the mirror, I practice smiling. I practice until I feel confident I can fake it.

There's no reason for a scene tonight. It doesn't help anyone. We leave for the camping trip tomorrow, and I can figure it out then. The space will be good. I'll be there, and he'll be here... with *her*.

Passing the classroom, the door is closed. They must have either realized it was opened, or they are back at the dance.

Weaving through the dancers, I spot James back at our table. He's talking with Josh, Kasey, and Quint who is wearing teal suit pants and matching vest which complements Kasey's silver gown.

Kasey's hair is done up in a French twist with silver star pins spread throughout. Everyone seems to match each other except me and James.

Now I can see why. Black and red match perfectly. He didn't want to match me, he wanted to match her.

I force myself not to scan the gym for her. I don't want to give anything away.

"Where did you disappear to?" James asks once I reach the table and sit next to him, avoiding both James and Josh's eyes. I'm not sure I'd be able to without shame settling deep in my chest. James slides a plastic cup of lemonade in my direction, and I gratefully swallow it in one gulp.

It is ridiculously hot.

Just needed some fresh air." My thoughts go back to what happened and I take another shaky breath. "Where did you go? I was looking for you."

"I was talking to Lisa. I wanted to get some pointers on how to handle her dad since I start tomorrow."

Truth within a lie.

"Oh," I say looking at the floor. "Okay."

"Dance with me," he takes my hand and pulls me towards the dance floor. I've been waiting all night for a dance, but now I just want to go home. The thought of his hands touching Lisa just minutes ago has me feeling nauseous.

"I thought you said you had two left feet and weren't going to dance." I try to keep my tone light and my expression neutral.

86

"I never said I wasn't going to dance." He smirks. "You deserve at least one dance from me with no complaint."

Oh, how thoughtful.

The song is slow and James places his hands on my waist which leaves me no other option than to put my hands on his shoulders. This is painfully awkward, but looking at James' face, he doesn't seem to feel the same.

I think back to dancing with Josh – how easy and safe it felt. My body tingles, and my brain is fuzzy with excitement.

I peek over James' shoulder towards our table. Rees and Josh are the only two at the table now. Rees is hunched over the table looking at something on his phone, the light shining off his face.

Josh is leaning casually back in the chair surveying the different couples.

He does look rather handsome in that suit.

He seems to be purposefully avoiding us, because not once does he look in our direction.

Why won't he look at me? Did I upset him?

When the song ends, I drop my arms and step back a little too quickly.

"Is everything alright?" James reaches towards me.

Please don't touch me.

I'm..." I pull back. "I'm just a little tired. Can you take me home?"

I don't wait for an answer. I head to our table, grab my bag, avoid the questioning looks, and step outside, wishing more than anything it was Josh following me instead of James.

87

Chapter 11

Josh

She's in the middle of the dance floor when I spot her –
not the center, but enough that the light catches her hair,
warm and gold.

She's laughing at something, her fingers laced with Kasey's
as they both spin like kids who forgot the world was watching.

And for a moment, I *do* forget the world's watching.

I freeze, something hitching in my chest.

Abbi.

She looks *free,* lighter than I've seen her in a while.

James isn't with her.

I scan the edge of the room, but there's no sign of him. Not
holding her coat, not hovering with that half-bored look he
wears when he's pretending to care.

The song is coming to an end.

I scan every inch of the gym, and he is unmistakably not there.

Why bring her to the dance if you don't plan to dance?

The music fades into something softer. The kind of song that leaves people glancing at their partners.

The crowd shifts, and pairs form.

Abbi is left standing alone in the middle of the floor. She turns to leave the dance floor, and I find my feet moving to stop her.

She deserves to dance.

"Would you like the dance?" I smile and hold out my hand.

When she turns around, the air escapes my lungs.

She is so beautiful.

Abbi takes my hand, and I pull her to me. I place my left hand around her back and hold her slender left hand in my other.

Where's James?" I'm watching her face for any sign of something being wrong. She has the most beautiful eyes. They're the kind of eyes you have to look twice to really see. Most people see them as blue, but when you look closely, they are green with only a hint of blue near the pupil, and flecks of gold spotted around the edges of her iris. In honesty, beautiful doesn't quite cover it.

A frown tugs at her mouth, a furrow to her brow. "I have no clue." She begins scanning the crowd, probably in another search for James.

How many times has she done this tonight?

I fight the anger rising in me and try to keep the conversation from taking a dark turn.

"His loss," I shrug and spin her out and around which makes her laugh. The anger and stress have left her face leaving behind a smile and glistening eyes that I could get lost in forever.

I pull her back to me and she surprises me by closing the space between us and resting her head against my chest.

My heart stumbles, just slightly. Her weight is barely there, but I feel it everywhere.

I lower my chin, letting it rest gently against the top of her head. Her hair smells faintly of lilac and whatever hairspray she used earlier.

"Thank you." I open my eyes, but don't move my head.

"What are you thanking me for?"

She raises her face up and my breath catches in my throat. Her eyes are shining. "For just being here."

It lands heavy, but not in a bad way. It's just like something meaningful slipped out before she could second-guess it, like she needed me to know that showing up wasn't nothing.

I should kiss her.

The thought lodges itself in my chest and refuses to move. I don't even realize I've stopped swaying. I'm just holding her, barely breathing, staring at the space between us like it's daring me to cross it.

She's so close now – warm and real – like every song before this one feels like background noise. My hand is at her back, the curve of her shoulder tucked beneath my palm, and all I can think about is how easy it would be to tip my head forward, just a little, and find her lips with mine.

The longing is so bad it's making my chest ache. But I don't move.

What if I'm reading it wrong. What if she's just being kind? What if this isn't what it feels like?

My head is spinning, stuck somewhere between *don't ruin this,* and *don't miss your chance.*

And then the music changes. It's like a light flipped on too bright. The moment breaks, and I step back automatically, clearing my throat.

She looks up, a little dazed, like maybe she felt something too – but I don't ask.

I'm too busy trying to catch my breath.

Chapter 12
Abbi

The car ride home is quiet. I have no desire to break the silence.

This was not how tonight was supposed to go.

When we pull up to the house, everything is routine. It's muscle memory by now. James parks, climbs out, and opens my door, just like always. However, when I step out, I can't bring myself to lean in – not tonight.

He waits for it, the kiss, the usual goodbye. I just can't force it. I step back instead, and he gets the hint.

He looks disappointed – not upset, or surprised, just a little let down. But he doesn't say anything. He doesn't ask.

He's got Lisa. He's good.

I close the door and bolt up the stairs to escape any questions or comments from Dad as to why I'm home so early. I just want to hide in my room and think.

I need to think.

Sitting in front of my vanity, I begin pulling out the flowers twisted into my hair. I can't stop replaying everything in my head.

James barely looked at me. Left me all alone. Then Josh... and now this?

I stare into the mirror and catch the frown etched across my face. I look tired, almost raw. I'm not the glowing girl who left a few hours ago.

I take a deep, slow breath and reach for my earrings. One clatters on the vanity before I can catch it. I gently place them back in their box, trying to focus on the motions – clean up, wind down, pretend everything's fine.

My brain disagrees. It races ahead, loud and insistent.

James cheated. There's no pretending otherwise. But, maybe...maybe I just keep it to myself. Don't tell anyone. Not Cienna. Not Lily. Not even Josh.

If they find out, they'll hate him. They'll hate me. I can't be the reason for their hate.

I blink hard, jaw tight. My chest feels too full and too empty at the same time. The image of Lisa and James in the classroom, as vivid as if it were happening right now.

I huff in frustration and hope a shower will calm my mind.

On my way to the bathroom, I grab my pajamas from the drawers, and catch a glimpse of my CD's. *Twilight* juts from the stack, just enough to catch my eye.

And just like that, I'm back there.

Last Sunday.

The way we laughed at the store, the purple daisies, the warmth on the couch.

A pang hits my chest. Josh pulled away at the dance. If there was something there, he wouldn't do that.

Would he?

Once the water hits my face, I'm already back to thinking about Josh. We have been friends our *entire* lives. He is always one of the first people I tell anything to. When I started dating James though, Josh and I seemed to grow a little distant. We stopped spending so much time together. I was uncomfortable talking about his best friend in a romantic way. In what world would you want to hear mushy details about your best friend from the person they're dating? I know I wouldn't. I'd *never* ask Jared to talk about Cienna like that. It would make me so painfully uncomfortable.

I close my eyes and picture Josh in my mind. I picture his face, and how flawlessly sculpted it is. The curve of his cheekbones, and the shape of his grey eyes. The way his eyes would change from grey to green to sometimes blue made my heart pound in my ears. I imagine how his dark copper hair falls into his eyes and how he would run his fingers through his hair to pull it from his face. I picture his perfectly sculpted jaw and his broad shoulders.

I shut off the water and jump out of the shower, drying off with my towel to stop myself from imagining any more.

What's the point if he doesn't feel the same?

Chapter 13

Abbi

By the time we pull off the gravel road and into the clearing, the sun's high and unforgiving. Shoes hit the dirt and the chorus starts.

"I'm starving." Cienna whines.

"I found a protein bar." Don holds up a dark blue bar – probably blueberry.
He starts unwrapping it, but Cienna grabs his wrist. "Hand it over and no one gets hurt."

"How about I make some sandwiches," Kasey laughs. She tosses her duffel onto a shaded rock and heads straight for the cooler. Quint's not far behind, already rolling up his sleeves like it's a full-contact sport.

The rest of us split off without needing to be told. It's the same patch of pine and packed soil we've been setting up camp on since elementary school. Luckily, the muscle memory does the heavy lifting.

Dad and Alec have staked their claim at the far edge, tucked behind a row of trees. Just far enough to escape our usual first night chaos.

The girls' tent sits nearest the water. To the left, Don, Rees, and Quint are still arguing over who gets the sleeping spot furthest from the zipper. Someone's already tossed a sock into the bushes in protest.

Josh and Jared's tent is on the right, just past the firewood pile, a little quieter, a little less crowded.

I'm grateful James didn't request a later start date. I need a break after last night. I spent the night tossing and turning, thinking about what I needed to do.

When we get back, I'm calling it quits.

If *I* do it, he won't be seen as the bad guy. I'll just take the questions and answer, '*we want different things for the future.*'

The certainty of it makes my chest feel tight and weirdly clear at the same time.

"Who wants fishing duty?" Dad asks after the trash has been thrown in a bag in the back of Alec's truck. Rees, Kasey, Quint, and Alec raise their hands. That means the rest of us are on kindling duty.

While wandering through the trees, I listen to the way the wind makes the leaves dance. I breathe in the smell of pine and quaking aspen.

This is true peace.

I find my favorite boulder cool under the shade of the trees. Sitting down, I close my eyes and take in the sounds and smells nature has created around me. I let my worries slip away. I just focus on being here and now.

"Can I join you?" My eyes pop open and Josh is standing in front of me, a small bundle of branches in his arms. He's wearing a grey flannel button-up over a black T-shirt even though it's seventy three degrees outside. I'm wearing a pair of capris and a faded blue tee. Sweat pools beneath my arms, trickling down my back. I nod, closing my eyes again.

I hear the crunch of branches as he drops the bundle beside us, and I feel his warmth as he sits next to me on the boulder.

There are those butterflies again.

"You're insane," I tell him, trying to distract my mind from how close we are.

"Why?"

"How are you not roasting right now?"

Josh laughs and I peek over at him. His eyes are closed, just as mine had been, but I'm now hypnotized by the curve of his mouth, the way the left side is slightly higher than the right.

"You forget your body temperature is always hotter than mine."

I roll my eyes. He's not wrong. Anything above sixty and I feel like I'm in a sauna.

"Yeah, I keep forgetting you're one of the lizard people," I joke, enjoying the way his smile widens. My heart thuds in a double beat.

"Careful, you never know if one of them is listening, ready to snatch you away," he teases, giving me a playful shove. His eyes never open.

The thought slips in–quiet and uninvited–before I can stop it.

What if I just lean in and kiss him right now?

My stomach twists.

It wouldn't be that different from what James did to me.

A choice, a moment, letting someone else fill a space that doesn't belong to them.

Only... It doesn't feel *wrong*. It feels simple and safe, like I wouldn't have to question if I was enough.

I blink hard and shift my gaze towards the trees.

I feel guilty, but I don't regret it.

After a while of sitting with our eyes closed, just enjoying the peace, Josh breaks the silence. "I'm sorry James couldn't make it this weekend." A twinge hits my heart. Not because of James, but because Josh thought I missed him.

If only you knew.

"Don't be," I say quietly. Josh places his hand on mine and says nothing. The heat rises in my face, and I'm grateful his eyes are closed. I like the way his hand feels in mine. It feels warm, safe, and utterly perfect.

"There you two are," Cienna huffs, breaking the silence. We pull our hands apart, shifting to the furthest edges of the rock. Cienna is carrying a large pile of kindling, some of the twigs tugging on her sweater as she struggles to carry it all. "Rees caught enough fish for dinner, and John's already cooking."

"John's cooking? We better hurry back then before it's all gone."

Josh stands and offers me a hand. Cienna's lips are pursed, her eyes darting between me and Josh.

I shake my head.

"You guys go ahead. I'm not hungry."

"Here," Cienna thrusts the sticks into Josh's arms and brushes leaves and dirt from her sleeves before disappearing towards camp without another word.

Josh shrugs and follows her through the trees, leaving me alone to my thoughts.

***

Cienna and Kasey are both out the moment their heads hit their pillows. Cienna's breathing is soft and steady. Kasey's curled deep into her sleeping bag, dead to the world.

I lay in the tent, staring up in the dark. My mind's a mess, caught between what I want to believe and what I'm terrified is all my imagination.

Josh.

The way he sat next to me earlier, like it meant something. Like *I* meant something. But... *what if I'm wrong?*

Realizing sleep isn't in the cards for me, I slip on my shoes, grab a blanket, and climb out of the tent. Dad and Alec have been out for hours now. From the sound of it, the guys all zonked as fast as the girls. I can hear snoring from the tent to my left, but to the right is complete silence.

I quietly zip up the tent, listening for any change from the others. My sneakers crunch softly on the gravel as I tip toe over to the makeshift log bench.

The feeling of Josh's hand on mine. The way he looked at me at the dance. The warmth of his arms around me last Sunday. It felt peaceful. It felt like home.

The moon is full and high, making the dark water shine. A small breeze causes the water to ripple, the light almost blinking like the starlight above. This was one of my favorite parts of camping.

"You're still up," I jump as Josh comes around the bench. He'd been so quiet.

"So are you," my heart beats faster.

"Couldn't sleep." He sits next to me, and we watch the water as the lake glimmers, soft and silver. After a while he scoots closer and asks, "Why are you still up?"

When I look over, he's in a grey t shirt and black and grey plaid pajama bottoms. "Aren't you cold?" I ask to avoid answering his question. He chuckles softly.

"First it's too hot, now it's too cold." He shakes his head, smiling. "You are a fascinating creature, Abbigail Thompson." I shiver, but it's not the cold affecting me now.

I open my oversized blue blanket, and he slides close. The warmth of him hits instantly. His shoulder brushes mine, then his thigh. Now he's everywhere. The blanket envelopes us, a shield from the cold.

"You never answered my question."

"I couldn't sleep either," I finally say after trying to find an excuse but coming up empty.

"Want to talk about it?"

I know James is your best friend and all, but I saw him having sex last night with Lisa. That isn't even the worst part. The worst part is that I like you, and all I can seem to focus on is how badly I want to kiss you.

"Do you?" I say keeping my voice even.

"Touche," he smirks. I rest my head on his shoulder, and his gently lowers on top of mine. We gaze around in the dark.

The bench creaks softly beneath us every so often, like it's trying to breathe with the wind. Somewhere in the vast trees, a fire crackles faintly. A pop and hiss now and then. Someone laughs distantly, echoing all around. A zipper zings shut. Then nothing.

It's quiet in that perfect way nature sometimes is. We don't speak. We don't need to. My eyes start to droop, and I yawn involuntarily.

What time is it?

As if reading my mind, Josh pulls out his phone. When his screen lights up, I focus on his background. It's a picture Mom had taken from the last camping trip we had before the accident.

We are all in our swimsuits, goosebumps and sunburns in progress, standing at the edge of the water. Mom shouts, "Say cheese!" And, naturally, we shouted every cheese we could think of.

"Cheddar!"

"Brie!"

STRING CHEESE!" Kasey screams, practically elbowing Jared in the ribs with her excitement. We were all a mess of limbs and laughter.

Mom rolls her eyes, like she always did when we push a bit too far, but the smile was real. She snaps the picture and says, "Okay, go be psycho."

Everyone screams and runs into the water, but I hang back.

I want to see the photo. So I trailed after her. She handed the camera to Dad and Alec.

When she hands me the camera she leans into both dads and whispers not too quietly, "Look at Josh and Abbi. Aren't they just so cute together?"

Now, sitting beside him under the stars, wrapped in the same blanket, the memory feels heavier. Maybe she saw something before either of us knew how to look for it.

Maybe she was right.

"It's two in the morning, we should probably try to get some sleep." Josh unfolds himself from the blanket, stands up, and holds his hand out to me, just as he had done earlier. This time I take it.

My hand tingles from the contact and I don't want to let go. We hold hands until we reach the tents. When he drops his hand from mine, the empty feeling is detestable.

He wraps his arms around me in a tight hug and then disappears into his tent, leaving me standing there staring at the closed tent flap.

Reluctantly, I slip back into my own tent. Somehow, I manage to fall fast asleep.

***

"Good morning sunshine," Dad announces when I stumble out of my tent groggy. The others are already dressed and ready to go. Most of them are at the picnic table eating the last bit of their breakfast. I spot Josh over by the trucks. He's busying himself with packing the backpack for our hike.

Dad gets up from the table and walks over with a steaming thermos. "Rough night?" I nod and take a small sip. Apple cider, yum. "Do you want to talk about it?"

"Maybe later," I take another sip, and he escorts me over to the picnic table, my feet still heavy with sleep. I sit between Don and Jared. Kasey slides a bowl of oatmeal with berries in front of me. I'm really not hungry, but I force it down and finish readying myself for the hike.

When we set off, the group naturally splits into pairs, like always.

Alec leads the charge with a dramatic stretch and a grin over his shoulder. "Alright nature nerds. Let's go find a bear to *not* pet."

Josh snorts. "You first."

He and Quint fall in behind him, mock arguing about whose backpack has better snack-ration logic, even though Josh packed them himself.

Kasey and Rees trail after them, already halfway through a debate about whether trail mix should include raisins.

"It's filler," Kasey insists.

"It's tradition," Rees fires back.

Don and Jared follow, deep in a conversation involving conspiracy theories and squirrel hierarchies, while Cienna and I bring up the rear. Dad follows behind like he's herding us all with invisible cattle prods.

The hike winds along the edge of the lake. It's more of a scenic stroll than a real trek, but once we get to the far side, the trail dips and climbs like it couldn't make up its mind.

"Your face is doing that thing again," Cienna says, side-eyeing me as she adjusts her baseball cap.

I frown. "What thing?"

"You know. Staring off into the distance like you're narrating a sad music video."

I roll my eyes. "I'm fine."

"Mmhmm." She doesn't press, just flashes a grin and jogs a few steps ahead, calling over to Jared. "Hey, Jare, did you remember to bring my water bottle or should I start blaming dehydration on you?"

He turns and raises his hands innocently. "If you must know, it's in your side pocket – but isn't that supposed to be *your* responsibility?"

"Not when I have you to take care of me." She loops her fingers through his and he kisses her forehead.

"Penny for your thoughts?" Dad matches my pace.

I let the silence sit a beat longer before answering. "I'm just tired."

He nods, like he's heard that a hundred times before, but isn't going to call me on it. "You don't have to talk about anything you don't want to."

"I know," My eyes are fixed on the trail ahead.

"Just… make sure you're not trying to carry something alone that you don't have to." His voice is gentle.

I bite the inside of my cheek. "I'm fine, Dad."

He doesn't respond right away. He just walks with me a little longer. "Alright. Then let me just walk with you. In case *fine* gets heavy."

That part gets me – much more than I want it to.

"Why is love so hard?" I whisper without meaning to. I clench my fists, allowing my nails to dig into my palm, and I pray he didn't hear me. The silence drags, but before I release my fists, Dad speaks up.

"Love should be easy."

"There is absolutely nothing simple about this," I groan.

"Does this involve a certain red head from next door?"

Ooh, you just love that don't you.

I squint over at him. "Maybe."

"I still stand by what I said."

He hums, smug like he's already won the conversation. "Just sayin', I've seen the way he looks at you."

I glance down at my boots, kicking a rock off the trail. "Maybe he's just nice."

Dad snorts. "Sweetheart, plenty of people are *nice*. That boy would walk through a thunderstorm carrying a metal umbrella if it meant the chance of sitting next to you someday."

I can't help it. My mouth twitches into a tiny, reluctant smile. "That's dramatic, even for you."

He chuckles, pointing between us. "Apple. Tree."

We keep walking, our steps crunching quietly over the trail. The trees open just enough to let a shaft of light spill over the path, warming my arms.

"So what's the complicated part?" He asks, more gently now.

My eyes drift up the trail to where Cienna's walking beside Jared. Her braid bouncing lightly with each step. She's laughing at something he said, elbowing him in the ribs like she's done a hundred times to me.

I watch her a beat too long.

Because *that's* part of it, too.

What if she hates me for walking away from James? What if I lose her, too?

"I think I'm just...scared," I finally say, eyes still on Cienna.

Dad doesn't rush me. He just gives a small humph of agreement beside me.

"It's not just about one person," I murmur. "It's all the people connected to it."

"Hearts don't break clean, do they?"

I shake my head. "Not even close."

Chapter 14
Abbi

The fire snaps and hisses, throwing sparks into the night like it's trying to set the stars on fire.

I sit next to Josh, close enough that our knees brush whenever one of us shifts. He's warm, solid, and pretending not to notice. Or maybe he *is* noticing and pretending not to care. I'm not sure which is worse.

I can feel their gazes across the circle.

Kasey's grin is all teeth and barely-contained glee. Her eyebrows wiggle the second our eyes meet. I glare, but it's useless. She just bites her lip to keep from laughing and turns her attention to the marshmallows.

"Here," Josh grabs another marshmallow from the bag and hands it to me.

"Thanks," I place it on the end of my roasting stick and lower it into the fire. I'm mesmerized by the way the flames dance around the marshmallow. The once white outside turning slowly to a golden brown gooey delight. Once it begins to darken and bubble I pull it out and squash it between the graham crackers and chocolate.

Looking up, Josh has some marshmallow dangling from his chin. I reach over with a laugh and wipe it away. "All better," I say turning back to my own s'more.

Cienna is quiet. Her arms are wrapped around her knees. Her face is half-lit by the firelight. She doesn't say anything, but I can feel the worry in her eyes. I shiver, the guilt rising.

Josh leans towards me, nudging gently with his shoulder. "You cold?"

"No," I lie, no longer wanting my s'more. I toss the plate and its contents into the fire, watching as it disappears into ash.

Don and Rees are the first to leave the fire. They value their sleep more than the rest of us.

Quint strolls over to Kasey and kisses her before disappearing into the tent after them.

Jared is next to leave, but not before pulling Cienna aside, whispering by the trucks.

Pretty soon it's just Josh, Alec, and me. Once Alec is sure the fire is out, he scans the campsite for any missed trash before retiring for the night.

A minute ago, I thought I might head to bed too. Sitting here though, with nothing but the stars, plans change.

I glance towards the tree line, then across the clearing. Dad's old red Chevy stands out like an invitation.

Perfect.

I reach into my tent and grab my blankets, sleeping bag, and pillow before climbing into the bed of the truck and laying everything out.

I get comfy and cozy under my pile of blankets, grateful I packed my fuzzy purple hoodie for just an occasion as this.

I find the Big Dipper and begin tracing different patterns like a crazy connect-the-dots. Looking up at the dark sky when there were clouds in the way was terrifying sometimes. It made me feel like I was in a black nothing. When the stars were visible, I felt like I could dance around them.

"Is this seat taken?" Josh asks startling me. He's holding several of his own blankets. Including the one blanket I never expected to leave his room.

My furry green blanket – the one that lives permanently draped over the back of his desk chair, even though we both know it's mine the second I sit on his bed and pretend I'm just there to study.

I shake my head and bite the inside of my cheek. He spreads it across both of us like it's nothing, like we do this all the time. Maybe we do.

Tonight though, it feels different.

I hold it close and when I take a breath, Josh's scent of cypress and leather drenches my thoughts.

We lie together pointing out different shapes – the occasional bunny or dragon popping up. It's not the real constellations, but if I had to pick my favorite part of this trip, it would be this.

Does tomorrow have to come?

I glance over at Josh, and in the moonlight his eyes are the exact shade I love – soft storm clouds, quiet and familiar. His face is relaxed, peaceful in a way that makes my chest ache.

The yearning catches me off guard. I want him to kiss me. Gosh. I *wish* he would kiss me.

I wish we could do this every night, just us.

He turns his head then and catches me looking, and smiles.

My whole body exhales. I didn't realize how tense I was until that moment. It's like my bones melt a little. I scoot closer, nestling into his side without thinking, letting my eyes drift shut.

He runs a hand gently through my hair, fingers slow and steady. I shiver.

Without a word, he tugs the green blanket tighter around me.

"Josh?" I whisper. I don't even know what to say.

"Hmm?" he murmurs, still gazing up at the sky.

I turn my head, wanting to see his face. But the words get caught somewhere between my heart and my throat. He glances at me when I don't answer, waiting patiently.

I bite the inside of my cheek.

Should I tell him?

"Thanks," I say finally, because it's the only thing that makes it out.

He smiles again, small and warm, then turns his eyes back to the stars.

I press in closer and close my eyes, grateful for the cold and the dark. It hides the flush blooming across my cheeks.

Nice going, Abbi.

***

I wake up to birds chirping their songs and Josh's arms wrapped around me with me curled up against him, my head on his chest. His breathing deep and even.

Oh no!

I sit up fast, my heart fluttering as I realize what happened. Sure, we only fell asleep... but we'd *never* hear the end of it.

Luckily, the sun hasn't fully risen yet, which means no one else is up yet.

Looking down at Josh, a knot forms in my stomach. He's so peaceful, his features soft and gentle.

I have no choice. Please forgive me.

"Josh," I shake him. When his eyes open, he too shoots up and begins scanning our surroundings. The chairs around the campfire pit are empty, and the pit itself is dark and cold. No movement is obvious from any of the tents, including our dads'.

"Crap, did we fall asleep?" I loved the way his hair looked after sleep. It's a mess of dark copper waves that stands in different directions. He rubs his eyes and stretches.

"We better be quick before anyone wakes up," I say gathering my blankets. Once we have everything rolled together into two giant balls, we quietly hurry back over to our tents, the gravel desperately trying to give us away with each careful step.

As silently as possible, we move the zippers an inch or two at a time, praying everyone stays asleep. Just as we duck into our tents, I hear the unmistakable sound of Dad's phone letting him know it's time to get up.

Chapter 15

Abbi

"Here, let *me* grab that tote," Josh reaches out and pulls the tote with the camping cookware from the bed of Dad's truck.

I step back, brushing a few pine needles off my hoodie. The driveway is full of movement. Car doors slamming, voices calling out, the clatter of coolers and sleeping bags being dragged across concrete. It's good to be home.

However, my stomach is already churning. I know what I have to do, and I don't like it.

"Thanks," I murmur, watching him hoist the tote over his head like nothing. My lips curl into a slight smile remembering the image of me with Josh's arms.

"Look who's here," Josh nods towards the street.

I follow his gaze, and my heart sinks. "Oh, no." The words escape before I can stop them.

"What's wrong?" Josh's tone instantly shifts. He sets the tote on the tailgate, his hand finds my arm, a small tingle of warmth growing from the contact.

"Nothing." I swallow hard, trying to smooth the panic from my voice. He doesn't say anything, but I feel his hesitation. His fingers linger just a second longer before he lets them fall.

"It's fine," I add, forcing a smile. "Really."

He doesn't push, but it's obvious he doesn't buy it either. I can see it in the way his eyes narrow.

I look back towards the street. James is leaning against his car, like he's been there a while, arms crossed, sunglasses pushed up into his hair. He's not smiling, or waving. He's just watching, like he's waiting.

Josh shifts beside me again...aware.

"Want me to take this inside?" he asks, voice low.

"Yeah. Thanks."

He heads towards the garage, and I stand there for a second too long, the weight of James' stare pressing against my skin like a sunburn.

I'm not ready for this – not even close.

With one last shaky breath, I move my feet. Each step feels heavier than it should.

James sees me coming and lights up. Like everything is perfect.

"Hey," he says, and before I can brace myself, he wraps his arms around me, tight and familiar. It's almost like he really *did* miss me.

I stand stiff in his embrace, my arms caught awkwardly between us. He doesn't seem to notice. He presses a kiss to the side of my head and exhales like this is the best part of his day.

It could just be my imagination, but I could swear there's that faint smell of vanilla again.

"Come on," I say softly, pulling back. "Let's talk."

He blinks in surprise, but nods. I lead him across the street towards the park. There are benches at the entrance, so I sit down on one, not wanting to go too far from the house. He hesitates but eventually sits down next to me.

"So," he nudges my knee. "What's up?"

I stare at the ground for a second, then look up at him. "Where do you see us?"

He tilts his head. "What do you mean?"

"I mean... in the future. Where do you see this going?"

He laughs, like it's a silly question. "I don't know. College, maybe? You and me... figuring it out together. I mean, we're good, right?"

I nod slowly. "That's what I thought."

He smiles again, easy and sure.

"I don't see us going anywhere anymore," my voice is barely above a whisper.

His smile falters. "What?"

"I've been trying to," I continue, forcing out the words before I can lose my nerve. "But I don't think anything's going to change how I feel. I don't want to keep pretending."

He stares at me, stunned. "Abbi-"

"I'm sorry," I say, and I mean it. "It's just- "

"I love you Abbi, please don't do this. Give me one more shot. I promise to try harder and be better." I'm not buying it.

"I'm sorry." I stand up and walk away. I don't look back, but I can hear him. His footsteps thud against the concrete. Each step sounds too loud, like he's chasing something that's already gone. But that's his fault. Not mine.

"Abbi-wait. You're not even giving me a chance to-"

"James, don't," I say, not turning around.

113

"Don't what? Ask why my girlfriend just blindsided me?"

I keep walking, but faster now. I just need to get inside. All I want is space and quiet.

"Abbi!" he calls again, louder this time.

Then Josh is there.

He steps in without hesitation, intercepting James like he's been watching the whole time. His voice is calm, but there's steel under it. "She said stop." I turn, feeling steadier now that I'm around the others.

James pulls up short, eyes narrowing. "This doesn't concern you."

Josh doesn't flinch. "It does now."

James laughs, but there's no humor in it. "Of course. Of *course* you'd be right there. You've always been right there, haven't you?"

"James," I warn, my voice sharp.

But he's already stepping forward. "What? You didn't think I'd notice? The way you look at her? The way she looks at you?"

Josh's jaw tightens, but he doesn't rise to it. "This isn't about me."

"No," I say, stepping between them. "It's about me. And I'm done."

James looks like I've slapped him. "So that's it?"

"Yes. That's it."

Why is this getting so ugly?

He stares at me for a long second, then shakes his head and backs away, muttering something under his breath I don't catch.

But Josh does.

His whole body tenses beside me, like a wire pulled too tight. "What did you just say?" His voice is low and dangerous.

James smirks. "You heard me."

114

Before I can ask what's wrong, he's already moving.

"Josh, wait..."

But it's too late.

His fist slams into James' face with a sickening crack. James stumbles back, stunned, but recovers fast and lunges forward, shoving Josh hard.

"Hey!" Alec's voice cuts through the air. "Knock it off!"

Everything explodes at once - Kasey drops the sleeping bags, Rees and Jared rush forward, and Dad's voice booms from the garage, *"Enough!"*

He goes unheard by Josh and James.

James swings again, wild and reckless. I step between them without thinking. His fist connects with my face, just above my eye. White hot pain radiates through my face. I stumble back, gasping, my hand flying to my brow.

"Abbi!" Josh's voice is raw. He's at my side in an instant, catching me before I fall. "Are you okay?"

"I'm fine," I whisper, even though my eyes are watering and I can feel the warmth of the blood trickling down my fingers and face, around my eye throbbing.

Cienna is there in a heartbeat, her voice tight with panic. "Let me see... Abbi, let me see."

"She got in the way," James snaps, defensive. "It was an accident."

"You hit her," Josh growls, stepping forward again.

But Alec and Don are already between them, holding Josh back.

"Back off, man," Don says firmly. "You're not helping."

"Everyone just – *stop!*" Dad's voice cuts through the chaos like a blade. "This. Ends. Now."

James glares at all of us, then turns and storms off down the street, muttering something I still can't hear.

Josh watches him go, fists still clenched, chest heaving.

Dad crosses the driveway in long purposeful strides, his eyes scanning me. First my face, my posture, then the way Josh hovers in front of me like a shield. His jaw tightens when he sees the red leaking through my fingers and down my arm and face.

"It's honestly not that bad. Face injuries just bleed more. It's a fact." I try to comfort everyone with that little fact I learned in biology, but it lands on worried stares that don't go away.

"You alright, kiddo?" Dad's voice is low but firm.

I'm still shaky, but I reply, "Yeah, I'm okay."

He doesn't press. Instead he just kneels beside me, his hand hovering near my shoulder.

"I saw what happened," he says, glancing towards the street where James disappeared. "You shouldn't have had to step in like that."

"I thought I could stop it," I whisper.

He exhales through his nose, steadying himself. "You shouldn't have had to."

Dad turns to Josh next who's still tense, fists half-curled. "You good?"

Josh nods. "Yeah, I'm sorry. I didn't mean for it to get that far."

Dad studies him for a long moment, then gives a short nod. "I know. But next time, you walk away. You hear me?"

"Yes, sir."

Then Dad turns to the rest of the group. "Give her some space." His tone isn't unkind, but it carries enough weight that everyone starts to back off.

Everyone, except Cienna.

She stays beside me, quiet and unsure, until Dad gives her a small nod too. Permission to stay, maybe.

He finally looks back at me. "You want to come inside?"

I glance at Josh, then Cienna. "In a minute."

He stands. "I'll be right inside if you need me." His gaze falls to Josh. "Let's go."

Josh looks at me, waiting. I faintly smile in response, and he follows Dad into the house.

Cienna's arm hovers like she wants to comfort me, but it never quite lands. I can tell she's trying to figure out where she fits in this moment.

Rees hands Cienna a bottle of water and the first aid kit from the camping supplies.

I glance at her, and for the first time, she won't meet my eyes.

"I didn't know he'd…" she starts, then trails off. Her voice is small. "I didn't think he'd ever –"

"You don't have to explain for him," I say quietly, still pressing my hand to my brow. "I'm the one that stepped in the middle. It's really my fault."

Cienna turns to me, her brows pulling together. "Abbi, no. That's not –"

"I thought I could stop it," I say, my voice cracking some more. "I thought if I just got in the middle, they'd stop," I sigh," but I made it worse."

She shakes her head, eyes shining. "You were trying to protect them. That's not on you." She pours some of the water on a square of gauze and removes my hand.

The guilt still sits heavy in my chest. "You're his sister. I didn't want this to happen. I didn't want to hurt you."

Cienna dabs at my face, the contact with the actual cut stings, but I refuse to flinch. "You didn't hurt me." She points in the direction James left. "He did."

"You aren't mad?"

"At you?" She shakes her head, prepping a bandage. "No. At him?" She gestures towards the house, and I know she's referring to Josh. "Yes. At James? Definitely."

Cienna goes quiet while she closes everything up. Then she exhales, slow and deliberate.

"I really thought you and James were endgame," she says softly. "Like... forever."

I pause, then shake my head. "I didn't."

She looks up, surprised.

"I wanted to. I tried to. But deep down... I think I always knew we weren't."

Cienna's brow furrows. "Why didn't you say anything?"

"Because he's your brother," I say. "And I didn't want to disappoint you. Or make things weird. Or admit that something that looked so perfect from the outside didn't feel right on the inside."

She's quiet again, and for a second I wonder if I've said too much.

But then she nods slowly. "Okay. That makes sense."

She looks down at her hands, then back up to me. "It's still going to take me a minute to get used to the idea of you and Josh. I mean, I've spent months picturing the future with the two of you..."

I laugh softly. "You really went all in, huh?"

She grins. "I had a whole Pinterest board."

I groan. "Please delete it."

She nudges me with her shoulder. "Eventually."

Then her voice softens. "But you have my blessing... for what it's worth."

I blink, surprised by the sudden warmth in my chest. "It's worth a lot."

She leans her head against my shoulder. "Just... don't make out in front of me for a while, okay?"

"Deal."

Chapter 16

Josh

The adrenaline's wearing off, and now everything hurts.

My knuckles sting, my chest is tight, and my head is still spinning from the look on Abbi's face when James' fist connected.

She said she was fine – but I'm not.

I'm standing in the driveway, staring at the spot on the grass where she sits.

"I'll be right inside if you need me." John turns to me. "Let's go."

I look at Abbi, unsure if I should leave her, but knowing I need to listen to John.

The house is quieter than it should be. Everyone's still outside. I follow him through the kitchen, past the half-unpacked coolers and the smell of pine still clinging to our clothes, and into the den.

I brace myself.

He doesn't yell, he doesn't pace – he just stands there for a second, arms crossed, like he's figuring out how to say what he needs to without losing his temper.

"You hit him."

I nod. "Yes, sir."

"You started it?"

"He said something about her," I say, my jaw tight. "Something he shouldn't have."

"What did he say?" Just thinking the words makes me feel sick.

"He called Abbi a whore."

John flinches but continues to study me. "And you thought hitting him would fix that?"

"No," I admit. "I didn't think – I just... reacted."

He tilts his head, his eyes watching me intently. "That's what I figured."

I wait for the lecture, the disappointment, for the part where he tells me I'm not good enough for her.

Instead, he walks over to a photo of Abbi resting on his work desk against the railing connecting the den to the kitchen.

"She's strong," he says. "Always has been. But that doesn't mean she doesn't need protecting."

"I know."

He turns back to me. "If you care about her the way I think you do, then you don't get to lose control like that – not around her, and not because of her."

I swallow hard. "I wasn't trying to-"

"I know you weren't," he cuts in. "But you still scared her."

That hits harder than any punch I threw.

"I'd *never* hurt her," I say, voice low.

"I believe you," he says, "but I need you to hear this anyway."

121

He steps closer, and his voice drops into something quieter, something heavier – not threatening, just truth.

"If you're going to be in her life – I mean really in it, you don't get to be reckless with her. Not with her time. Not with her trust. Not with her heart."

I nod, throat tight. "I understand."

He watches me for a long moment, then finally exhales. "Good."

"She's been through enough." He says this part softer. He picks up a picture of Naomi now, his thumb running along the frame.

"I know," I say. "I just... I want to be what she needs."

"Then be steady," he says. "Be the one who doesn't make her flinch."

I nod again, and this time, I mean it with everything in me.

He claps a hand on my shoulder, "Go check on her. But give her a minute first."

John leaves me alone in the den.

I try to breathe through the weight of everything he just said. He isn't wrong – not about any of it.

I'd do anything to protect her.

But I didn't protect her. I let it get out of control. I let James get under my skin, and she got caught in the middle.

Footsteps jerk me from my thoughts. Dad stands at the base of the steps, leaning against the wall.

He crosses his arms. "You want to tell me what happened out there?"

I sigh and sink onto the edge of the couch. "He said something – something about Abbi. I just... I lost it."

"I figure it was something like that." He doesn't yell. He doesn't even sound angry. He just sounds tired, like he's seen this coming for a while.

"You know," he says. "I've seen you mad before. I've seen you frustrated." He sighs. "I've never seen you *snap* like that."

I stare at the floor. "I didn't mean to. I just... I saw her face. The way she looked when she came back from talking to him. Then he opened his mouth, and I just-"

"Reacted," Dad finishes.

"Yeah."

He walks over and sits on the ottoman across from me. "You've got a good heart, Josh. You always have. But a good heart doesn't mean much if you can't keep your hands – and emotions – steady when it counts.

I nod, my jaw tight.

"I'm not saying he didn't deserve it," he adds. "Honestly I probably would've hit him too if I were your age."

That gets a small, bitter laugh out of me.

"You're not just some guy in a fight, though," he continues. "You're someone she trusts – someone she might lean on. That means you don't get to lose it. Not when she's watching. Not when she's in the middle of it."

"I know," I say. "I know I messed up."

He leans forward, elbows on his knees. "You didn't mess up by caring. You messed up by letting him decide how you showed it."

His words drop like a weight.

I nod again, slower this time.

"I'm proud of you," he says. "Not for the punch – for the fact that you're sitting here owning it."

I look up at him. "I just want to be someone she can count on."

"Then start now," he says. "Be calm, be patient, and let her come to you."

"You've got this." He stands and claps a hand on my shoulder, the same way John had. "Make sure you don't forget who you are when it gets hard."

I nod, and this time, I feel it settle in my chest. "Thanks, Dad."

He gives me a small smile. "Go check on her – but like John said, don't crowd her."

"I won't."

Not again.

Chapter 17

Abbi

The swing creaks under me as I shift, pressing the ice pack a little tighter to my face. It's already gone a little numb, but the ache is still there.

Dad handed it to me without a word. He just gave me the kind of look that says everything and nothing all at once.

Everyone else is gone now. The driveway's empty. The house is quiet. Cienna drove James' car home. It's lucky he left the keys in the ignition.

I can finally exhale.

The door opens next to me.

"Hey, stranger," Josh says, his voice soft and a little unsure.

I glance over. He's standing in the doorway, his hands in his pockets.

I manage a small smile, the pain around my eye dull and pulsing.

"You okay?" he asks.

I sigh. "Yeah. Just... tired."

He half-smiles – like he gets it. Maybe he's tired in the same way.

I pat the empty spot beside me. He sits gingerly, like even gravity might hurt me.

I'm not porcelain, but I'm not sure I won't break.

"I'm so sorry." He looks up at me. Something raw in his eyes.

"You were trying to protect me." I reach over and take his hand squeezing it in comfort.

We sit in the kind of silence that feels like it's holding its breath.

When I lower the ice pack I glance at him. His eyes widen, just for a moment, before he resets his features. "You should see the other guy," I joke.

He huffs a laugh, and it's the first real sound of relief I've heard all day.

My heart flutters.

There's a new sensation thrumming through my body. It's like static under my skin. I don't know if it's adrenaline, or something else entirely, but it's warm and alive and terrifying in the best way.

Josh swallows. His touch is gentle, like he's asking permission even as he holds it. His thumb brushes over my knuckles, slow and steady.

"I'm not imagining things, am I?" he asks, his voice low.

I shake my head, barely breathing. "I hope not."

His eyes search mine for a beat longer, then he reaches up, slow and careful, tucking a strand of hair behind my ear.

The porch is quiet. The world feels smaller. Like when we danced.

Instead of pulling his hand back, he cups my face and leans in pressing his forehead to mine. His breath is warm and sweet. The pain around my eye causes a wince, and he pulls back, but only slightly.

"I've wanted this for so long," I breathe. The electricity amplifies. I lean in, our lips almost brushing.

"Me too." He presses his lips gently to mine. The electricity surges to our lips and I melt into him. He moves his hand to the back of my head and wraps his fingers in my hair. My hands reach up and hold his shirt, pulling him closer. The ice pack is forgotten on the ground beside us.

***

"So what does this mean?" I ask.

We're cuddled up on my bed, music playing softly from the radio in the corner of my room.

"What do you mean?" Josh asks, stroking my arm.

"What are we?" I'm a bit embarrassed to ask. I sit up so that I can see him clearly.

"I don't think that's just up to me," he muses. "I don't go around kissing just anyone." My face grows hot, and he laughs.

I don't know what else to say. Each time my mouth opens, the words get jumbled.

"Come here," he says with a laugh. I lay back down, my head resting on his chest. He continues to stroke my arm. The steady rhythm of his heart is mesmerizing.

"Knock, knock." We both look over at my bedroom door. Dad is standing there amused. We both sit bolt upright. "Are you guys hungry? I was going to order some Chinese."

"Sounds great." I fight the shaking from my voice. I don't know why I'm so nervous. Cuddling isn't a crime.

"Can I talk to you for a sec, Josh?" He doesn't wait for Josh to answer before walking away. Josh steals one more kiss before climbing off the bed and following Dad out of the room.

I pick up my phone and text Cienna and Kasey a smiley face emoji with hearts.

I slip my phone back onto the nightstand and swing my legs over the edge of the bed. My face still aches a little, but the ice helped.

So did Josh.

The house is quiet as I make my way downstairs. It's the kind of quiet that feels earned.

When I reach the kitchen, I pause in the opening. Josh is sitting on one of the bar stools, elbows on the counter, head tilted slightly like he's listening to something. He looks up when he hears me, and the corner of his mouth lifts. Just a little. Just for me.

Dad's leaning against the counter with the cordless phone pressed to his ear, the takeout menu spread out in front of him.

"Hi, yes, can I get your number two, number five, number eleven, and an extra side of egg rolls?" He spots me in the doorway. "Anything specific, Kiddo?"

I shake my head. "Surprise me."

Dad turns back to the phone. "Yeah, and two orders of potstickers. Thanks."

I walk over and slide onto the stool next to Josh. His knee bumps mine under the counter, but neither of us moves away.

"What did he want to talk to you about?" I lean in and whisper while Dad reads off his credit card to the person taking his order.

"He just wanted to know what I wanted to eat."

I sigh. "So you really want to do this? There's no turning back."

Are you trying to make him change his mind?

"I'm not going anywhere." He tilts my head up and gently plants a kiss on my lips.

Chapter 18
Cienna

"What is wrong with you?" I demand once I spot James at the kitchen table. He's holding an ice pack against his nose. I toss his keys at him, but they land on the table with a metallic thud.

"What are you talking about? *I* didn't start it." He snaps, taking the ice away from his face. His nose is red, with a little blood crusted around the bottom. Abbi gets a cut above her eye, but James just gets a bloody nose.

That's not right.

"Why did you have to flip out?"

"Hey! I was just trying to ask her a question. Josh is the one sticking his nose where it doesn't belong."

"Rich coming from the guy with blood around his nose. What exactly did she say to you?" I ease my voice. Attacking James isn't worth it.

He shrugs and looks away his voice level matching mine. "She said she just doesn't see a future with me." His voice begins rising again. "She acted like what we had wasn't real. It was real to *me*."

He stands up just as Mom and Dad walk through the garage door. They stop in their tracks. Mom's eyes widen with worry.

"What the hell happened to you?" Dad asks, his voice calm. But I can see his jaw clench, his hands curling into fists.

"Just a misunderstanding," I chime in. Dad *hated* violence.

"What happened?" Mom is already across the floor and examining James' face and body for any other injuries.

"I'm fine, Mom." He pulls away and puts the ice pack back in the freezer.

"Your mother and I asked you a question, James." Dad's voice is firm.

"Abbi dumped me, okay." He faces Dad, his face unreadable.

"Abbi did this?" Mom's hands fly to her mouth.

"What? No. Don't be stupid." James rolls his eyes. "It was Josh. He couldn't mind his own business when all I wanted was to ask Abbi why she didn't want to be with me."

"James, don't lie." I interject.

James' glare pierces through me.

"The truth, James." Dad's voice is like steel. James looks away and refuses to answer.

"He called Abbi a whore." I answer for him.

"James Matthew Jacobs!" Mom looks horrified.

"I didn't mean it." He storms up the stairs and we hear his door slam shut.

Mom and Dad turn to me. "What?" The color drains from my face.

Dad steps forward, his voice softer. "Tell us everything."

Chapter 19
Abbi

"How's James?" Rees asks Cienna, who is doodling in a notebook.

Jared is looking over her shoulder with awkward concentration.

There isn't a cloud in the sky, so we decided it was a picnic day. Blankets are stretched across the grass, shoes kicked off, and snacks are scattered in the middle like offerings to the sun.

Kasey's leaning back on one arm, sunglasses perched on her nose, with Quint's head resting in her lap. She's absently running her fingers through his hair while he hums along to the music playing from Don's phone.

Don and Rees are propped against the giant oak tree at the edge of our patch of grass – half in the shade, half in the sun. Rees has a bottle of lemonade balanced on his knee. Don's flipping through a comic book, but I don't think he's really reading it.

It's peaceful.

I lie back against Josh who's resting against a smaller tree opposite Don and Rees. My eyes are closed, and I enjoy the warmth of the day. My face still throbs but being around everyone helps distract from the pain.

I'm listening, still waiting for Cienna to answer.

"He'll be fine. He's mainly upset he let his anger get the best of him. I told him to give everyone a little more time." Cienna shoots a sympathetic look in our direction.

"Personally I think..." Kasey's comment is cut off by Quint who sits up and kisses her, his hands holding each side of her face.

"Did you seriously just kiss me to shut me up?" Kasey asks once Quint lets her go.

"No," he smirks. "You just wanted to talk when I really wanted to kiss you." He gives her a light boop on the nose.

"You're lucky you're so cute." Kasey's face matches the pink of her hair.

"I know," Quint tosses a grape in the air, trying to catch it in his mouth. All he manages is to hit himself between the eyes.

"Real lucky," Josh laughs, his arms wrapping tighter around me. He leans up enough to kiss my hair before resting back against the tree.

"Well I didn't think the PDA would be *this* intense yet." Rees jests.

"Yes you did," Don says bluntly.

"Hey, I was trying to pretend we didn't *all* see this coming." Rees defends.

"Not everyone," Jared elbows Rees, his eyes shifting back to Cienna. "Cienna, what are you looking at?"

Cienna is no longer doodling in her book. We all look in the direction of her glare.

A woman in black leggings and a fitted tank top is taking a sip from her water bottle before continuing her jog. Her blonde hair is pulled back into a tight ponytail that swishes behind her with each step, catching the sunlight like a blade.

"She's jogged by six times now, and each time she keeps looking at Jared." Cienna is still glaring down the path where the woman had disappeared around the corner.

"I don't think she's-" Jared gets cut off.

"I thought the first time was my imagination, but each time I see her, she isn't looking at anyone *but* Jared." She turns to Jared. "You know I could take her." Cienna says it like a fact. I envy Cienna's confidence.

"I love that you want to protect me and all." Jared brushes her hair from her face before continuing on, "I mean, don't get me wrong, it's cute. But you are half a foot shorter than me," Jared muses.

"What's your point?" Cienna picks up one of the chocolate covered strawberries and takes a bite.

"I love you," Jared kisses her hair before laying down on the blanket.

"I love you too." Cienna throws a grape at him.

He turns, scandalized. "*Rude.*"

Cienna's already grinning, her hand halfway into the fruit container like she's daring him to retaliate.

"You deserved it," she says sweetly.

"For what?"

"Breathing too loud."

She tosses another grape. This one flies over his head.

"Oh, it's on," Jared mutters, launching to his feet. Cienna's already up and running.

Jared takes off after her, tripping over the edge of the blanket in his rush. Cienna shrieks and darts around the swings, laughing so hard she nearly falls over.

The rest of us barely flinch.

"Place your bets," Kasey says lazily.

"Cienna's faster," Rees says without hesitation.

"Jared's more chaotic," Don counters. "He'll win by accident."

Quint snorts. "They're both going to trip and eat dirt."

Josh chuckles, and I look up at him. He's watching the chase with a soft smile, his arm absent mindedly stroking my arm.

Josh's phone vibrates in his pocket. When he pulls it out, his laugh fades.

His expression shifts. The corner of his mouth flattens and his brow furrows.

"What is it?" I ask.

He doesn't answer right away. Instead, he just stares at the screen.

Then he sighs and turns the screen towards me.

It's a text from James.

We need to talk

That's it – no punctuation, no apology – just those four words.

Josh locks the screen and sets the phone face-down on the blanket.

"Are you going to answer?"

He shakes his head. "Not right now."

The laughter from the playground drifts back towards us. Cienna's voice is high and breathless. Jared is yelling something about "grape warfare."

"I give it two months." Quint's voice cuts through our tension like a knife.

Josh blinks, his gaze shifting over to Quint. "What?"

Kasey lifts her sunglasses. "Two months until what?"

"Until Jared pops the question," Quint says, like it's the most obvious thing in the world.

Don snorts. "Please. I give it a week. He's probably already got the ring hidden in a sock drawer."

"Six months." Rees chimes in, stretching his legs out in front of him. "Cienna's gonna make him work for it."

Josh lets out a quiet laugh, and I feel the tension in his shoulders ease just a little.

I raise an eyebrow. "What's the prize?"

"Bragging rights," Quint says.

"Loser buys dinner," Kasey adds, already pulling out her phone to make a note. "And I'm writing this down, so no one tries to back out."

"Wait, wait," Don says, sitting up straighter. "Do we get bonus points if we predict how he does it?"

"Absolutely," Rees says. "But only if it's dramatic."

"Jared doesn't do not dramatic," I mutter.

Josh leans in close enough I can feel his breath on my shoulder. "What's your bet?"

I glance towards the playground, where Jared is currently hanging upside down from the monkey bars while Cienna throws mulch at his shoes.

I smile. "Three months. And he'll do it in the most ridiculous way possible."

Josh grins. "Like... flash mob ridiculous?"

"Worse," I say. "Like... skywriting and a mariachi band."

***

137

The twins have outdone themselves for game night. Their den buzzes with energy as we gather around the ping pong table, cups already set in place. The 'battleships' are arranged in neat little formations, each cup filled with a mystery liquid. Lemon juice, lime juice, water... and vinegar. The vinegar is the real villain here.

"Alright, ladies versus men," Don declares, twirling a ping pong ball like a weapon.

"You mean ladies versus crybabies," Cienna shoots back, flipping her hair over her shoulder.

"Crybabies who always win," Rees adds with a grin.

"Not tonight," Kasey flashes a smile, cracking her knuckles. "I've been practicing my bounce shot in the mirror."

Quint raises an eyebrow. "That explains the broken toothbrush cup."

"I'll be the sacrifice," Josh raises a hand and comes over to the girls' side. He grabs my hand and squeezes it with an easy smile.

"But... but." Quint stammers.

"It's only fair. Four versus four."

"Fine," Quint concedes.

We all laugh as Cienna steps up for the coin toss. "Heads!" She calls.

The coin lands – heads.

"Boom," she says, already lining up her shot. "Prepare to suffer."

She bounces the ball with laser focus and, *plop*, right into the far-right cup.

The other guys shove Jared forward. "Of course," Jared mutters. "Guess it's my turn to be the sacrificial lamb."

He takes the drink, pauses, then smiles. "Water. I live another round."

"Boo!" Kasey shouts. "We want vinegar tears."

Jared winks at Cienna before taking his shot. It arcs perfectly into our front cup.

Cienna groans. "You're too good at this."

She takes the drink like a champ, then makes a face like she's just licked something bitter. "Lime. Not the worst." Her eye twitch begs to differ.

Kasey's up next. She bounces the ball with a little flair and nails a center cup.

Rees picks it up, sniffs it, and immediately regrets it. "Oh no."

He drinks, gags, and staggers back like he's been shot. "I've seen the other side!"

I'm laughing so hard I nearly drop the ball when it's my turn. I aim for the center, but the ball veers left like it has a mind of its own.

Quint catches it mid-air. "Abbi, seriously? How do you miss every time?"

"I don't know!" I groan.

"It's a gift," Josh says from behind me, smirking.

Quint sinks a shot into our back corner. I sigh, grab the cup, and brace myself.

"Plug your nose," Kasey whispers.

I do.

Sweet, glorious water.

"Lucky," Rees mutters. "I'm still tasting vinegar."

The game goes on, cups disappear one by one. We're down to the final cup on each side. Cienna steps up, eyes narrowed.

"I can't," Kasey whispers, covering her eyes.

Cienna grins. "Watch and learn."

She tosses the ball. It bounces once, twice – *plop*. Right into the cup.

We scream, jump, and hug. We've never won before.

Jared runs over and spins Cienna in a circle. "That's my girl!"

Don groans and picks up the last cup. "If this is vinegar, I'm suing."

"You're the one that filled them," Rees glares.

It is in fact vinegar. His face twists, and he reaches for water like it's life or death.

"Who won?" Connie, the twins' mom, calls from the top of the stairs, peering down with her silver glasses glinting. Her short blonde hair frames her face in waves.

"The girls!" Don shouts, gasping between breaths as he continues chugging water.

"Woohoo!" Lance, their dad, yells from behind her. His bright red hair, thinning at the crown but still defiantly vibrant, matches Rees and Don's almost exactly.

Us girls file into the kitchen. Connie is already pulling out the ingredients for dinner. "Lasagna night, huh?" Cienna asks, eyeing the ingredients.

"Yes, Ma'am," Connie says.

The guys filter out one by one, the back door swinging open and closed with each exit. Laughter echoes from the yard. Don is shouting something about "revenge tackles", and Lance is daring Quint to outrun him.

Josh lingers near the fridge, sipping water, his gaze flickering towards the door, torn between calm and chaos.

Connie, still wiping her hands on a dish towel, catches the hesitation. "You're not going to let them have all the bruises, are you?"

140

Josh smiles faintly. "I'm debating it."

He glances towards the backyard again, where Quint is now yelling something about "unfair tackles." We can only see so much through the kitchen window, but we can see Rees doing cartwheels for no reason.

Josh chuckles, "They're ridiculous."

"Exactly," Connie replies. "Go be ridiculous with them. I can't gossip with you in here."

Josh hesitates one more beat, then sets his water bottle down and heads for the door.

"Tell Lance to go easy on Don," Connie calls after him. "He's still recovering from the rose bush incident."

Josh laughs as the door swings shut behind him, and I catch Connie's smile as she turns back to the stove.

"He needed that," she says softly.

The kitchen is alive with motion. Cienna is chopping cucumbers. Kasey is tossing cherry tomatoes in a bowl. I'm trying not to cry over the onions. Connie stirs the sauce, humming softly to herself.

She glances over her shoulder, her eyes twinkling behind her silver glasses. "So... are you and Josh official?"

I freeze mid-chop. Cienna snorts. Kasey drops a tomato.

Connie grins, casual as ever. "What? I'm not allowed to be curious? You two have been orbiting each other for months."

I feel my cheeks warm. "We're... Yeah, we're together."

Connie turns fully, her hands on her hips. "Well, it's about time. That boy looks at you like you hung the moon."

Cienna rolls her eyes. "He really does. It's kind of gross."

"Romantic," Kasey corrects, nudging Cienna. "Grossly romantic."

I laugh, trying to hide the way my heart flutters.

From the backyard we hear a loud shout, followed by laughter and the unmistakable sound of someone hitting the grass too hard.

Connie sighs, exasperated. "I'll go check on them before someone ends up in my ER."

As Connie steps out to check on the backyard chaos, Cienna slides the salad bowl towards me and leans against the counter. "Just so you know, if Josh tries to feed you a tomato like it's holy, I'm throwing one at him."

I laugh. "Noted. No tomato PDA."

Kasey snorts. "What about croutons? Croutons should be neutral territory."

"Croutons are safe," Cienna agrees, then adds, knowing I don't care for croutons, "But if he starts quoting poetry over the lasagna, I'm out."

"Josh doesn't do poetry," I grin. "He barely does full sentences when he's tired."

"True," Kasey laughs. "He grunts like a caveman after 9 p.m."

Cienna huffs a laugh, her tone lighter now. "Honestly, I *am* happy for you. I just need a little buffer zone – a no-smooch radius."

"Ten feet?" I tease.

"Ten feet and no dreamy eye contact during dinner." She points a carrot stick at me like a wand.

"Deal," I hold my hands up in surrender.

Josh walks in just then, cheeks flushed from the football game, hair even messier than before. He grabs a water bottle and leans against the fridge, catching my eye with a quiet smile.

"That's dreamy eye contact." Cienna tosses a carrot at Josh. "I saw that."

Josh blinks in surprise at the assault by carrot. "What did I do?"

"Nothing," I say quickly. "You're good. Just... no tomatoes." I can't help but smirk.

He looks even more confused. "Okay?"

Kasey pats his shoulder. "Don't worry. You'll learn the rules eventually."

Josh gives me a look, half amused, half bewildered.

Cienna rolls her eyes again but smiles. "You two are ridiculous."

Connie reappears from the backyard, brushing her short blonde bob back from her flustered face.

"Well," she says slightly breathless. "Looks like tackle football claimed another victim. Lance tackled Don into the rose bush again. I swear one of these days I'll have to start charging my own family for ER visits."

Josh grins. "Lance still hits like a linebacker."

She moves to counter, glancing between me and Josh with that knowing mom-look that makes you feel like she can read your entire soul without a word.

"So," she says casually to Josh. "You two finally figured it out?"

Josh blinks and clears his throat. "Yeah."

"No tomato feeding PDA," I add quickly, stifling a giggle.

Connie laughs. "Shame. I was hoping for some dramatic spaghetti kiss."

"Wrong pasta," Kasey says, tossing croutons into the bowl. "But I support the vision."

Cienna looks over, her tone light, but her eyes careful. "Just maybe keep the dreamy eye contact to a minimum during dinner."

Josh twists the cap back onto his water. "No dreamy eyes. Got it."

Connie gives a playful nudge. "You can't help it, sweetheart. You've got those, *'I'd build her the world'* eyes."

Josh flushes and I try not to melt.

Cienna coughs. "Just don't fight my brother again."

Josh nods, serious now. "I won't."

"Good." Connie pats his arm. "I like having all my boys in one piece."

Chapter 20

Josh

The park is quiet. The noon sun beats down intensely for a mid-June day. There's no breeze, making it feel hotter than it actually is.

James is already there, pacing. He sees me and stops, his jaw is tight and his fists balled.

I walk up slow, mentally prepping for retaliation for the fist to the face last week.

"You took your time," he grumbles.

I stop a few feet away. "You said noon."

He shrugs, sharp. "Guess I didn't expect you to actually show."

I don't answer.

He studies me. "So... what? This is you playing the good guy now?"

I keep my hands in my pockets. "You said you wanted to talk."

He laughs, short and bitter. "*Talk*. Right."

He takes a step closer. "You think you're better than me now? What–just because you have Abbi that makes you all high and mighty now?"

I shake my head once. "I'm not here to fight."

"Bullshit," he snaps. "You've been waiting for this."

He shoves me, but I hold my ground.

He shoves me again, this time harder. "Come on. Hit me. You did it once."

I stare at him. "I'm not doing this."

"You think she's yours now?" His voice cracks. "You think she doesn't remember everything we had?"

"She didn't forget," I say. "She just stopped acting like it was enough."

That does it.

He swings, but I barely manage to block it. He comes at me again. He's wild, angry, and has no aim. I dodge, grab his arm, and shove him back. He stumbles but catches himself. He charges towards me again. This time I don't hold back. I plant my feet and throw him off balance, my knuckles connecting to his face. He hits the grass with a grunt and rolls before scrambling back up.

His lip is bleeding and his eyes are wild.

"You don't get to win," he growls.

"This *isn't* a game."

He lunges again, but I sidestep. He crashes into the bench behind me, metal clanging.

I stand still.

He stares at me, fists clenched, blood on his teeth.

I remember Dad's voice.

Keep your hands steady when it counts.

And John's.

Be the one who doesn't make her flinch.

So I don't swing.

James is still breathing hard, but he's not swinging anymore. I stay where I am, my hands loose at my side. My voice is low. "You done?"

He doesn't answer.

"Because I'm not gonna hurt you, man. No matter how many times you try."

His jaw tightens. He wipes his mouth with the back of his hand. "What do you call this?" He holds up his hand, showing a smear of blood against his bronze skin.

"You attacked me."

"You think that makes you better?"

"No," I say. "It makes me tired."

He laughs, sharp and bitter. "You don't get it. She was everything."

"I know. That's why you're so angry."

He looks at me like he wants to argue, but the fight is draining out of him. It's slow, like a leak he can't patch.

I take a step closer. "Let me walk you home."

He scoffs. "What, so you can gloat?"

"No. So you don't do something stupid on the way. This doesn't mean we can't get past this."

James hesitates, only for a moment. Then, without another word, he turns and starts walking.

We don't talk much. There's only the sound of our footsteps on the sidewalk or the occasional car passing. His shoulders are still tense, but his hands are no longer fists.

When we reach his street, I spot them before he does.

Abbi and Cienna.

They're sitting on the porch. A half empty bottle of lemonade rests between them. Abbi's hair is pulled back in a braid, her eye still bruised. Cienna's arms are crossed, her eyes sharp even from here.

James stops walking.

I stop behind him.

He stares for a second, then mutters, "Of course."

"She didn't know I was coming," I say quietly.

He doesn't move.

Abbi looks up. Her eyes meet mine first, then shift to James. She stands slowly. Cienna's gaze follows hers, and she jumps up, her eyes wide with worry.

James shifts his weight. "I can't do this."

"You don't have to," I say. "Just go inside."

"What is *wrong* with you?!" Cienna scolds.

"Lay off it, will ya?" James dodges Cienna's attempt to grab his face. Without another word he storms inside.

"Are *you* going to tell me what happened?! I thought I told you *not* to hit my brother again!" Cienna crosses her arms.

"This time it was self-defense, I swear." I hold my hands defensively.

"You boys are so stupid," she huffs. She storms off after James before I can stop her, leaving me alone with Abbi.

"What happened?" she asks in a soft voice. She studying my face like she's looking for any sign of injury.

"I'm fine." I pull her into a hug and she melts into it. Her arms wrap around my waist, her forehead resting against my chest.

Her breath is warm through my shirt as she says, "I'm going to go talk to him."

I shake my head, my voice low. "I think you should give him some space."

She pulls back just enough to look up at me, her blue eyes shine–not just with resolve, but something softer – something for him. "He needs to hear it. I have to," she steps out of my arms. Her eyes are steady.

"Abbi-"

"I know," she cuts in gently. "But I still have to."

I know it's pointless to argue so I just nod.

She turns and walks up the steps, slipping through the front door without knocking.

I'm left staring at the grain of the wood on the front door, jaw tight, hands in my pockets, trying not to imagine what's being said on the other side.

Inside, I know James is still raw – still furious. However, she's not afraid of that.

I just hope he listens.

Chapter 21

Abbi

While climbing the stairs, each step feels like lead.

What am I going to say? What is he going to say?

I rub my fingers along my thumbs in a calming counting motion. Turning the corner at the top of the stairs, James is walking from the bathroom to his room across the hall.

I take one last calming breath and make my way to him.

I stop in his doorway and freeze. He's facing away from the door, pulling off his grass-stained shirt. My eyes travel from his tense shoulders to the muscles in his arms and back.

"I don't want to hear it, Ci. I just want to get in the shower and be left alone." He doesn't turn around. I'm still left speechless.

He crumples up his shirt and throws it towards his closet where it manages to make a thud.

Once he turns around, his eyes widen, his mouth going slack.

He's already cleaned up his lip, and now I can see it's smaller than what it seemed when he got home.

"Abbi..." The way he says my name gives me shivers.

"Yeah, I know." I take a step into the room, my hands in my back pockets so he won't see me fidget. "Are you okay?"

He shakes his head.

That's obvious. However, it's still more than he gave Cienna.

"Do you want to talk about it?" He isn't looking at me. His hands tense into fists at his side before he shakes his head again.

I don't know what else I can do, so I step towards the door. "I'm sorry. I'll go."

"Wait."

Turning back around, he's already crossed the space between us. His hands come up and cup my face, his lips crash down on mine. My heart leaps in my chest. The warmth of his body is pressed against me. His kiss tastes like peppermint and blood, sweet and sharp – layered, like a thread snapped inside him.

I pull back, my hands grabbing his and taking them away from my face.

"No," I say, trying to catch my breath.

I let go of his hands and step back into the doorway.

He slumps down on his bed, his head in his hands. "Do you love him?"

I open my mouth, then close it. I've never said it out loud before, not even to myself.

Now that it's here, hanging in the air between us, I know.

"Yes."

He stares at me for a long moment. Then his posture changes, as if something inside him just gave way.

"Then that's that."

He stands, walks to the closet, and starts flipping through shirts as if we've discussed which one is best for this type of weather. He pulls a red V-neck off the hanger and slips it over his head.

"I won't pretend I'm happy about it," he says, his voice flat. "But I can see nothing I do will change your decision."

I watch him, unsure what to say. There's nothing left to argue - nothing left to fix.

He's still facing the closet, adjusting the hem of his shirt.

I turn to leave, hand brushing the doorframe.

"I really am sorry about your face." He doesn't look at me when he says it. There's no trying to explain or excuses it. Instead, we let the words hang in the air, an unspoken resolve.

I nod, even though he can't see it. "I know."

And I do.

I open the door and step out into the hallway, the air cooler somehow, like I've crossed into something new.

Chapter 22

Abbi

The burgers are seasoned, the grill's heating up, and the backyard look like something out of a summer catalog. Fairy lights are strung along the fence. The flowers in full bloom gift us with their vibrant colors and smells. Two long picnic tables line the right side of the yard, each topped with a giant blue and white umbrella.

I'm just wiping down the counter when the door creaks open.

Cienna steps in first, arms full of chips and a stack of paper plates. "Smells amazing," she remarks, setting everything on the counter. She pulls me into a tight hug. "Anyone else here?"

"Nope. You're the first."

James follows next.

He gives me a small nod. "Need help with anything?"

I glance at the fridge. " Actually, yeah. Could you start setting out the toppings? Lettuce, tomato, cheese, pickles... all that?"

"Coming right up." He hustles to the fridge and starts pulling things out, setting them on the counter with quiet focus.

When Ryan walks in, he greets me with a soft smile and glances towards James. "Did you get the onions?"

"Already sliced," James says shaking the container I had prepped earlier.

Ryan claps him on the shoulder. "Good. Can't have a burger without onions."

They work side by side, laying out the toppings on trays like they've done this a hundred times. There's no tension. There's just rhythm and familiarity.

Lily is carrying her famous potato salad like she's afraid the herd will charge once they get a whiff, which they will. She sets it down and pulls me into a hug.

"They promised their best behavior," she murmurs. She pulls back and cups my face. "And your face is healing beautifully."

I busy myself with washing the freshly emptied containers when the doorbell rings.

I wipe my hands on a dish towel and hurry to open it.

Lisa stands there, smiling. She's holding a tray of pre-packaged fruit – the kind with too much cantaloupe and unripe watermelon.

"Hey! James said I could come. I hope that okay."

My stomach drops.

I blink. "Oh. I... Yeah... Sure."

"Great!" She steps inside, breezing past me like this isn't wildly inappropriate.

"Your house is beautiful. I absolutely love the fox stained glass."

"Lily, James' mom, actually made that."

I glance towards the kitchen. James is still at the counter, laying out slices of tomato like nothing's wrong. He smiles when he sees Lisa, then he glances at me. His expression worry, but... *curiosity*?

He didn't tell me she was coming. He never even ask if it was okay.

Cienna goes still, Ryan's hand pauses over the pickles, and Lily's smile falters.

Lisa sets the fruit tray on the counter next to the potato salad and starts chatting about her plans for the next week. I nod along, but my chest feels tight.

It's been six days. Six days since everything cracked open.

Now she's here – in my house.

The door swings open again, this time without a knock.

"Smells like heaven in here," Don says, stepping inside with Rees right behind. They're both carrying bags of salad and foil wrapped pulled pork sandwiches. Barbeque sauce and comfort.

Lance follows close behind, balancing a giant white box and a massive Tupperware container. "I brought cookies." He says. "And Connie made sure to make that fancy cake with the cheese and berries that Kasey loves."

"Mascarpone," Rees mutters, like he's been forced to recite it many times before.

Lance just grins. "Fancy cheese."

155

The kitchen is full now. Lisa's voice still floats above the others like she belongs here, even though every glance says otherwise. James is pretending not to notice, Cienna's gone quiet beside me, and Ryan's keeping busy with the condiments like they're the only interesting thing in the room.

The door opens again.

"Hope we're not late!" Kasey calls, stepping inside with a giant bowl of pasta salad and a grin that could light up the whole room. Her smile manages to reach her eyes this time.

Moira, Kasey's mom, follows right behind, balancing a tray of deviled eggs and wearing a pair of oversized sunglasses and a green ombre braid that brushes her shoulders. She looks like she walked out of a music festival and into my kitchen.

Kasey's pink-tipped curls bounce as she sets the bowl down. "We brought the good stuff."

"Pasta salad?" Lily asks, already reaching for a spoon.

Obviously." Kasey laughs. "And Mom made the eggs."

Moira gives a mock bow. "You're welcome."

Their energy shifts the room, even if it's just a little. The tension doesn't vanish, but it softens around the edges. Now it feels almost like someone opened a window and let in a breeze.

Kasey gives me a quick hug, then glances around. Her eyes land on Lisa. Her smile doesn't falter, but her eyebrows lift just slightly.

I don't say anything, and neither does she. Her look lets me know she clocked it.

Moira, meanwhile, is already chatting with Ryan about the best way to keep deviled eggs from sliding off a paper plate.

Jared is next to arrive, a grocery bag in each arm.

"I come bearing buns and ice cream."

156

"Bless you," Lily jumps up immediately, taking one of the bags. "You're saving the root beer float tradition. I completely forgot to grab ice cream."

He grins. "Figured someone had to."

"My hero," Cienna kisses Jared cheek, and he looks like the whole world just became right again.

He sets the bags on the counter and starts unloading - two packs of hamburger buns, a tub of vanilla ice cream, and a box of waffle cones he clearly couldn't resist.

"Where's Louis?" Ryan asks.

"Dad's at the ER," Jared says, not missing a beat. "He and Connie got called in. Mom's still overseas until next month so... just me today."

There's a beat of silence, but Jared fills it before anyone can say anything heavy.

"I'm claiming double dessert privileges in her honor," he adds, holding up the ice cream like a trophy.

The room relaxes again.

He catches my eye and gives a small, familiar smile.

I respond with my own.

"I think it's getting too crowded in here. Let's take this out back." Lily starts shooing the others down into the den and out the doors.

Suddenly the kitchen is too quiet. I grip the edge of the counter, staring at the tray of burger toppings like they've personally offended me.

How dare he.

How dare James bring her here. To my house. To my dad's barbecue like it's nothing... Like I'm nothing.

My throat tightens, and I blink hard, refusing to let the tears fall.

They're not sad tears – they're angry, and embarrassed. Everyone saw it. Everyone felt it – the shift when she walked in – the way no one knew where to look. James just stood there like it was fine – like *I* should be fine.

I press the heels of my hands into my eyes.

Quietly, stubbornly, another thought slips in.

I wasn't exactly innocent either. Josh and I... we were already something. Not officially or physically, but something real. It was something that mattered. And it started before James and I ended.

I didn't cheat, but I didn't *stop* it either.

Is it really that different?

I take a breath and let it out slowly.

I don't want to be the girl who makes this harder than it has to be. I don't want to be bitter. I don't want to be cruel.

I stand up and smooth my hands over my shirt.

I'm going to be nice...

Even if it hurts.

I grab the pitcher of lemon water from the counter and head outside, focusing on the simple rhythm of it – set the table, pour the drinks, breathe.

The backyard is buzzing now. Voices, laughter, and the sizzle of the grill all make a strange yet beautiful song. I weave through the crowd towards the table, careful not to spill.

I turn too quickly and my shoulder clips someone. The pitcher jerks in my hand, and suddenly, I'm soaked.

Cold lemon water splashes down my front, seeping into my shirt and clinging to my skin. A slice of lemon slides down my arm and lands with a wet *plop* on the grass.

I gasp, more from the shock than the cold.

"Oh my gosh!" Lisa says, stepping back. "I'm so sorry. I didn't see you there."

"It's okay," I say quickly, trying to calm the shaking in my voice. "It's fine."

"Let me grab you some towels –"

"No, really," I cut in, forcing a smile. "I was planning to change anyway."

She hesitates, then nods and hurries to James at the other end of the yard.

I stand there, dripping, humiliated, and trying not to let it show.

Of *course. Of course this would happen.*

I take a breath, square my shoulders, and carry the pitcher to the table like nothing's wrong.

I said I'll be nice and I meant it.

As inconspicuously as possible, I slip inside, letting the door swing shut behind me. My shirt clings to my skin, cold and sticky with the lemon water. I head straight for my room, shutting the door gently behind me.

I don't cry. What would be the point?

I just stand there, dripping on my white carpet, trying to breathe through the sting behind my eyes.

A soft knock breaks the silence.

"Abbi?" Cienna's voice is muffled but gentle. "Can I come in?"

"Yeah."

She slips inside and closes the door behind her. Her eyes sweep over me and her expression crumples.

"I'm so sorry," she says, stepping closer. "I had no idea James invited her. I swear if I'd known –"

"It's okay," I say quickly.

"It's *not*," she says. "He should've told you. Or at least warned you. And Lisa just... showing up like that? I wanted to throw her fruit tray at her head."

That pulls a laugh out of me. It's small, but real.

Cienna softens. "You've been handling this like a freaking queen. I would've lost it."

"I almost did," I admit, "in here just before you came in."

She crosses to my closet and starts flipping through hangers. "You need something dry. Something that says, *'I'm fine actually, and I also look better than you.'*"

She pulls out a white dress with delicate green embroidery along the hem. "This one."

I take it from her. My fingers brush the soft fabric. "I forgot I even had this."

"Well, now you remember, and you're going to look like a meadow goddess. You're welcome."

I laugh again, fuller this time.

"Thanks," I say.

She squeezes my arm. "I'll be outside. Take your time. And if Lisa says one more word about her trip to Europe next month, I'm faking a wasp attack."

When she leaves, I change slowly. The dress fits like a breath a fresh air. It's light and clean, like the perfect reset.

And when I look in the mirror, I don't see the girl who got soaked in front of everyone. I see someone who's still standing.

I'm smoothing the skirt of the dress when there's another soft knock on my bedroom door.

"Abbi?" Josh's voice is quiet.

"Come in."

He opens the door cautiously, like he's not sure what he's walking into. The second he sees me his shoulders drop a little.

"You okay?" he asks.

I nod. "Just needed a minute."

"Want to talk about it?"

I shake my head. "Not worth the time."

His eyes flick over me. There's a hunger there that awakens something deep inside. "You look…" He exhales. "Beautiful."

I roll my eyes, but my smile gives me away. "I dumped lemon water all over myself."

He steps closer. "Still beautiful."

I look up at him, and for a second, everything else fades – the noise outside, the sting in my chest, the ache of trying to be okay.

He leans in. It isn't fast, or dramatic, but it is perfect. A soft, careful kiss dances between our lips. My eyes flutter shut. I forget everything. I forget about Lisa and James – I forget about everything except being here, right now, with him.

When he pulls back, he doesn't speak – He doesn't have to.

I reach for his hand. He takes it right away.

"Ready?"

No," I sigh. "But let's go anyway."

The French doors swing closed behind us as Josh and I step back outside, hand in hand.

The backyard's louder and fuller now. The grill's going, the table is half set, and someone's already opening the chips.

Quint and Alec have made their appearance. A massive red cooler sits near the patio, lid propped open and ice spilling over the sides. Cans of root beer, cream soda, and something neon and probably radioactive are already floating inside.

"Delivery complete," Quint announces from a lawn chair, holding up a neon can like a trophy. "And yes, I carried that thing myself. You're welcome."

"You carried one side," Alec says, stacking Solo cups with quiet precision. "I carried the other, and the ice, the cups, the —"

"Details," Quint waves him off. "What matters is hydration."

Josh snorts beside me. "They've been here five minutes and he's already claimed the shady spot."

"Seniority," Quint calls. "And superior instincts."

"Or maybe everyone else is actually helping," Alec chides.

By the time everyone's seated, the table is a patchwork of paper plates, half unwrapped foil, and mismatched condiments.

Someone already spilled lemonade near the napkins, and the burger buns are slowly drying out in the sun. It's messy... Loud... *Real.*

Josh and I end up at the far end of the table, *directly* across from James and Lisa.

What else?

Lisa's laughing at something James just said, her hand brushing his arm like it's the most natural thing in the world. He doesn't pull away, but I catch him glancing towards Josh and me with that same curious glance from before.

I try to focus on my plate. Josh's knee rests lightly against mine under the table, his hand gently brushing mine where no one can see. It's calming in a way I didn't know I needed.

Cienna's across from Jared, who's already halfway through his burger but is pretending not to be engrossed in everything she does. If *she* moves, *he* moves. They are completely in sync. Kasey and Moira are arguing over whether the pasta salad needs more salt, Rees is trying to stack chips into a tower while Don's pretending *not* to help.

"So... is volleyball still happening? I've got a score to settle." Lance stares down Quint with a playful glare.

"Yes!" Quint cries immediately. "Parents versus kids!"

"Losers clean up," Lily adds, pointing her fork like a judge.

There's a ripple of groans and laughter.

"Wait," Lisa says, glancing around. "That's not fair. There are, what–six parent, and ten of us?"

"Seven if you count me," Rees grins, leaning back against his chair, his arms behind his head. "I've accepted my fate."

"Still." Lisa presses, "That's almost double. Shouldn't we even it out?"

I stare at her. She's not wrong.

"We can rotate players," I say. "Make it work."

"Or give the parents a handicap," Ryan mutters. "Like no jumping."

"Speak for yourself," Lily says. "I've got a wicked spike."

The table erupts into laughter again. The normalcy is reassuring.

James leans back in his chair, arm draped casually behind Lisa. "Lisa and I will take the parents' team," he announces.

Lisa smiles, a little surprised but not embarrassed. "I mean, I'm not technically a parent –"

"We're honorary," James says, grinning. "Just for today."

I take a sip of my drink and focus on the feeling of condensation sliding down the side of the cup.

I said I'd be nice.

I meant it.

Even now.

"Well, what are we waiting for?" Lance says, standing up and brushing crumbs off his jeans. He's already halfway across the yard before anyone else moves.

We follow him over to the net, dragging our feet, our stomachs full. Someone grabs the volleyball from the shed.

Ryan serves first.

Rees dives for it, arms flailing, and somehow keeps it in play.

But when Alec spikes it, clean, fast, and brutal, we all just kind of... watch it hit the grass.

We're doomed.

The game is complete chaos. Lily trips over Moira, Jared and Cienna keep getting distracted by each other, and Quint insists on narrating every play like it's the Olympics. Josh is still really good, but even he can't save us from Alec's laser-accurate serves.

Still, we rally.

By the end, it's close – too close – but still the parents win.

"A bet's a bet." Don concedes, wiping sweat from his forehead.

After the match we collapse into lawn chairs and picnic blankets, passing around plates of cookies, cake, and melting ice cream. Someone finds the root beer, and the floats are sticky and perfect.

Quint reaches for Kasey's Mascarpone cake, but she swats his hand away. "No one touches my cake. Not even you."

Cleanup is a breeze. It helps having eight people working together. There's laughter, teasing, and a lot of bumping into each other as we pass dishes and folded chairs.

For a little while, it feels like we're all on the same team again, even if some of us are still pretending.

Chapter 23

Kasey

The air is warm, but it feels lighter today. The lavender is in bloom all over the backyard. Mom insisted we plant it last year when she learned it helps calm anxiety as well as ward off bugs. There's even a few small bushes of white sage to ward off *'evil spirits'*.

Abbi sits across from me on a baby pink blanket we pulled from my closet so we could paint our nails outside on the grass.

Jared promised Cienna a "bonding experience" at a retro roller rink, even though neither of them know how to skate.

"Sometimes it's nice not having everyone around." Abbi sighs. She dumps the bags of nail polish onto the blanket and starts sorting them by color. "Don't get me wrong though," she continues. "I love having everyone around, but it can be a bit chaotic for every day."

"Totally," I agree. She has no clue just how spot on she is. These new meds have helped so much, but there's still times when everything is just... *too much.*

"I'm thinking..." she hovers over the green section but then reaches for a navy blue. "This one. Josh will love it."

She twists the cap and starts applying it to her toes.

"You are completely and utterly smitten," I laugh.

My phone buzzes and when I check it, it's a message from Quint.

Beauty or Beast?

This is Quint's way of checking on me without the constant *'How are you feeling?'* after a therapy appointment.

I respond:

Beauty.

When I turn back to Abbi, she's got one eyebrow raised, a smile playing on her lips.

"What?"

"Oh nothing," she goes back to painting her toes. "You were just smiling. I could tell you were talking to Quint."

"I was *not*." I try to play it off with a laugh.

"Sure." She screws the lid back on and starts fanning her hands to dry the polish.

"Is it always that obvious?" My cheeks turn a darker pink than my hair.

"Why does that have to be a bad thing? He *loves* you. Josh is always telling me how Quint *never* shuts up about you. It's sweet." She's scanning the bottles again for another color.

I reach for a neon green. It's a color I wouldn't have chosen a few months ago, but now it somehow feels just right.

"I recommend painting white over it first," Abbi holds out a white bottle. "It helps the green pop."

"I didn't know you had so many colors."

"Hey. Half of these are yours."

"Yeah, the darker half."

"Well at least *some* part of you doesn't always have to sparkle. Simple is beautiful too."

I smile, thinking back to how my therapist said pretty much the same thing. Therapy today, though, was less about sparkle, and more of just being able to breathe without feeling like I'm too loud.

"How have things been since I last saw you?" Kyle's sitting in his usual beige chair, a soft smile on his lips.

"It's actually been really good." I cross my legs on the couch and grab a small handful of chocolate covered peanuts he keeps on his coffee table.

"Anything particular that you think contributed to that?" He scribbles in his notebook.

"I don't know. I mean, I don't feel as heavy as I used to. We had a party about a week ago and I actually had fun. We had a barbecue and we played volleyball. It was nice."

"That's great." He scribbles some more.

"Mom's on a new kick now."

"What is it this time?" He chuckles.

"Rocks. She thinks stones have healing properties. She has all different types spread out around the house. Last night she did this weird 'moon charging ritual'."

"Do you think it could help?"

168

"Right now? I think anything is possible."

"Hey you two!" We look up and spot Don walking across the yard. "I need to pick your brains."

"Uh oh, we're in trouble now." Abbi murmurs.

"What's up?" I ask, my voice more chipper than I'm used to, catching me slightly off guard.

"I need dating advice." Don sits down between us on the blanket.

"Only if we can paint your nails," I jest.

"Agreed." His face is serious.

Abbi and I exchange looks, trying to keep our expressions neutral.

"Okay," he crosses his legs and leans in towards us, holding his hand out for Abbi. "Teach me the art of flirting. I am but an unpolished stone."

Abbi's eyes grow wide. "You want us..." she points between the two of us, "to teach you... how to flirt?"

"Yes. Preferable without causing emotional whiplash."

I hum thoughtfully, while coating my nails in the white polish Abbi handed me. "First rule is... flirting is 87% vibe." I'm honestly just rambling, but it sounds legit.

"That's not quantifiable."

Abbi grins. "Exactly."

Don squints. "Okay... So... *vibe*. Got it. But what do I actually *say*?"

I exchange a glance with Abbi, who's already rifling through her mental playbook.

"Example," she says while brushing on pink glitter polish onto Don's fingers. "Let's say a cute girl is reading on a bench.

You don't just say, 'nice book'. You say, 'should I be reading that, or are you gatekeeping masterpieces today?'"

"Flirty with a hint of tension," I add.

"Or," Abbi continues, "you can go the chaotic route. 'What's your go-to apocalyptic survival skill? Mine is crying artistically.'" She says with a flourish of her hand.

Don whips out his phone with the hand not being painted and starts typing. "This is gold. So flirting is like... being weird on purpose, but in a seductive way?"

"Exactly," Abbi says. "Weird but curated. Like a museum of your best quirks."

Don switches hands, his eyes closing. "I am ready to unleash mild confusion with emotional sincerity."

Mom emerges from the sliding glass door, arms full of satin pouches and tiny velvet boxes. Her hair's braided with twine and dried lavender. She's wearing mismatched socks, a kaftan, and a determined expression.

We're definitely in trouble now.

"*These,*" she announces, dropping a pouch onto the blanket with a thud, "are freshly recharged. The moon was in Pisces last night, so obviously, the emotional cleansing potential is high."

Don jumps slightly as a heart-shaped stone rolls onto his knee. "What... what does this one do?"

Mom beams. "That's rose quartz. It enhances love energy, self-worth, and sometimes encourages impulsive decisions. So if you find yourself texting your ex, then it's working."

"Definitely not for me, thank you." Abbi pushes the rocks away and twists the cap back on the pink polish.

I pick up a jagged chunk of obsidian. "This looks like something you'd throw at a ghost."

170

"Yes," She says seriously. "It's for protection."

Abbi coughs into her gold-polished hand. "Protection from who? The HOA?"

"Spiritual enemies," Mom settles cross-legged beside us. She begins arranging the rocks in a loose spiral around Don's feet like she's crafting a tiny emotional force field.

"You're trying to flirt right? These will help you manifest your romantic aura. But also don't text 'wyd'. That stone isn't strong enough to protect you from bad choices."

Don stares as she places a chunk of amethyst on his forehead like a third eye installation.

"I think I'm in love already," he mutters.

Mom winks. "That's the rocks at work."

I lean over and whisper just loud enough for Abbi to hear, "Does all that stuff you said actually work?" All Quint had to do was smile and I was head over heels.

"I have no idea," She continues smiling at Mom and Don ogling over the different stones. "It would be a great experiment to see in action."

Chapter 24
Abbi

One second the TV's humming in the background, and the next, silence. It's the kind that makes you sit up straighter and shadows feel heavier, especially when you're home alone.

Stumbling my way to the kitchen, using the flashlight on my phone, I find a candle in the drawer by the sink. Once I light it, the flame flickers like it's nervous too.

The house lights up around me. I try to count, but I don't get past one. The rumble is so loud, I'm afraid it'll break the windows.

Too close.

Three knocks echo from the front door.

I freeze.

"It's me," Josh calls. His voice is muffled, but familiar.

I open the door.

He's standing there in a rain-soaked grey hoodie, flashlight in one hand, and a bag of marshmallows in the other. "Hey, stranger."

"You came over here for *s'mores*?"

"I came over because I know you hate storms, and I know your dad is out," he says, stepping inside. "The marshmallows are just a bonus."

I close the door behind him. "You're soaked."

Josh shrugs, "Had to make sure you weren't alone in the thunder. It's worth the soggy socks."

I smirk, "You could've texted."

"Wouldn't help the part where I wanted to see you."

Another rumble rolls through the sky, I curl into Josh's arms until the sound passes.

After digging out a water jug from the pantry, we haul it up to my room. We sit cross-legged on my bed, a blanket shared between us. The flashlight is pointed at the jug of water which lights up the room bright enough to convincingly pretend the power hadn't gone out.

Josh opens the marshmallows and tosses one at me.

I catch it just before it can hit my nightstand.

"Nice hands," he teases.

"I was distracted."

"By what?"

I glance at him. "You, obviously."

He grins. "*Obviously*."

We sit in the quiet for a while, listening to the rain.

Eventually he says, "You ever think about what you'd do if you weren't here?"

"Like... in life?"

"Yeah. If you could go anywhere – no rules, no money problems – just... go."

I think about it. "Somewhere green. With trees, and a lake. And no cell service."

"Off grid?"

"Off everything."

He nods. "I'd go to Iceland."

I blink. "That's specific."

"Hot springs. Northern lights. Fewer people."

"Fewer people sounds nice."

He leans back on his elbows. "You sure you wouldn't get bored?"

"Why?"

"Wouldn't you miss your books?"

"I'd bring them with me."

He smiles. "Fair."

Another crack of thunder rolls through, causing me to flinch. Josh shifts closer, his fingers brushing my knee.

"You okay?" He asks.

"Yeah."

"You sure?"

"You being here helps."

He doesn't say anything to that. Just reaches over and hands me another marshmallow.

Eventually, we're lying on our sides, the blanket pulled up to our chests. Even though it's summer, the chill from the storm feels like it's seeping through the house.

That's when there's a soft knock on my door.

Dad pushes it open just enough to peek in, flashlight in hand.

"You two alright? He asks.

174

"Yeah," I say. "Just waiting out the storm."

His eyes flick to Josh, then to the blanket, then back to me. He doesn't look mad. He just looks tired, maybe a little amused.

Josh sits up a little. "Sorry, sir. I didn't mean to –"

Dad waves a hand. "Relax, I know you're not stupid."

Josh blinks. "Thanks?"

Dad leans against the doorframe. "No funny business."

Josh holds up both hands. "None. I swear."

He lingers for a second longer, then nods. "I'm making tea. If either of you can't sleep, come grab some."

"Thanks, Dad," I say.

He nods again, then closes the door behind him.

Josh lies back down beside me, and I follow suit.

We don't talk after that. Instead we just listen to the rain. Somewhere between one breath and the next, I fall asleep.

Chapter 25

Josh

The rain's still coming down, but it's softer – now a steady rhythm against the windows.

Abbi's breathing has evened out beside me. She's curled towards the dresser, one hand tucked under her cheek, the blanket pulled up to her chin. She looks so peaceful and safe.

I slip out of the bed as quietly as I can, grab the flashlight, and head out into the hall and down the stairs.

John is in the kitchen, leaning against the counter with a mug in his hand. The kettle hisses softly behind him.

He doesn't look surprised to see me.

"Couldn't sleep?"

I shake my head. "Didn't want to."

He nods, then gestures to the second mug on the counter. "Tea?"

"Yeah, thanks."

I take it, wrapping my hands around the warmth. We stand in silence for a moment. It's the kind of silence that doesn't feel awkward, just quiet.

When John finally speaks, his voice isn't more than a whisper. "She trusts you."

I glance at him. He's not smiling.

"She trusts easy," he adds. "Always has. That's her weakness."

I nod slowly. "I know."

"She sees the good in people even when they don't deserve it."

"I know that too."

He studies me for a long moment, not hostile, just... protective.

"You planning to be the exception?"

I meet his eyes. "I already am."

John raises an eyebrow but doesn't interrupt.

I continue, a little quieter now. "She's... she's the kind of person who makes you want to be better. Not because she asks you to, or because she's watching. It's because she believes you already are."

I look down at my tea, then back up.

"I don't take that lightly. I know what it means to be trusted by her. I know what it would mean to break that."

John's expression softens... just a little.

"I care about her," I say. "More than I've ever cared about anyone. And not just because she's kind, or smart, or funny, or beautiful. It's because she's real, and she lets me be real too."

John exhales slowly, then nods.

"Alright," he says. That's what I needed to hear."

He picks up his mug again and heads towards the stairs.

"Get some sleep," he says over his shoulder. "You're making breakfast in the morning."

I smile. "Deal."

Chapter 26

Abbi

I wake up to the smell of bacon.

For a second, I don't know where I am. The light is soft, filtered through my curtains, and the air smells like rain and cypress. My room is quiet... Still.

Josh is gone. But the blanket beside me is rumpled, and his hoodie is draped over the edge of the bed. I remember the storm, the flicker of the power going out, the way he showed up with flashlights and marshmallows.

I hadn't meant to fall asleep.

I sit up slowly, wincing at the stiffness in my neck. My phone says it's barely past seven.

The smell of bacon pulls me from my bed.

I pad down the stairs, cloaked in Josh's hoodie, and find him in the kitchen. He's barefoot, and his hair's a mess, but it's a sight I wouldn't mind seeing more often. He's flipping pancakes.

Dad's leaning against the counter, coffee in hand, watching him with a look of something between pleased and impressed.

"You're up early," I say, my voice still thick with sleep.

Josh doesn't look up right away. "Didn't want to wake you."

When he does look my way, he pauses, the corners of his mouth growing to a full on smile.

"What? Do I have something stuck in my hair?" Even with the hoodie on, I shiver.

"That suits you."

"Okay, you two. I'm still here, and this is my house." Dad jokes.

Noted.

"You made breakfast?"

He shrugs. "Figured it's the least I could do after stealing half your bed."

Dad raises an eyebrow. "I might start charging you rent."

Josh laughs. "Only if it comes with unlimited bacon privileges."

I slide onto a stool at the counter, watching him move. He's calm and focused, like he belongs here.

He does.

He sets a plate in front of me -pancakes, bacon, scrambled eggs – the works.

You didn't have to –"

"I wanted to," he says, sitting beside me with his own plate.

Dad sips his coffee. "Seriously, kid. You ever think about moving in?"

Josh smirks. "You offering?"

Dad grins. "We'll talk after I finish this bacon."

I shake my head, smiling into my orange juice.

It's not a big moment – it's not dramatic or life-changing – it feels real.

It feels perfect.

"After breakfast, I have somewhere I want to take you." Josh takes a bite of bacon and smiles at me.

"Where?" I set my orange juice down and enjoy how fluffy the scrambled eggs are.

"It's a surprise. Just make sure you wear good shoes. It's outside."

"Didn't it rain last night? Or was that my imagination?"

"It's July. By the time we get there it'll be fine."

***

Josh won't tell me where we're going.

He just shows up at the door with his huge smile and a cooler in the bed of the truck.

The truck smells like sun-warmed leather and cypress. The air is warm after the storm. We drive with the window cracked enough to let in the breeze. The radio hums with something soft and old – a song I don't know, but don't want to turn off.

My head rests on his shoulder, the leather warm beneath me, his shirt is soft where it brushes my cheek.

He doesn't say anything, but he shifts slightly, like he's setting into the weight of me.

Outside, the trees blur past in streaks of green and gold. The road curves gently.

I close my eyes, enjoying this feeling. It feels like home. The hum of the engine – the rhythm of the tires, the steady rise and fall of his breath – home.

If I could bottle this moment, I would.

Then, quietly, so quietly I almost miss it, he says, "I think this is my favorite version of you."

I don't move, don't open my eyes, but my heart does something I can't name.

Josh turns off the engine, and the world exhales around us.

The low *whir* of cicadas rises in the heat. A breeze stirs the trees, rustling the cottonwoods like a whisper. Somewhere in the distance, a bird calls, sharp and clear, almost like it's announcing our arrival.

I start to reach for the door handle, but he's already out of the truck, walking around to my side. He opens the door and offers his hand.

I raise an eyebrow. "You know I'm capable, right?"

He grins, "I know. Doesn't mean I don't want to."

I take his hand.

When we step into the sun, I breathe in deep. The air smells like dry grass and pine.

Josh grabs the cooler from the back and leads me through a narrow break in the trees.

The path is overgrown, but not wild. Someone's definitely been here before, just not recently. Burrs cling to my jeans, and I brush them off absently, still thinking about what he said in the truck.

I think this is my favorite version of you.

I don't know what that means exactly, but I know how it made me feel – *seen.*

We step into the clearing, and I stop.

It's small, tucked between a ring of cottonwoods and willows, the grass soft and patchy beneath our feet. A plaid blue blanket is already laid out in the center, with a small wooden box, and a cloth bound book resting on top.

I blink. "You did all this?"

Josh shrugs, suddenly sheepish. "I know how much you love being outside. And I figured... you deserve a place that feels like you."

I walk to the blanket and kneel beside the box. It's hand-carved and a little rough around the edges, but beautiful. I lift the lid.

"Did you make this?"

"I had a little help from your dad," he confesses.

Inside there is a collection of tiny things. A dried sprig of lavender, a feather, a smooth stone shaped like a heart, a folded scrap of paper with a sketch of a tree with the words, "*our tree*" written in black ink. It's the one we fell out of when we were little.

In the center is a small, pressed daisy.

My fingers hover over it, careful not to disturb anything.

"These are all..." The words catch in my throat.

Josh sits beside me, his voice low. "Little things that reminded me of you... Of us." He looks down a little sheepish again. "Moments I didn't want to forget."

I close the lid gently, like I'm afraid the pieces might scatter if I breathe too hard.

Then I reach for the book.

It's green, cloth-bound and soft at the edges, like it's been handled a lot. It's not just a book, it's a scrapbook. I open the first page.

There's no photo, no caption – just a single flower, pressed flat and centered on the page. It's a very pale yellow, nearly white, with tiny, clustered petals like lace. The stem is thin, the leaves feathery and delicate, almost fern-like.

I brush my fingers over the edge of the paper. "What flower is this?"

Josh leans in beside me. "Yarrow."

I glance at him. "Is that what it's called?"

He nods. "It grows everywhere around here. Most people don't notice it."

I look back at the page. "It's beautiful."

"It means healing," he says softly. "It also means protection and endurance."

The words settle in my chest like a warm weight.

"You started with it."

"Felt like the right place to begin."

I turn the page.

A photo with slightly faded edges is taped in with care. We're maybe six or seven, sitting in Alec's backyard, both of us covered in mud.

I'm grinning like I just won the lottery. Josh is mid-grimace, mouth open, eyes wide with betrayal.

I laugh out loud. "Oh my gosh. This was mud pie day."

Josh groans beside me. "You dared me."

"You *agreed*."

"You said it had healing properties."

"It had a dandelion on top. That's practically medicinal."

He shakes his head, but he's smiling. "Dad took that picture right after I took a bite. I remember the taste. Gravel and regret."

I laugh harder, and for a second, it's like we're right back there. Barefoot in the grass, sunburned and fearless, daring each other to do something ridiculous just to see if the other would.

Taped beside the photo is a tiny, pressed dandelion. It's petals are still faintly yellow.

I run my fingers over the page, softer now.

"You kept this," I say.

Josh shrugs again. "It was the first time I realized I'd do something stupid just to make you laugh."

I turn the page.

The photo is quieter this time. We're older. Maybe ten or eleven, sitting on the porch steps at my house. My knees are pulled up to my chest. Josh is leaning forward, focused on something in his hands.

I remember this.

We'd spent the whole afternoon braiding bits of string and twine we found in the junk drawer. I'd told him I was making friendship bracelets. He said his fingers were too big for that kind of thing, but he tried anyway.

Taped beside the photo is one of the braids. Its faded now, the color dulled with time. There's blue, green, and a thread of pink running through the center. The edges are frayed, but it's still intact.

I brush my thumb over it, careful not to tug it loose. "I can't believe you still have this."

Josh nods. "You tied it around my wrist and said it was for luck."

"You wore it for weeks."

"I didn't want to take it off."

I glance at him, and he's not smiling. There's something softer in his eyes. Something that makes my chest ache.

"You said it would keep me safe," he adds.

I look back down at the braid. "I meant it."

I turn one more page.

This photo is different.

It isn't old or faded. It's from about a month ago. The Sunday before everything changed. When Josh made me feel important.

We're sitting at the kitchen table, mid game. The worn box of *Scattergories* is pushed to the side, a timer frozen in the middle of the table. Josh has one hand buried in the popcorn bowl, his other hovering over his answer sheet. His lips are caught mid-word.

Probably arguing that 'penguin' counts as a household pet.

I'm beside him, head tilted back in a full laugh, a fistful of popcorn in my hand, like I was about to take a bite until Josh stopped me with his antics.

My brows furrow. "Where did you get this?"

Josh smiles. "Your dad took it. He said he liked the lighting."

I shake my head, but I'm smiling too. "He's such a liar."

"He emailed it to me the next day. I almost didn't print it. It felt like it wasn't mine to keep."

I look at the photo again. The way we're leaning towards each other. We look unguarded. *Happy.*

Taped beside it is a pressed white peony. The petals are soft and layered, still holding their shape like they've been frozen mid-bloom. The same kind he gave me that day, wrapped in brown paper and handed over like it wasn't a big deal.

"You remembered," I said.

Josh doesn't ask what I mean. "You said they were your favorite. They looked like they were always on the edge of blooming or breaking."

I run my fingers along the edge of the page. "I didn't think anyone was listening."

"I always listen to you."

The peony seems fragile, but it's held its shape – almost like it was meant to be here, like it's been waiting.

I close the scrapbook gently, fingers lingering on the cover.

When I look at Josh, he's watching me. There's no expectation. He's just...there, as solid as always.

Something shifts between us. The air feels heavier, but also electric.

I lean in first.

Or maybe he does.

It doesn't matter.

Our mouths meet in a soft tentative kiss.

His hand finds my cheek, thumb brushing just beneath my ear. I melt into him like I've waited to do this for years. His fingers slide to my hair, and everything changes. The kiss deepens, unraveling into something hungrier, more certain.

I move closer, knees brushing his, one hand fisted in the fabric of his shirt. He tastes like summer and memory, and something I don't have a name for yet. Something warm and wild, and entirely his.

It's not careful anymore.

It's real.

I don't want it to stop.

Josh pulls back slowly, like it costs him something. His forehead rests against mine. His eyes are closed, jaw tight.

"I don't want to push you," his voice is low and rough. "Not like this."

I don't answer right away. I just breathe him in while trying to catch my breath. His warmth and restraint fills the air between us.

That's when it hits me.

He's perfect.

It isn't in the polished, untouchable way, but in the way that matters – in the way he waits – the way he *sees* me.

I press my hand to his chest, right over his heart. The thud of his heart under my fingers is quick – excited like I'm excited.

"You're not," I whisper. "You're not pushing me."

He opens his eyes.

"I just…" I swallow. "I want this. I do. But I want to do it *right*. You know?"

He leans in, kissing the corner of my mouth. "So we wait."

The corner of my lip curls into a small smile. "For now."

"I have one more surprise."

My eyes widen. "There's more?"

He leans back and reaches for the cooler behind him. "You didn't think I'd bring you all the way out here and not feed you, did you?"

My stomach grumbles at the mention of food.

I watch as he unpacks it, one item at a time.

First, a small container that's still warm. He lifts the lid, and the scent hits me – crispy, golden, and just a little smoky.

"Chicken Cordon Bleu," he says. "I had to call in a favor to get it right."

I laugh, stunned. "You *made* this?"

"I helped. Mostly I hovered and annoyed Dad until he let me bread the chicken."

Next comes a glass jar, the top sealed with wax paper and twine. Inside is a pale gold liquid with a few slices of peach floating near the surface.

"Fresh-squeezed Peach lemonade," he says. "I even strained it – twice."

I shake my head, grinning. "You are ridiculous."

"And finally…" He pulls out a small, chilled ramekin, the top glistening with caramelized sugar. "Crème Brulee. Don't worry, I didn't torch myself. I know my limits. Connie helped with that."

I stare at the spread, then at him. Something in my chest goes soft and full all at once.

"You remembered *everything*."

Josh gazes at me, his eyes shining. "Of course I did."

I sit down slowly, my legs folding beneath me on the blanket. The warm, buttery smell of chicken cordon bleu drifts up, but I don't reach for it.

Instead, I press my palms to my knees and stare at the space between us.

"I don't know what to do with this," I say quietly.

Josh tilts his head. "With what?"

"This." I gesture to the food, the scrapbook, the grove. "You. All of it."

He doesn't speak, just waits.

I swallow. "I've never had someone do things like this for me. Not because they had to. Just because they wanted to. I've never felt…" My voice catches. "Seen. Not really."

Josh's brow furrows and he shifts closer, his voice low and steady. "Abbigail Marie Thompson."

I shake my head, but he keeps going.

"You are the most *seen* person I know. You walk into a room and people breathe easier. You make Quint laugh when he's trying not to. You remember how your dad takes his coffee and that Cienna hates the sound of ticking clocks. You carry everyone."

He reaches for my hand, lacing his fingers through mine.

"And I see you," he says. "Not just the strong parts, or the brave or funny or stubborn ones. I see the parts you don't show anyone. I see you in the ones you think you have to hide."

My throat tightens.

"To me you're not just someone I care about. You're the person I look for first in a room. You're the one I want to tell things to first – the one who makes everything feel like it matters."

I blink hard, but the tears come through anyway.

Josh gently tilts my chin up, "You don't have to do anything to earn that. You just have to be you."

Chapter 27
Abbi

The backyard at the twins' house is already a mess of folding chairs, mismatched plates, and the smell of something slightly overcooked on the grill.

"Where's James?" Don asks, poking at the grill like it might bite him.

Cienna doesn't even glance up from her phone. "Europe."

Rees blinks. "What?"

"With Lisa," she adds, like it's no big thing.

Quint, crouched beside the cooler, looks up. "Wait... they *actually* left?"

"Yep." Cienna scrolls with the intensity of someone trying to summon a demon. "She's already posted twenty-three Instagram stories today. I know because I watched them all, against my will."

Josh raises an eyebrow. "You okay?"

"She narrated her entire airport breakfast," Cienna mutters. "*'Croissant is mid, but vibes are high.'* I swear if she says 'mid' or 'vibes' one more time, I'm reporting her to cybercrime."

Don flips a burger. "I kinda like her."

Josh and I exchange looks.

Cienna looks up, stoically. "You also think *Fast & Furious 9* deserves an Oscar, so..."

Quint grins. "She's not wrong."

Josh leans towards me," Should we tell them?"

Kasey turns towards us, leaning in close. "Tell us what?"

He straightens, clears his throat, and raises his voice just enough to get everyone's attention.

"I have an announcement," he says solemnly.

Everyone freezes.

Josh takes my hand, pauses for dramatic effect, then delivers it like a eulogy. "Don thinks ketchup is too spicy."

The silence lasts half a second.

Then Don lunges. "I told you that in confidence."

Josh yelps-actually yelps- and scrambles to his feet just in time to avoid a flying spatula.

"Oh, it's like that?" He shouts, already hoofing it across the twins' backyard.

Don barrels after him, apron flapping, tongs still in hand. "Come back here and say it to my face, you condiment coward!"

Josh laughs so hard he nearly trips over a lawn chair. "You're proving my point!"

Quint's doubled over, wheezing. "This is better than cable."

Cienna is back on her phone. "I hope he catches him. I want to see blood."

192

Josh tears across the yard, barefoot and laughing. Don is hot on his heels shouting threats that definitely violate some kind of neighborhood noise ordinance.

Quint shades his eyes with one hand. "Ten bucks says Don wipes out before he catches him."

Cienna doesn't blink. "Fifteen says Josh trips over the sprinkler head."

I arch an eyebrow. "You guys are betting on injuries?"

"We're betting on inevitabilities," Quint corrects. "Also, I have twenty on Don pulling a hamstring."

Josh loops around the garden bed, narrowly dodging a lawn flamingo. "You're all monsters!"

Don, panting but determined, screeches, "I'm gonna end you!"

I lean back on my elbows, smiling at the chaos unfolding in front of me. "Twenty bucks says Josh wins by climbing a tree."

Quint whistles. "Ooh, bold move. You taking side bets?"

Kasey's already pulling out her phone. "Hang on, I'm making a bracket."

Josh veers towards the old oak at the edge of the yard, Don still thundering after him.

"No way," Rees mutters, standing now.

Josh grabs the lowest branch and hauls himself up.

Cienna gasps. "He's climbing the tree. He's actually climbing the – *oh my gosh*."

Don skids to a stop at the base of the trunk, hands on his knees, wheezing. "You coward! Get down here and fight me like a man!"

Josh grins from his perch, about ten feet off the ground, legs dangling. "I *am* fighting. Strategically."

"You're hiding in a tree!"

"I'm *winning* in a tree."

Quint's doubled over laughing. "I owe Abbi twenty bucks."

Cienna's already filming. "This is going on the group chat."

I shake my head, smiling so hard it hurts. Josh catches my eye from the branches and gives a lazy salute, like this was all part of the plan.

And somehow... it kind of was.

Josh lounges across a thick branch like he's posing for a Renaissance painting, one arm draped dramatically over his forehead.

Kasey squints up at him. "Do you live there now? Is this your origin story?"

Josh props himself up on one elbow. I have transcended your mortal squabbles. I am one with the canopy."

"So you're a tree goblin now?" Rees laughs.

"I prefer *arboreal prince*, but sure."

Don, still catching his breath. "You're lucky I don't bring the hose."

Josh grins. "You'd have to aim upward. That's a lot of effort for someone who just lost a footrace to a guy older than you."

"By *one* year. *I* didn't get held back in kindergarten."

Cienna tosses a pretzel at him. It flies wide, missing the tree completely. "Speak, oh goblin of the leaves. What wisdom do you bring?"

Josh strokes an invisible beard. "Beware the girl who narrates her croissants. She is chaos incarnate."

I'm laughing so hard now that I nearly spill my lemonade. "You're never coming down, are you?"

Josh looks down at me from the tree, legs swinging, hair a mess, grinning like he's king of the backyard.

"Only if you ask nicely," he says.

I don't say a word.

I just look at him.

Something in his face shifts.

It's subtle, barely a flicker, but I see it. His grin softens, his shoulders drop, like I've just told him something without opening my mouth – because I have.

I don't need to tease him or roll my eyes or play along with the bit. I just look at him like he's ridiculous, brave, and mine – and somehow, he understands all of it.

Josh drops to the ground with a soft thud, brushing bark off his hands. He doesn't look at anyone else. He just walks straight back to me and sits down beside me.

Our hands find each other in the grass, fingers brushing, then curling together like they've done so many times these past weeks.

Quint groans. "Ugh, she didn't even say anything. That's not fair."

Cienna smirks. "That's called emotional dominance, Sweetie. You wouldn't survive it."

Quint shoots her a look. "*Please*. If someone tried that on me, I'd be immune."

From across the yard, Kasey raises an eyebrow.

She strolls over, slow and casual, sipping from a can of lemonade like she's got all the time in the world. She stops in front of Quint, tilts her head, and says, "Hey."

He glances up. "Hey."

She doesn't say anything more.

Just looks at him.

One eyebrow slightly raised, her lips curved in the faintest, most infuriatingly confident smile. The one that says I know exactly how to undo you.

"Wait..." Quint swallows.

Cienna snorts into her lemonade, "Told you."

Josh leans towards me, whispering, "This is better than the tree."

Quint stares at her like she's just short-circuited his entire brain. "Okay, that's not fair. That's *weaponized silence*."

Kasey just keeps looking at him.

And Quint... Quint, who's been dating her for two years and still thinks he's the one in control, stands up without a word and follows her through the gate next door to her house.

Jared claps once. "Iconic."

"It's official," Don concedes. "I'm scared of her now."

"You should be," I grin.

"I love this group," Josh sighs.

"How come you never do the look with me?" Jared asks Cienna.

Cienna turns to him, smile blooming wide, her dimples deep on each cheek. "After six years, you still have no clue."

Jared blinks. "Wait...What does that mean?"

She just pats his cheek like he's adorable and hopeless. "Exactly."

Josh leans towards me again. "I give him ten minutes before he spirals."

"Make it five," I whisper back.

Chapter 28

Josh

It starts like a hundred thoughts I've had before. This time, however, it sticks.

The job site is buzzing. Twenty guys move like clockwork – nail guns are firing, someone yells for more plywood from the truck, the air smells like pine, sweat, and sunburned steel. I'm right in the center of the organized chaos, but I'm not in it.

I'm standing on the second floor, nail gun in hand, watching the frame of the house take shape. And all I can think is, *I want this.*

I want this life... with her.

When we break, Dad and John peel off from the crew, and I follow them around the side of the house where it's quieter. Don and Rees are off with Jared driving to get lunch, leaving us alone in the quiet.

We sit on Dad's tailgate, taking cold water bottles from the cooler.

"I think I'm gonna ask her."

Dad looks over, his eyebrows raised in question. "Ask her what?"

I glance up. "To marry me."

He blinks. "You're serious?"

"Yeah," I say. "I really am."

John is quiet, his face unreadable.

"You're young," he says finally, taking a sip of water.

Dad leans back, arms crossed. "You sure this isn't just adrenaline from using the nail gun?"

I huff a laugh. "No, I've known for a while. I just... wanted to be sure I could give her something real. Something that means *something*."

I turn to John. "I respect the hell out of you, and I want to make sure I do this properly." I take one final breath before there's no going back. "May I have your blessing to marry your daughter?"

His expression softens. "You have it. You've had it since the day you started showing up for her without needing to be asked."

I take in the breath I didn't know I was refusing. It's settled something in me.

Dad grins. "Good. Now maybe we can finally get you out of the house."

John snorts. "*Please.* He's been at mine more than yours lately. I'm starting to think he likes my cooking better."

I laugh. "I plead the fifth."

Dad shakes his head. "Eighteen years of parenting and I lose him to a casserole?"

"Don't forget bagels," John jokes.

Dad raises his water bottle. "To young love and borrowed sons."

I clink mine against theirs, my heart pounding.

I can't wait to get started.

I'm going to ask her, and I'm going to make sure I do it right.

I hop down off the tailgate and walk to my truck for some privacy.

After pulling out my phone, I dial the number and hold it up to my ear.

The phone rings twice before Lily picks up.

"Lily's phone," she answers, voice clipped like she's still mid-task.

" Hey." I clear my throat. "It's Josh."

When she speaks again her voice is softer. "Hey, sweetheart."

"I –" My fingers tighten around the phone. "I was wondering if you had time to meet, about something... important?"

Another pause. "Come by after I close. Back door'll be open."

"Can we keep this just between us?"

"My lips are sealed."

***

The sun's just dipping behind the buildings when I pull into the alley behind her shop, the light for 'Jacobs Jewelers' is switched off for the night. The front windows are dark and the sign is flipped to CLOSED. When I reach the back door, it's cracked open, warm light spilling out like an invitation.

I knock once and step inside.

The place smells like metal and cedar polish. Lily's at her workbench, sleeves rolled, glasses low on her nose, a tiny flame still flickering in the soldering lamp. She doesn't look up right away, but finishes what she's doing, sets her tools down, and turns to me.

Her eyes flicker over my face. She doesn't smile.

"So," her eyes bore into mine. "You're really doing it?"

I nod back.

She gestures to the stool across from her. "Sit."

Neither of us speak. The only sound is the soft tick of the wall clock and the hum of the cooling lamp.

Then she says, "You love her."

It's not a question, but I answer it anyway.

"I do."

Her eyes don't leave mine. "And you're sure this isn't about fixing something? Or proving something?"

"No. It's about choosing."

She leans back with her arms crossed. "You know what she's been through – losing her mother, the drama with James…"

"I do."

"You know what it means to carry someone else's pain."

I nod. "I've seen it, I've held it, and I still want to be the one beside her."

Lily is quiet for a long time. Then she continues. "You were three when your mom left. You used to sit on that stool and ask me if I thought she'd come back."

I swallow. "I remember."

"You don't flinch easy," she says, "but you feel everything."

"I learned that from you."

That gets a smile, even if just a flicker. When it fades, she glances towards a photo resting on her desk. It's a family photo from one of their trips to India to visit Lily's grandmother. Cienna is hugging Ryan and James has his mother wrapped in a tight hug.

"He's still my son."

"I know."

"I don't excuse what he did. I don't defend it. But I don't stop loving him either."

"I wouldn't ask you to."

Her eyes soften, and for the first time tonight, she looks like the Lily I've always known – the one who kept a drawer of snacks under the counter for me when I was little. The Lily that never made me feel like I was missing anything, even if I was.

"I'm not asking because I doubt you," she admits. "I'm asking because I love her like she's mine. And I love you like you're mine too. So I need to know... I really need to know this isn't just a beautiful idea in your head."

"It's not," my gaze is steady. "It's a life, one I want to build with her, one I want to earn."

Lily watches me for another beat, then she sits back.

"Okay," she smiles. "Let's make a ring."

Lily flips open a sketchpad and sets it between us. The pencil she grabs is short, worn smooth from use.

"Tell me what you're thinking," she says gently.

I glance down at the blank page. "I want it to feel like her."

She nods. "Go on."

I shift in my seat. "Silver -not gold. She likes shine, but not all the time. She wears bold stuff when she wants to feel strong, or when she's trying to keep people at arm's length. But this... this should be something she can wear when she's *just her*.

Lily starts sketching a simple band. I watch her hand move, and something loosens in my chest.

"She fakes it sometimes. She pretends she's fine when she's not, but she's a terrible liar. Her voice gets tight, she won't meet your eyes, she even does this cute finger counting when she's trying to hold herself together." I show it with my own fingers as an example.

Lily's pencil slows, but she doesn't stop.

"She doesn't always see what's wrong," I add. "Not because she's blind to it, but because she wants to believe the best in people. She brushes things off, giving second chances even when they aren't deserved, sometimes even third chances. She gets hurt because of that, yet she still does it."

I lean forward, elbows on my knees. "She's been through hell, and she still shows up, not because she has to, but because she chooses to.

"She likes quiet – not silence - p*eace*. She likes when the wind moves through the trees, or when the light hits the floor in the morning. She likes things that feel *earned*."

I stop, suddenly aware of how much I've said. I blink. "Sorry. I didn't mean to–"

Lily smiles, soft and full of something I can't name. "You didn't ramble. You described *her*."

I look down at the sketch. The band is simple, but the leafwork curls up around the setting like it's holding something precious. It's not delicate, just... alive – something that knows how to hold on.

But something is *still* missing.

I lean in. "Can we add stones on the sides? Small ones. Not to make it flashy, just something extra."

Lily glances up. "You have something in mind?"

"Maybe four?" I'm not sure if I'm asking myself or Lily. After a quick contemplation, I decide. "Four on each side." One for each of our friends.

"And the stone?"

"Oval diamond," I answer without hesitation. "Not too big. Just enough to catch the light. Something she can wear with a hoodie or a dress and still feel like herself."

Lily nods, already adjusting the sketch.

I sit back, heart thudding.

This isn't just a ring, it's *her*, and it needs to be perfect.

Chapter 29

Josh

The note sits tucked beneath her pillow like a secret, like it's half-hidden, half-begging to be found. My fingers brush the edge before I pick it up. Her handwriting's a little crooked, like she scrambled to write it.

Josh,

Happy birthday old man!

If you woke up hungry, there's a chocolate kiss beside you.

If you woke up grumpy, there's a real one waiting for you at the end of the day.

Spoiler: You get both!

Now get kidnapped properly.

-I love you!

A chocolate kiss waits beside it, glistening slightly in the morning light. I smile and let it melt in my mouth slowly, the way I want the day to move. I slip the note into my wallet next to a photo of Abbi.

The house is quiet. It isn't the eerie quiet though... peaceful. It's the peaceful quiet of sunrise when the world breathes a sigh. I gaze around the room. My hoodie is draped over her reading chair. Abbi's claimed it for her own, the same way she's claimed my green blanket. I love it though, the way her smile grows just a hint brighter when she uses them.

The knock on the bedroom door isn't gentle. It's the kind that says, *'we're coming in whether you answer or not'*. I'm still sitting on the edge of Abbi's bed, her note tucked into my wallet like a charm, when the door bursts open.

"All hail the Tree Goblin King!" Jared is first through the door, holding a party hat aloft like a crown.

Rees trails in behind him, draped in streamers and holding a bag. He tosses the bag to me and I chuckle. Orthopedic insoles. "They'll be good for you," Rees plops down on Abbi's reading chair. "You're aging out of bowling form."

Don lingers in the doorway, studying the room. "It's so..." he scrunches his nose, "*Purple.*"
Quint bursts through the door, knocking Don further in. "When you said you were staying here, I thought it would have more... well... you."

"Yeah, how did you manage to persuade John in letting you stay here?"

I shrug, not really sure of the answer myself.

"I need pointers. Ryan and Lily have Cienna's room on lockdown." Jared groans. "It's infuriating."

"Food?"

"Was it from Mount Olympus?" Rees smirks.

"No... I... well..."

"Fine, fine. Keep your secrets."

"Do you at least have clothes here?" Jared inquires.

I slide off the bed and saunter over to the dresser. Abbi cleared out the bottom drawer for me a week ago. I took that opportunity to bring some of my clothes over. For two weeks I was going home just to change my clothes.

"So... not to be nosy, but are things like, 'officially official?'" Jared uses air quotes, "emotionally... and uh, logistically?"

I shrug again, blushing just a little. "We're taking it slow."

"Slow?" Jared exchanges a look with Rees and smiles. "You're practically *living* here. You have drawer space. If that's slow, then Rees is a snail dating a shadow."

"Hey!" Rees says defensively but then shrugs, pulling a streamer from his hair. "Rude, but fair."

"I just want to make sure it's... *right*."

Quint tilts his head thoughtfully, "Yeah. You can tell when it's right. It doesn't have to happen fast."

"And you're speaking from experience?" I ask.

He clears his throat. "Well, I'm not gonna *lie*. I've been with Kasey two years. I let her take the lead."

Turns out I *really* didn't want the answer to that.

"Some of us are still waiting on that kind of '*right*'," Don responds softly.

"Not that we're bitter." Rees argues. "Just romantically under-employed."

"Now get dressed and let's get out of here. We've got a busy day ahead. And Cienna will have *my* head if we don't skedaddle."

Chapter 30
Abbi

"A little more to the left," Cienna's holding her hands up like she's framing in a photo. Kasey is on one of the bar stools from the kitchen. She's next to the back door holding up one edge of the navy blue banner we painted. I'm standing on the arm of the couch holding the other. We move the banner slightly, our arms shaking from holding it up for so long.

"How's that?" Kasey grunts. She's on her tiptoes, one arm braced against the wall, the other on the banner.

"The *other* left." Cienna closes one eye, moving her hands further from her face. We move the banner towards Kasey, and she can finally lower herself off her toes.

"Perfect!" We tape the ends to the wall and pray it doesn't fall. "I'll blow up the balloons and Kasey can be in charge of streamers."

"Ooh, yay!" Kasey digs through the bag from the party store and studies the room, strategizing the best places to put them.

I make my way back into the kitchen to finish adding the whipped topping to the French silk pie, and I check the clock. We've got one more hour until they get back.

"You look like love and domesticity." Cienna leans against the kitchen table while holding a blue half-inflated balloon. "You disgust me."

"Yeah right. As soon as you pick out your ring, we all know you'll be walking down that aisle in a heartbeat."

"True," she smiles and finishes blowing up the balloon. "But it's only been a month and a half and he's *living* here."

"What's your point?" I pull out a knife and cutting board from the pantry and walk them back to the counter.

"Have you had sex yet?" My step falters on the way to the fridge.

"Way to be blunt," I say flatly, grabbing out the variety of fruits for the salad.

"What? It's perfectly normal."

"How are we having this conversation? You told me you didn't want to hear this stuff about him."

"James has moved on." She shrugs. "He's in Vienna right now." She pulls out her phone and shows me a photo of James and Lisa standing in front of a gorgeous castle. Lisa is grinning ear to ear while James kisses her cheek. I'm surprised by how much the picture doesn't bother me. I think back to just a month ago when I was upset he brought Lisa over here without a heads up. Now looking at it, I'm actually glad to see how happy they are. It's nice knowing that we've both moved on.

"I still thought you didn't want to talk about my relationship."

"I didn't. But seeing you two this past month has really shown me how much *happier* you are now. *Both* of you."

"Thanks, Ci."

"So have you?" She twirls the balloon's tail between two fingers.

"Why do you want to know?" I set the knife down and glare at her. Not angry, just... *annoyed*.

"Oh my gosh. You haven't have you?"

"He wants to wait."

"Do *you*?"

I bite the inside of my cheek.

"What do you guys do every night? Just cuddle and sleep?"

"Well... yeah." I blush.

"Have you thought about it though?"

"I'm *not* having this conversation."

"Okay, fine." Cienna groans and drags herself back down into the den where she picks up another balloon. "I hope you put this much effort into my birthday next week."

"Don't worry. I got your spreadsheet."

I lean against the counter and open Jared's messages. There's a string of photos from the day.

The first one is of Josh with a crooked birthday crown blowing out nineteen candles in a stack of donuts while Rees sobs dramatically beside him.

Another photo shows Josh front and center, wearing last year's faded sash that originally read, "18 on the 18th." The first "18" is scribbled out and replaced with a lopsided "19" in permanent marker. The ink is smudged slightly. Quint leans in from the side, flashing a thumbs-up with his best "*I fixed this*" expression. Behind them, Don is mid-somersault.

The next photo shows the back of the sash. Someone taped a glittery sticker on it that says, "*Some restrictions may apply*".

The final photo is from the escape room Jared signed them up for. Quint is wielding a foam sword. Rees is slumped dramatically beneath a puzzle poster. Josh is laughing with Don while holding up the remaining timer: 0:02.

Cienna pops a balloon in the other room and I jump, laughing under my breath as I tuck the phone away. One more hour and he'll be back.

I sure hope he loves it.

***

A chorus of car doors closing is met with all five boys yelling and laughing, the sound growing closer with each passing second. Then, there's silence. I smooth my hair, yank off my apron, and come around to the entry way to the kitchen, hiding what I can of the food display behind me on the table.

I made sure to make all his favorites. Steak, sauteed mushrooms, corn, and my rainbow fruit salad. Everything from that Sunday - the Sunday everything changed. The day my heart decided where it wanted to be.

Josh told me it was his favorite. I remember how he went back for seconds and thirds of the salad and was sad when he realized we only picked up enough steak for one each. I made sure to get him two this time.

The joy in my chest wants to burst free when the knob turns, but I press my heels further into the ground, pretending it will keep me in place.

Josh steps through the door. He's framed by sunlight and noise, his waves a mess from the shenanigans of the day. My heart flutters when his eyes find mine and he smiles.

"Hey, Stranger." He crosses the room in a few short strides, his arms enveloping me. I wrap my arms around his waist and squeeze. When I look up at him, he leans down, his finger tilting my chin to his, and he kisses me.

It's deep and intoxicating. It's the kind of kiss that says, *"I've missed you and I need you now."*

The back door clatters open and Quint's voice slaps through the silence. "Do I need to avert my eyes so I can get some food? We're starving back here. Rees is staring at his shoe like it's a piece of pizza."

Josh laughs against my forehead, and just like that, reality tiptoes back in. He takes my hand and lifts it to his lips, causing a tingle to ripples up my arm. He rotates my arm and kisses the inside of my wrist. I swallow. My heart forgets how to beat.

"Anyone?" Quint urges.

"Yeah, you guys can come in now." I manage to choke out. My skin is humming. I touch my wrist. It's warm from his kiss.

The others flood in. I hear their voices, their footsteps, the clattering of dishes, but I'm barely aware of them.

I feel it before I understand it – the way his gaze settles, the way my pulse stumbles. The blue in his stare deepens, stormy and still, like he's holding something back, something he wants to be known.

Then he leans in and whispers. "Every time I think I've memorized you, you show me something new."

I feel it, not just on my skin, but somewhere deeper. His words are stitching themselves into memory.

"We *are* still here, you know." Quint claps both of us on the shoulder, shaking us back to earth. I blush and turn away, scrambling to find something for my fingers to do – filling everyone's glasses, getting out some more napkins, *anything*.

Josh just laughs a quiet laugh and shoves Quint away with a, "buzz off," before sitting himself down at the table.

I stay standing.

I'm still dizzy from how he looked at me. My wrist still burning from the places he touched, and I try not to smile too obviously while pretending the water jug *absolutely* needs rearranging.

Chapter 31

Josh

I've walked the same ten feet of grass at least fifty times.

Back and forth, back and forth – like if I keep moving, I won't explode.

The lights are up, soft and low, strung between the trees like stars that decided to stay close tonight. In the middle of it all, I laid out her favorite green blanket. The one she always grabs when she's cold. The one she wraps around her shoulders like armor when she's tired or overwhelmed.

The ring is in my pocket. I've had it for three days.

It took almost a month to make. Three weeks of quiet planning. Three weeks of sketching with Lily - of checking and rechecking every detail at the shop after hours. Everything is finally perfect.

I check my phone again. There are no message or missed calls – just the time.

She will be here soon.

I run my hands through my hair, then stop and do it again because it doesn't feel right. I've never been this nervous in my life. – not during finals, not the first time I kissed her, not even when I asked John for his blessing.

This is different.

I pull the ring box out of my pocket and open it again, even though I've looked at it a hundred times. The silver band catches the light just enough. The leafwork curls around the diamond like its cradling something alive. The eight tiny stones on the side give it the something extra – something to let her know she is never alone.

It's not just a ring – it's *her*.

I close the box and tuck it back into my pocket. My hands won't stop fidgeting. I crouch down and smooth the edge of the blanket even though it's already perfect, then I stand up again. Pace – stop – breathe.

I'm not scared she'll say no.

I'm just... full – like my chest can't hold all of this at once.

I hear the rustle before I see her, soft footsteps on the path, the brush of fabric against leaves.

When she steps into the light, I forget how to breathe.

She's wearing a long, dark green dress with a tie in the front. It's the kind of dress that moves like water when she walks. It clings and flows in all the right places, like it was made for her.

Her hair catches the light, just enough to glint, a golden waterfall cascading in curls around her face. Her eyes – *God* – Her eyes find mine, and I feel everything in me tighten and unravel at the same time.

It's like something out of a movie, one of those slow aching romance scenes where the music swells and the schmuck just stands there, stunned, because he knows he'll never see anything more beautiful for the rest of his life.

That's me -I'm the schmuck.

I try to swallow, but my throat's tight. My chest aches, and my eyes sting. I blink hard, but it doesn't help. The tears are right there, pressing up, trying to choke their way out of me.

She smiles, soft and unsure, and tucks a piece of hair behind her ear like she doesn't know what she's doing to me.

"Hey, Stranger," she murmurs.

I open my mouth to answer, but nothing comes out.

I swallow hard and try again.

Still nothing.

She takes a step closer, and the dress shifts with her, soft and slow. It feels like the whole grove is holding its breath.

I press a hand to my chest, like maybe I can steady it, like maybe I can keep everything from spilling out too fast.

"I –" My voice cracks. I laugh shakily. "Sorry. You just…" I shake my head and clear my throat. "You look like a dream I don't want to wake up from."

Her smile deepens, but she doesn't speak. She's waiting.

"I didn't plan a speech." The words come out rough and uneven. "I tried, but none of it felt right."

I reach a shaky hand into my pocket and pull out the ring box. "So I'm just gonna say it."

I drop to one knee, the blanket protecting my suit pants.

She draws in a breath.

"I love you." My voice is steadier now, but my heart's pounding. "I've loved you for so long I don't remember what it felt like not to. I don't want to go another day without knowing I get to keep choosing you, over and over, for the rest of my life."

I open the box.

"Abbigail Marie Thompson, will you marry me?"

For a second she just stares at me with wide eyes. I watch as her lips parted and her hand flies to her mouth.

She nods once – then again, faster. Her eyes fill so quickly it nearly undoes me.

"Yes," she breathes, voice breaking. "Yes – of course I will."

I don't realize I've started crying until I feel the tears hit my hands.

She drops to her knees in front of me, and I fumble with the ring, laughing through the tears, trying to get it on her finger without shaking too hard.

It fits like it was made for her – because it was.

She looks down at it, then back up at me, and her face... her face is everything. Lit by the soft glow of the lights, frame by that dark green dress. Her eyes shine like she's never been more sure of anything.

I cup her face in both hands and kiss her.

It's not rushed or desperate, but full, like a promise.

"You really did all this?" she whispers.

I'm still breathless, but I manage to sound calm. "I wanted it to feel like us."

She smiles, and it's the kind that makes my chest ache.

"It does," she says. "It really does."

Chapter 32
Abbi

The ring is still settling on my finger, but I already feel it like a heartbeat.

Josh is kneeling on the blanket in front of me, his eyes glassy. His lips are parted like he's still catching up to what I just said, like he can't quite believe I meant it.

I did.

I *do*.

I always will.

I kiss him. Every nerve is electrified – intoxicated.

He kisses me back like he's been holding it in for weeks. Maybe he has. I can feel it in the way his hands slide to my waist, in the way he exhales like I just gave him permission to breathe again.

I pull back and look at him.

"You okay?" I whisper.

He meets my eyes and gives me a barely-there smile, like he's dizzy. "You're gonna marry me."

"I am," I grin.

I shift closer, knees brushing his, and the blanket rustling beneath us. That's when I really look at him.

He's in a suit, and he looks... unfairly good.

I reach up and smooth the lapel, fingers brushing the edge of his shirt. "You wore a suit?"

He gives a breathless laugh. "I didn't want to show up in jeans."

I shake my head, eyes lingering on him. "You didn't have to."

My hand rests lightly on his chest, feeling the steady thrum beneath the fabric. "You in this..." I pause, my voice barely above a whisper. "It's *sexy*."

His breath hitches – just a flicker, but I hear it and smile.

"You're the one in that dress. You walked into the light and I forgot how to stand."

His eyes search mine like he's trying to memorize the exact way I'm looking at him.

Then he leans in, slow and deliberate. Almost like he's trying to give me time to change my mind.

I won't.

I kiss him slow at first, then deeper, hoping he can feel everything I'm not saying – the longing, the ache, the way I've never wanted anything more.

I clutch at the lapels of his suit jacket, pulling him closer. His hands skim my arms, and I shiver, every nerve alive under his touch.

"I'm ready," I whisper, pulling back just enough to meet his eyes. My voice trembles, but I've never been more certain.

His jaw tightens. He swallows hard, lips parting like he's about to speak but can't find the words.

"Love me," I breathe.

He brings his hand to my cheek and kisses me again – deeper this time. The blanket cradles us beneath the trees, soft and familiar. The lights above flicker gently, casting gold across his face. His hand brushes through my hair, and he hesitates.

"Are you sure?" His voice is rough and unsteady. His eyes search mine, fierce but full of care.

A quiet shock ripples through my ribs. *"Please."*

That's all it takes.

His lips find my neck, and I feel the world tilt. The sensation is new, electric. He moves lower, fingers finding the tie at the side of my dress. He pauses, just for a breath, then begins to undo it, slowly, reverently.

My heart pounds in my ears, but I can still hear our breathing, growing heavier with each kiss.

I slide my hands beneath his jacket, pushing it off his shoulders, then tug his shirt free. His muscles tense beneath my touch, and something inside me melts.

He eases the dress from my shoulders, and for a moment, he just looks at me. He sucks in a breath before he can stop himself. A smile tugs at his lips, soft and awed. The joy in his eyes sends a fresh wave of shivers through me.

No more waiting.

He kisses me again, and this time, he takes my hands in his, fingers laced, muscles taut, and I feel everything in that touch.

"I love you," he whispers, lifting my hands above my head as he kisses me like he means it.

Like he always has.

Chapter 33

Abbi

The mall is loud in the way only malls can be. Music bleeds from every store, there are kids shrieking near the escalators, and the scent of cinnamon pretzels and fried food hanging thick in the air.

Josh brushes my hand as we walk, and I gaze up at him. He's in a hoodie and jeans today, casual and relaxed, but his fingers keep twitching like he wants to reach for mine, so I let him.

Cienna's already ten steps ahead, dragging Jared toward the jewelry store. "Come on, I want to see what's new in the window."

"Your parents *own* a jewelry store," he says flatly.

"Exactly. I need to keep them humble."

"Or she's trying to give him a message," Josh whispers.

"I think he's gotten it loud and clear." I smirk.

We pass the bridal shop, and I slow without meaning to. The dresses in the window glow softly under the lights. Lace, satin, tulle, every shade of white you can think of. One of them has sleeves that remind me of something out of a fairytale. The lace is elegant, the body slim.

Of course Josh notices.

"You like that one?"

I let the moment stretch, then offer a small smile. "It's pretty."

He doesn't say anything else, but his hand tightens around mine.

Ahead of us, Kasey lets out a dramatic gasp. "Hot Topic. Quint. Now."

Quint gives us a helpless look over his shoulder as she grabs his arm. "Help," he mouths before disappearing into a sea of black and neon.

Josh snorts. "He won't make it out alive."

We peel off from the group near the food court, just for a minute. Josh says he wants to check out the new arcade remodel, but we don't make it that far.

The hallway behind the photo booth is quieter. It's the kind of space that smells like old popcorn and floor wax, but also something sweet from the candy kiosk around the corner.

Josh slows and I match his pace.

He glances over his shoulder, then back at me. His hand finds mine again, fingers lacing like it's second nature.

I lean into him, shoulder to shoulder, and he turns just enough that I feel the shift in his breath.

His eyes flick to my mouth.

I don't wait.

I press up on my toes and kiss him softly at first, just enough to feel the shape of him. He exhales against my lips, and his hand slides to the small of my back, pulling me closer.

The noise of the mall fade to nothing but the hum of the vending machine behind us. I love the warmth of his palm through the fabric of my dress, the way he kisses me like he's still not used to being allowed.

I smile against his mouth. He kisses me again – and again. When we finally pull apart, I'm breathless and a little dizzy.

"Hi," I whisper.

He grins. "Hey, Stranger."

He leans his forehead against mine, and for a second, neither of us moves.

His thumb brushes the inside of my wrist, slow and steady before bringing my wrist to his lips, his kiss gentle and slow.

"I still can't believe you said yes," he murmurs.

I nudge his chest with a smile. "You asked me in a grove strung with fairy lights... In a suit... With a ring that fits like it already knew me."

He laughs, low and quiet. "Okay, yeah. I did kind of go all in."

I trace the line of his jaw. He closes his eyes like he's soaking it in.

The sound of footsteps echo in the distant, but they're getting closer with each step.

Josh sighs. "We should get back."

I smile, but I don't move yet. I press one last kiss to the corner of his mouth, then step back, smoothing my dress. He straightens his hoodie, runs a hand through his hair, and gives a look that's all warmth and wonder.

We walk back to the group side by side, not saying much, but his pinky hooks around mine. Cienna and Jared are still at the jewelry store, faces pressed to the glass. She's pointing at something, and he's nodding along.

After Josh picks up some fries and pizza, we join Don at our table. Rees is leaning against a pillar near the pretzel stand, watching a girl in a denim jacket walk by. He straightens, runs a hand through his hair, and flashes a smile. She glances at him, then keeps walking.

He turns back to us, unfazed. "She's clearly intimidated."

Don doesn't even look up from his drink. "By what? Your cologne or your confidence?"

Rees scoffs. "You think you could do better?"

Don shrugs. "I think I could do *less* and still do better."

Rees narrows his eyes. "Alright, then. Go on. First girl you see."

"You're serious?"

"Dead serious. Let's see the master at work."

Don scans the crowd, then stands. "Fine."

He walks over to a girl waiting in line at the pretzel counter and says something. She laughs. He gestures to his phone, and she takes it, types something in, and hands it back.

He returns, sipping his drink like nothing happened.

Rees stares. "No way."

Don holds up his phone. "Her name's Talia. We're getting coffee next week."

Rees blinks. "What did you even say to her?"

Don shrugs. "I asked if the cinnamon pretzels were worth the line."

Rees throws up his hands. "This is rigged."

Don smirks. "Maybe she just wasn't intimidated." His eyes catch mine and he winks. I give him a subtle thumbs up.

It does work.

Cienna and Jared arrive back, mid-argument. Both carrying a smoothie.

"I'm just saying," Jared teases, "If you already know what kind of cut you want, why are we looking at rings *here*?"

"Because I like to keep my options open," Cienna replies, sipping her smoothie. "And because your taste is questionable.

"My taste is *flawless*."

"You once said mood rings were '*underrated*'."

"They are."

Cienna rolls her eyes and flops into a chair.

A second later, Kasey comes striding up triumphantly, dragging Quint behind her.

Quint looks like he's just lost a bet.

He's wearing a black T-shirt with a giant kitten on the front with pink glitter glasses and a rhinestone collar.

Josh stares. "Dude."

Quint sighs. "She said it was this or the fishnet tank top."

"That's what you get for making fun of my store." Kasey crosses her arms. "Besides, you look adorable."

"I look like I got mugged by a Lisa Frank folder."

Rees snorts. "You're pulling it off though."

Quint stares. "I hope you get rejected again."

Don raises his drink to his lips. "Too late."

Rees glares. "We're not talking about that."

"Pretty sure we are," Don snickers.

Cienna pulls out her phone and scrolls. "Okay, everyone look alive."

"No!" Quint cries in horror.

Josh is mid-laugh. Rees is throwing a fry at Don. Kasey's pointing at Quint's glitter kitten shirt while smiling ear to ear. Jared's pretending not to smile. I'm leaning into Josh, my hand on his knee. The ring catches the light. I don't even notice it right away. I'm halfway through a fry when my phone buzzes.

Then again – and again.

I glance down, thumb swiping instinctively. Cienna already managed to post the photo to Instagram. I tap the screen and my stomach flips.

@ciennawild: Mall rats forever (also someone's fiancé era is showing)
@moira.rose: Wait is that a ring??
@sydwrites: fiancé ERA???
@kasey.chaos: I knew first. Everyone calm down.
@jared.exe: I look amazing. thank you for noticing.
@quintverse: I'm deleting the internet.
@don.notnow: I warned you.
@jacobs.james: ?

Josh squeezes my hand under the table. I look over at him, his smile a little nervous and a little proud. I squeeze back.

***

We don't go straight home after the mall.

Josh turns right at the light instead of left. The truck is quiet, now just the low hum of the engine and the faint scent of cinnamon from the pretzels we didn't buy.

Neither of us found anything worth taking home today.

The cemetery is still, with a few cars parked along the drive. A groundskeeper in the distance is trimming hedges. It's only 3p.m, but the light's already starting to shift.

We stop at the florist cart at the entrance. I pick out a bunch of purple asters. They're bright and a little wild, like they grew just for her.

Josh pays for them and holds my hand as we walk the familiar path.

Her headstone is clean. Someone's already left daisies. I crouch down and start pulling the weeds that have crept in around the edges. They're tiny things, stubborn and wiry.

Josh kneels beside me, brushing away a few stray leaves. I set the aster in the vase and smooth the grass around the base, then I sit back on my heels and look at the stone.

"Hey," I say softly.

Josh stays quiet beside me, letting me talk.

"We've got some news." I hold up my hand. "We're engaged."

I glance at Josh. He gives me a small smile, then looks back at the stone - at her picture.

"He asked me in the grove, with lights and everything. You would've loved it."

I pause, picking at a blade of grass.

"I wish you were here," I add. "But I think you already know."

Josh clears his throat. "Hi, Naomi," his voice is a little rough. "I'll take good care of her, just like I promised."

I reach for his hand. We sit there for a while longer, just the three of us. The aster shifts gently in the breeze, and the sun keeps moving.

Then I stand, brushing the dirt from my knees, and say, "Okay."

Josh squeezes my hand once before we turn back towards the truck.

***

The house smells like mint tea and new paper. Josh is in our room humming off-key while packing for his night out.

My phone's still buzzing every few minutes with congrats and heart emojis. It's been like this since this afternoon when Cienna posted the photo.

Everyone knows now, and weirdly, I'm not hiding from it. Each notification excites me.

Dad grabs his keys from the dresser by the door. Alec just pulled up to take him to poker night. After picking up the poker chips from next to the front door, he pauses, eyes narrowing like he's trying to sense a trap. "You two have everything you need for the night?"

Josh straightens. "Yeah, I'm heading out in a bit. Boys night thing."

Dad's eyebrows climb. "You're leaving her alone?"

Before Josh can answer, I tap the top of the bridal magazine in my lap. "I was just telling Josh about the twelve-part checklist for venue selection. We've only completed three. And don't even get me started on the shade of ivory vs. cream."

Dad blinks, the color draining from his face like a man staring down his own mortality. "Right," he mutters. "Well... Goodnight."

Josh's shoulders shake with silent laughter as Dad slips out the door. We hear Alec's voice—something about someone cheating last week—then the car pulls away.

The house settles. It's just the two of us now.

Josh walks over slowly, like he can't stay away even if he tried. He slides onto the arm of the sofa and takes my hand without saying a word. His thumb drags over the ring, lazy and reverent.

He's quiet for a long moment, then leans in brushing his thumb along the edge of my jaw like he's memorizing it. The ring on my hand pressed lightly into his palm as his fingers lace through mine.

"I'm so glad you said yes," he murmurs.

I smile. "I'm glad you asked."

His lips brush mine once, and then again, this time slower. The kiss is familiar and new at the same time. It's not rushed. It's not dramatic. It's just him, solid and warm, pulling me closer like he doesn't want to let go – like kissing me still feels like a discovery.

I let my hands settle at the back of his neck, my heart ticking a little too fast in the quiet. He deepens it, just a little, and I melt into him.

HOOOOOOONK.

We both flinch, bumping noses and breaking apart with a laugh. Josh groans, forehead dropping against mine.

"Jared," he mutters like a curse.

"You should go," I whisper, even as my fingers stay curled in the hem of his shirt.

"Yeah," he says, but he doesn't move.

Another honk, two sharp blasts this time.

"Fine, I'm going," he grumbles, stealing one more kiss before dragging himself to the door.

I collect the magazines and carry them up to my room like sacred scrolls and not glossy paper full of $9,000 dresses I'll never wear. A fresh mug of mint tea steams in one hand, bridal tower in the other.

I'm not sure how Cienna managed to find so many so fast. I've only been engaged since last night. It's like she's been hoarding them in secret. She's had her wedding planned out since she was six. Down to the last detail is in these magazines.

She plopped them in my lap earlier with a serious face.

"You're gonna want to hydrate," she said. *"There's a whole section on napkin folding that changed my whole worldview."*

Honestly, I thought she was exaggerating, but now I'm staring at this stack and realize... she wasn't. There are *so many.*

Glossy covers, tiny dog ears where she already marked things "for inspiration", each magazine is stuffed with tiny tabs of neon pink and yellow, and absolutely *none* of them are mine.

I curl into my reading chair, blanket wrapped around my legs, one leg tucked beneath me the way it always ends up. The stack of bridal magazines looms beside me on the floor. I set my tea on the nightstand, meaning to sip it, but then the page in my lap distracts me. Before long I'm invested in an article about fabrics and the emotions they're supposed to hold.

Silk: Grace and clarity.

Satin: Devotion.

Organza: Strength hidden in softness.

I smile, letting myself imagine being adorned in a *real* dress, walking down a *real* aisle. The tea is already cooling behind me, completely forgotten. My thumb grazes the edge of a page, trailing over a sentence print in soft italic type.

"Lace is tradition made visible. It's delicacy a symbol of devotion, its threads a map of memory."

I read it twice.

Lace – that intricate, barely there kind of beautiful. It shouldn't hold together but somehow does. I don't know if it's suits me, but I can't stop staring at the picture.

My phone buzzes against my thigh, and I nearly drop the magazine. Opening my messages, I see that Josh has sent a photo and I snort.

Josh is flanked by chaos. He's shirtless, grinning, and his body is streaked in red and silver paint. Jared's wielding two pool noodles like crossed sabers. Rees has smeared blue on his chest in the shape of... possibly a dinosaur? Don's attempting a Viking glare but mostly looks like he's about the sneeze. Josh, at the center, has one arm outstretched like he's leading them into a noble cause. His expression is absurdly serious. The pool noodle across his back does not help.

The caption reads:

Victory is imminent.

I laugh and text back:

You look like a rejected boy band from a post-apocalyptic summer camp.

Three dots appear, Then:

We're calling ourselves Savage Tenderness.

Please don't.

Too late. We're dropping an EP.

I shake my head, smiling so hard it hurts a little. I save the photo and immerse myself back into the magazines.

Outside, the light shifts from gold to gray. I barely register it. At some point, I tuck the blanket around my legs tighter, but I don't remember when. I stop noticing how long it's been since Josh texted.

There's a weird comfort to the quiet - to the soft scratch of pages turning, and the sound of my own breathing in this room where I still half expect life to interrupt me.

But it doesn't, so I keep flipping pages, the night slipping past me in whispers. The pages in my lap blur slightly. It's the kind of blur that comes from too much focus. Somewhere between tulle diagrams and symbolic florals, I lost track of time. The stack beside me has slumped. My cold tea is staring at me from the nightstand like it knows I'm never finishing it. I reach for another magazine, fingers skimming one of Cienna's tabs.

The knock doesn't sound like a knock. It's three heavy smacks against the front door.

I blink up from the magazine, still caught between lace silhouettes and Cienna's notes about what color "photographs well in candlelight." For a second I think I imagined it – but then it comes again.

BANG. BANG. BANG.

I grab my phone. 10:02p.m.

Josh is still out and Dad's cards won't fold before midnight. No one's supposed to be here.

Still curled in my T-shirt and sleep shorts, I climb out of my chair and stretch. My engagement ring flashes as I brush my hair out of my eyes, still tangled from leaning over magazines all night. The stack beside me looks like it's been raided by a paper hurricane.

I flip on the stairs light before I head down, enjoying the way the carpet feels under my feet. I open the door with the same soft smile I've had all night – lace still on my mind and Josh's dumb text still warming my chest.

232

When the porch light hits him, I'm frozen – confused. He's unkempt. I recognize the red button-up before I process anything else. It's slouched open over a grey t-shirt with dark splotches all down the front. From the smell, I can only assume it's alcohol.

His eyes aren't focused. They're wandering, and glossy, but not in the way that means wonder or awe. The second he sees me, they snap sharp–too sharp–and I feel it, cold and sudden, straight though my spine.

My voice is a breathless whisper, "James."

Chapter 34
Abbi

He steps towards me, and I instinctively step back, forgetting about the door. He pushes his lips to mine and shoves me against the dresser across from the door. My lower back hits the edge, causing an instant throbbing ache, the dresser thudding against the wall – the contents on top scatter.

What is happening? Is this real?

It takes all my strength to push him off. "What are you doing?" I wipe my hand across my mouth, the taste of alcohol bitter on my lips.

"Why?" He steps towards me again, but I shove him back. This time he hardly budges.

"Because you're drunk," I snap, reaching for the door. James bats my hand away and places his own hand on the edge of it, blocking any chance to leave through it.

"I gave you everything," he slams the door, the latch makes a resounding final click. The air inside the house changes. His eyes don't move from my face. "I waited patiently, and you…" he grabs the sides of my face firmly and speaks through gritted teeth. "I know you gave it to him. Why else would you have a ring?" There's a fire in his eyes, his nostrils flared.

You need to get him out of here.

I take his hands into mine and pull them from my face. His muscles fight against me like stone and fury. "You need to leave," my voice trembles.

I sidestep, allowing some distance between us. I should've stayed still. His hands are in fists now, his breathing is heavy. His mouth turns into a deeper frown, making my stomach churn.

"It was supposed to be *me*," he steps forward. I take another step towards the kitchen, *praying* he'll stay back.

"*You* cheated on *me*," I say venomously. I never intended to let him know that I knew, but he doesn't even flinch. It's like the words mean nothing to him, and even after months, that stings, just a little.

"I could have any girl I want." The way he's looking at me causes the world to tilt – and not in the good way. The floor feels suddenly uneven.

"What do you want from me?"

Maybe I can talk him down from whatever he feels he needs to do. This isn't him. He's better than this.

"You aren't that beautiful, but I chose you." His words are a slap. "You should be grateful." He leaps at me, but I dodge him. I race towards the front door, but he grabs me by my hair and jerks me back, causing me to fall.

I crash through the coffee table. A piece of the metal frame lodges into my side.

Air explodes from my lungs like someone reached in and yanked it out by the root. The world doesn't spin now, not exactly. It folds. I open my mouth, but nothing comes out, just a hollow ache for breath that isn't there. Glass cuts into my back, the pain from it dull compared to the panic and pain in my side.

Before I can regain myself, he's grabbing for me again. This time, he holds onto my hair, hoisting me to my feet. My hands work desperately to pry my hair from his grip. He throws me on the couch.

Just get to the door.

He steps towards me, the sound of glass crunching under his shoes. I draw my right arm back, but he stops my attempted punch with his own blow to my gut. I fold in on myself, coughing, desperate for air.

"You owe me," he hisses through gritted teeth. He grips my hair again and holds my face next to his.

"Why?" I yelp. My body doesn't know which pain to focus on first.

He stares down at me, and I can feel his grip loosen on my hair.

Now!

I stomp on his foot with all the energy I can muster. He doesn't grab for his foot, but he releases my hair. I make a run for it up the stairs to my room where my phone is.

Get help!

Before I can reach the first landing, James has a hold of my shirt and pulls me back. I flip down the steps, a sharp pain flaring in my left shoulder.

I can't stop now!

I stumble to my feet as James reaches for me. Ducking away from his next punch attempt, I make another shot for the stairs. This time I make it to the top.

Locking my door, I rush to my chair in search for my phone, but I don't see it. James is banging on the door. My tears burn my eyes.

I can't let him win.

I'm fumbling through the scattered magazines, searching for my lost phone. My tears blur everything, making it impossible to find my phone. It's just gone.

With one final **BANG,** the door swings open. I bolt for the bathroom. When I reach to close the door, James manages to wedge his foot in and blocks me from closing it.

Why does everyone have to be stronger than me?

The fire in his eyes burns brighter, and he forces the door open.

I spot my can of hairspray by my sink. Before I can get the lid off, his arm snaps around my throat like a vice. I drop the can trying to get his arms away from my throat. I choke on the first breath I can't get. My fingers scrambling for leverage, for space – *anything.* My vision starts to blacken at the edges.

Don't give in!

He drags me to the bed and flings me onto it like a rag doll. When he releases me, I cough and gasp, greedy and grateful for the air.

As the lights come back into view, he has my pants off and is ripping at my shirt. The sound of the fabric tearing echoing in my ears.

"Please," my voice is barely audible, the effort painful. "James, you don't have to do this," I sob.

James is undoing his pants, his eyes focused on his hands.

Now's your chance!

I roll to my left, but the pain in my shoulder is too strong, causing me to hesitate.

He grabs me by the hair again and throws me back onto the bed. His right arm pulls back, and his fist connects with my face.

I let out a scream as the sharp stabbing pain fills my vision.

He covers my mouth, muffling the sound, and places his face close to mine. His breath scorches my face, sour with alcohol.

"If you scream, I *will* make it worse," he hisses.

How could it possibly be worse?

His pupils feel too dark. His jaw is tight. I continue to kick and claw, but he manages to place both knees on my thighs, forcing my legs apart. His hands grip my wrists. He pushes harder on my left arm sending more white-hot pain through my arm and back.

My vision starts blackening around the edges again. I whimper in pain, but he stops it with a kiss.

He forces his tongue down my throat, making me cough with surprise and disgust. The remnant of alcohol is bitter and horrid.

The ceiling blurs. My hands aren't mine anymore. I let go of everything I know. As James enters me, the pain swells, wrapping around my ribs, my throat, my lungs, until there's nothing left but dark.

Chapter 35

Josh

The second I walk in, something feels...off.

The door wasn't locked. Light pours from the upstairs hallway like Abbi just stepped out for a second. But the air's wrong – still – like it's holding its breath.

I step into the living room and stop cold at the crunch under my feet. Glass litters the floor. The coffee table is destroyed – tempered glass shattered and scattered like someone dropped a body on it. A twisted chunk of the silver frame is speared through one of the couch cushions while another chunk looks like it's been coated with a dark liquid. Whatever happened here – it wasn't small.

There's a hole in the drywall across from the staircase. Bigger than a fist. *Violent.* The sight of it lands somewhere deep in my chest.

I don't call her name, I just move.

The stairs creak beneath me as I take them two at a time.

Her door's half off the hinge, busted inward like someone kicked it hard and didn't stop until the wood gave.

I push it open– and everything in me stutters.

She's on the bed, her body sprawled. Her left arm sits at an awkward angle, like it's been detached from the socket. Her shorts are on the carpet beside the bed in a forgotten heap. Her shirt ripped down the center and pulled away from her body. There's blood across her body and sheets.

My eyes scan her face. Her lip is split and bloody. A bruise is already blooming at her temple. Her face is swollen and darkening around her eye. There's a smear by the edge of the mattress that looks like a handprint, and blood in droplets on the white carpet.

My heart just... drops – like it left me behind and I haven't realized yet.

"*Abbi.*"

I'm across the room in two steps. Dropping to my knees beside the bed, I reach for her, but my hands are shaking too badly. I don't want to touch her wrong.

She doesn't move. I'm not even sure she's breathing.

I fumble with my phone. I don't even remember dialing. I just keep saying the address over and over like that'll make them get here faster.

My eyes stay on her the whole time. I can't look away. I don't know if I'll ever forgive myself for not being here when she needed me most.

I don't look away, not once – not when I see the bruises, not when I see what was taken from her. I keep my eyes on her face. She deserves *that*. She deserves to be seen like she still matters – like she's still human.

The sound of sirens grows closer. I know they'll be here in seconds.

I'm letting strangers walk into this room and see her like this.

I spot it in the corner, on her chair. The green blanket. The one that used to be mine until she claimed it without saying so. I grab it with both hands, barely noticing the way my fingers clutch the fabric too tight. It's soft, familiar – s*afe.*

I kneel beside her bed again.

Don't look at the bruises. Don't look at the blood. Just her face.

Her lashes are stuck together like she cried herself unconscious.

I cover her with our blanket – the only thing I can think to do because I was too late to stop whatever happened here.

I lay it gently over her shoulders, draw it down over her chest and her legs. I tuck the edge under her bare bruised thighs, carefully – like maybe if I do this right, she won't flinch the next time someone reaches for her. It's the only thing I can give her right now that hasn't been ruined.

Boots crash through the entry downstairs. Voices yell out, commanding and clipped. "Fire and EMS! Anyone inside?!"

I shout back, my throat raw. "Upstairs! First door!"

Their feet pound the steps like thunder. The hallway fills with noise, but still I don't leave her.

They burst through the bedroom doorway, first responders already reaching for gloves, for vitals, for answers I don't have. Orders are barked in tight, practiced rhythms.

"She's breathing. Weak pulse. BP's low."

"Sir, we need you to step out."

I don't move until they physically guide me from the room. It's only a few feet, just outside the door, but it feels like another world. One of the officers leans in, voice gentle but firm. "Name?"

241

"Josh Anderson." The words feel strange coming out of my mouth. Like I've forgotten what they mean. The officer writes it down while EMTs work behind him. I can hear gloves rustling, vitals called out, plastic snapping open.

Josh Anderson, who was supposed to protect her.

Josh Anderson, who arrived too late.

"What time did you arrive?"

"Five minutes ago? Maybe ten? I don't... I'm not sure." I rub my face. "The front door was unlocked. The living room was destroyed. Her door was broken in. And she was – " I swallow hard. "I found her like that."

The officer nods, jotting everything down. "Did you touch anything?"

"Just her. Just to check she was breathing. And the blanket. The green one."

He steps back to make room as more medics crowd the doorway.

And then I hear it.

"Josh?"

I turn just in time to see John at the top of the stairs, Dad right behind him. Both of them are frozen in the chaos. Their eyes fall to me, then past me – to the room. To her.

John shoves past the officers trying to stop him. *"Abbigail!"* His voice breaks open like glass. He stumbles into the room, falls to his knees beside her bed. "No. No, no, no, baby, no..."

Dad doesn't say anything. He silently leans against the doorframe. His fists are clenched, his eyes too wide.

I try to go to them, but another uniform gently blocks the way.

That's when Chief Blake Matthews arrives. The towns tall, steady, Fire chief – and Kasey's dad.

He steps up onto the landing, radio crackling at his shoulder. I see it hit him like a sledgehammer. The busted door, the blood, John sobbing on the carpet.

He stops. No one has to say anything. He already *knows*. I watch him as the blood drains from his face.

The EMT on scene tries to speak, gently. "Unconscious female. Signs of trauma. We're prepping transport to County General."

Blake nods once, his voice hoarse. "I'll escort."

Then his eyes find me. And for a long second, he just *stares* – *n*ot as fire chief, not even as Kasey's father - just as a man.

"You riding with her?"

I swallow and nod.

"Then come on. Now."

And I follow – because there's nothing else left to do.

Chapter 36
Abbi

Beep... Beep... Beep...

The sound drills straight through my skull.

I try to reach out, to turn off whatever is making that sound, but my body–it doesn't move right.

Everything aches – deep, twisting, *wrong*.

My shoulder throbs like it doesn't belong to me anymore. My rib grinds with every breath. My side feels like it's being split open. My lip stings, and one eye won't open all the way.

I open my mouth, but what comes out is more of a whimper.

There's a movement, then a hand. It's not mine. It's warm.

"Abbi?" His voice shatters through the static in my brain. "Hey. I'm here. You're safe."

Josh.

He's sitting next to me, his eyes glassy, voice soft. He's trying so hard not to scare me. It's too bad something's already broken.

I want to move closer, to find the pieces of me that don't feel like mine anymore, but even the smallest shift lights every nerve in my body on fire.

"Where..." My mouth is dry. I taste blood and something chemical. My throat barely works. "Where am I?"

"Hospital," he says gently. "You've been out a while. But you're here. You're okay."

'Okay'?

His words don't make any sense. *Why wouldn't I be okay?* That's when it hits me.

A memory.

A hand.
The slam of a door.
The way his breath smelled.
The anger in his eyes.

I shut my eyes, as tightly as I can, ignoring the throbbing in my face.

No.

Josh's hand squeezes mine, bringing back into the room. I cling to it.

I want to tell him – I do, but shame floods every crack in me faster than air. It coats my throat like tar.

So when he asks, his voice trembling, "Abbi... do you remember who did this?" I lie.

"I don't know..."

Because if I say the name, I'll never stop hearing it.

The door clicks, I tense, my pulse spiking. My grip tightens around Josh's fingers.

"It's me."

Connie.

She steps into the room like she's been doing it all her life. Like hospital tiles don't dull her warmth.

She's in maroon scrubs and sneakers that squeak a little when she moves, but she still somehow looks like Don and Rees' mom before anything else. Right now, that might be the only reason I don't burst into tears.

"Hey, Sweetheart," she says, her voice gentle and even. "Still raising hell I see."

It's a joke, but not a good one, and she knows it. Her eyes are soft and red-rimmed. Her hands move with muscle memory–checking the monitors, adjusting the IV drip–but her focus never really leaves my face.

"I came as soon as I could," she says.

I believe her.

"Your scans look clean," she goes on, pulling my chart. "Your dislocated shoulder's back in place. That gash on your side" she points to something on the chart, "you got lucky. It missed anything major. Four broken ribs, one with a hairline fracture, which, unfortunately just means breathing is going to suck for a while."

I huff something that's not quite a laugh. It still hurts.

She leans in and brushes my hair back the way moms do when they don't want to say they're heartbroken. I flinch, the pain in my scalp still feels fresh, the sensation of being dragged hurts more than my head. "You're going to be okay, Abbi."

They keep saying that. 'Okay' – as if it means something to me. How could I possibly be okay?

My voice shakes when I ask, "Does everyone know?"

Connie's smile fades to something more solemn.

"They all know. And they love you. *We* love you."

I nod. I nod until my ribs remind me why that's a bad idea, and I wince.

She doesn't press. She just rests her palm briefly on the side of my head and says, "He didn't take anything that can't be rebuilt – Piece by piece, breath by breath."

She lets the silence settle before adding quietly, "You want me to kick out this boy for a while so you can nap?"

When I look at Josh, he's pretending to breathe normal even though his hands haven't stopped shaking since I woke up.

"No," I whisper. "He stays."

Connie nods, and I watch as her lips twitch. It's not quite a smile... Not yet.

"Then I'll go find you some juice that helps with the chemical taste I bet you've got." She squeezes my foot through the blanket and slips out the door.

Josh hasn't moved. He's close enough that I can feel him watching me without pressure, without blame – his hand still in mine.

I shift slightly, ignoring the fire along my ribs. My shoulder aches and my throat feels scraped raw.

When he speaks, his voice is barely louder than the beeping behind me.

"Abbi..."

He pauses, worrying the inside of his lip. "I know you said you don't remember, but if you do... if there's something..."

His eyes are pleading.

I swallow, the pain in my throat unsure if it wants to retreat or intensify.

I could tell him. I could say the name.

Then I'd watch the warmth leave his eyes, let him carry the truth I'm dragging behind my ribs like barbed wire.

But I can't – because once it's spoke, it's real, and once it's real, it's his too.

So I do the only thing I can to keep him from that knowledge, I lie... again.

"I don't know," I say, staring at the edge of the blanket where a blue thread is coming loose. "It was dark. I think I passed out."

He's silent for a while, his eyes searching my face.

"Okay," he says quietly. He doesn't ask again.

The door swings open like someone forgot what gentle means.

"I swear to God, Alec, if one more nurse tells me to breathe, I –"

Dad stops mid-sentence.

His eyes lock on mine. My lip is split, my shoulder bandaged. The machines beep like tiny lifelines. Josh's hand is still tight in mine.

Dad's holding a hospital coffee cup, the lid askew like he dropped it on the way here. Alec's behind him, looking contrite and exhausted, mouthing '*sorry*' before slipping away.

"Kiddo..." Dad steps forward like the air's thicker than he expected. "You're awake."

I try to nod, but the muscle in my neck pulls on my shoulder.

He moves closer, standing just beside the bed but not touching anything. His fists tighten around the coffee cup.

"I was gone five minutes," he hisses. "Five. Alec said I should get some air, that it would help. I come back and you're–you're looking at me like..."

"I'm okay," I whisper. Now it's my turn to use that word. It tastes so metallic in my mouth. Then again, it could also be the drugs they're pumping into me.

His shoulders drop. "I missed you opening your eyes," he mutters.

Josh shifts beside me, quieter than the machines, but enough to be noticed. Dad doesn't turn to him. His gaze lingers on my black eye, on the edge of the blanket pulled high over my ribs. Then he finally meets Josh's eyes.

"I'm glad you stayed," his voice is flat.

Josh squeezes my hand. "I'll always stay," he replies. He doesn't look at me when he says it, but his words sink in, my heart fluttering even though it feels heavy. I know he means more than just today.

Dad exhales – not quite forgiving, but it's something close enough to let the tension ease.

He crouches beside the bed and gently places the coffee cup on the tray. Then he touches my hand, just two fingers against my knuckles.

"You want me to find them?" he asks, voice low.

My breath hitches in my throat, my heart speeding up, the monitors matching with its *beeps*.

"No," I say. "I don't know who it was."

He watches me - watches me *want* to say more.

"Okay," he looks away, and I know what that cost him. He isn't going to push. He's going to rage in silence. But right now – he stays.

The door opens with a soft knock, and then two people step in.

The woman's blazer is charcoal grey, her hair pulled back in a tight twist. Her eyes scan the room like she's cataloging everything, her fingers holding up her badge draped around her neck.

The man beside her wears a badge clipped to his belt and a look that says he's seen too many rooms like this.

"Miss Thompson?" the woman says. "I'm Detective Condie. This my partner, Detective Lawrence. We're here to follow up on the report."

Dad straightens beside me, his jaw clenched. Josh's hand tightens around mine under the blanket.

"Can't this wait? She just woke up," Dad says, his voice threateningly low.

Detective Lawrence steps forward, calm but firm. "We understand. But we need to ask a few questions while the details are fresh."

'Fresh'.

Like blood. Like pain.

Detective Condie's tone is soft, gentle, like she sees right through me. "We can come back later if you'd prefer, but if you remember anything, anything at all, it could help."

Josh glances at me. His eyes ask the question he promised not to say out loud.

"I don't remember." I know it's a lie, but it's the only one I know how to live with. "And I don't want to pursue anything."

"Abbi..." Dad tries to intervene, but I cut him off.

"No. I just want to forget this happened and move on."

Detective Condie nods slowly. "Okay. We'll leave our card." She sets it on the tray beside the untouched coffee. "If you remember anything, or change your mind, feel free to call us." Then they both turn to go.

Dad's footsteps echo against the tile.

Back and forth.

Back and forth.

He's not yelling. He's not even raising his voice – but every time he turns, I feel the gravity shifting.

"I wish you would tell us." His tone isn't angry. Just...pleading - like the words might unlock something if he says them enough.

Josh's hand is still wrapped in mine beneath the blanket. He hasn't moved, hasn't spoken, but I feel him watching Dad, watching *me,* like he's trying to hold both of us together with nothing but silence.

"I wish you'd let me help," Dad says, stopping at the foot of the bed. "I'm your father, Abbigail. I'm supposed to protect you."

I close my eyes.

"You *have* protected me," I whisper. "You're here."

"That's not the same. Being here *after* doesn't fix what happened *before.*"

"I don't know who it was," I repeat, trying to keep my face unreadable.

He stares at me, and I can see it. His eyes don't believe me.

"I wish you would tell us," he says again. This time, his voice cracks. My tears come spilling out fast, like something cracked from the inside and didn't ask permission.

I curl into Josh's hand, breathing through the pain in my ribs, the pull in my shoulder and side, the ache that lives everywhere else.

Dad goes still before he takes one look at me—just one—and he breaks.

He turns without another word and walks straight to the door with footsteps that sound more like a retreat than an exit.

The door clicks shut behind him, sounding too final.

Josh doesn't let go. His hand holds mine tighter, anchored in this mess, his earlier promise thrumming in my heart. He shifts a little closer, arm brushing my side gingerly. Just enough to let me feel what I can't say.

I cry into the space between breaths.

He doesn't speak, yet somehow, that saves me more than words ever could.

Chapter 37

John

I don't even realize I've left the hospital room.

I guess I walked out, but I couldn't say how. My body moves, but my mind stays behind. I don't notice the hallway or clock the nurses, I don't even register the elevator. I'm sick from watching my daughter sob without being able to help.

Now I'm in the parking lot. My hand is on my truck door. I open it, get in, and sit down, the weight in my chest heavier than the jostle of the cab.

It's quiet – too quiet.

Then it's not.

I scream – the kind that empties your lungs and still leaves something behind clawing at your chest, raw, desperate. I continue even after my voice gives out.

I slam my fists against the edge of the steering wheel until pain shoots through my arms, although it doesn't matter. It doesn't stop me.

"That's my daughter," I croak. "That's my baby. My baby, and I couldn't–"

I can't finish the sentence. I can't lose her too. Not after her mother–

I think about Naomi, about the crash. How one drunk driver took her from us, from *me*.

I promised I'd protect Abbi. I swore I wouldn't let her hurt again. I swore nothing would ever hurt my baby girl.

But here I am. She's hurting, she's scared, and she lied to me.

She knows. She knows who did this. She has to.

I couldn't stop it – not this monster, not the night, not the scream that lives in her eyes now.

I lean forward, resting my head against the wheel, my hands feeling heavy, my chest aching.

I lost Naomi.

I could have lost Abbi.

What am I supposed to do? What's left when I couldn't do the only thing that mattered?

Chapter 38

Cienna

It's been three days since Abbi was attacked. We don't know more than that. No one will tell us anything. Alec asked us to come in and clean it up before Abbi gets released. We don't ask questions. We know we won't get any answers.

The air hits me the moment I turn the knob. It's stale and metallic, like dust and something sharper underneath. Jared's behind me. Don and Rees follow, slower. No one speaks.

The front room is shadowed, the only light coming from the kitchen window. The curtains in the front room are closed tight, like the house itself wants to hide.

I reach for the switch near the door. My fingers hesitate– just for a second–then flick it up.

The light floods the room, and everything sharpens. Glass litters the floor. It's not just a few shards– it's *everywhere*. Glittering like ice crystals. The table's base is a twisted mess of silver metal, curled into itself like it tried to fight back and lost. One piece looks as though it was painted in blood, the red against the silver–eerie, macabre, *wrong*.

The couch beside it is ripped wide open, it's stuffing exposed, fabric torn where the metal must've hit. It looks like something exploded.

"Damn," Rees says quietly. The horror sits heavy around us like smog.

Don doesn't speak. He's staring at the hole in the wall. It's bigger than someone's head. The drywall's cracked around it like a spider web. Wide red streaks are marked beneath it, where it pooled near the base of the wall.

I step forward, glass crunching under my shoes too loudly – too final.

This isn't just mess. This is pure violence – and we're standing in the middle of it. I turn towards the stairs.

The stairs rise in front of me, steep and narrow. I've climbed them a hundred times – but not like this. The light grey carpet is stained with deep red and brown. A bloody handprint claimed the banister like it was daring someone to forget.

Jared stays close behind me. I hear Don and Rees shifting downstairs, but I don't look back. I'm staring at the wall straight ahead at two red smears. That's all I can see–parallel, deliberate, jagged at the ends–like her fingers skidded. Not the kind of mark you leave when you fall. It's the kind you leave when you're bracing for impact. It didn't feel random. It felt like her body was trying to stop something–maybe gravity. Maybe *someone*.

Halfway up, I pass the family portrait on the ground. The corner stabbed through the drywall, leaving a puncture, like the house itself couldn't hold the memory anymore. The frame's face-down.

It's Abbi, Naomi, and John – smiling like nothing could ever trouble them.

I want to pick it up, but I don't. I keep climbing.

That's when I see the bedroom door.

It's not just broken, it's *disfigured* – splintered down the center, the knob twisted, around it bloody. The frame is warped like someone hit it with everything they were.

Only real anger could do that.

Who would be this angry?

I don't know what I'll find inside – I don't know if I want to. I reach for the handle anyway, trying to avoid the blood framing in the knob. I push the door open and it groans on its twisted hinges, splintered near the top where the wood buckled inward.

The room hits me instantly.

Viscerally.

The air hangs thick and humid with something primal. It's like a space that was left raw and never recovered.

The mattress is bare.

There is no bedding, no comforter – just the shape of something awful.

I don't know what was taken–sheets, clothes, pieces of her– but I know it's missing.

The mattress wears its evidence like a confession. It's soaked, not just in streaks–not in splatter–just heavy, dark blotches that sag into the padding like the bed itself has been wounded. The blood seeped deep, especially near the left side, where color pressed outward in slow, deep red, uneven blooms. It doesn't make sense. There's no pattern, no logic, just blood–too much of it, in too many places.

The carpet didn't escape it either, it's white fibers stained red.

My stomach flips.

Across the room is her reading chair.

On it and scattered on the floor around it, are the bridal magazines I lent her. Runnels of red thread towards the chair, towards the wall, halting in places that make no sense until you realize they aren't supposed to.

The magazines aren't just tossed or scattered. The pages are bent and torn, the gloss paper wrinkled and stained like someone tried to crush joy with their bloody fists.

All I see is chaos.

And her bridal magazines–*my bridal magazines*–thrown like trash.

I reach for one of the magazines on the floor. The pages are bent and curled.

The fear in my stomach turns heavy. The edges of it don't just ache–they press against everything soft inside me. Like I want to cry, but it's stuck.

I smooth the page uselessly, knowing but hoping it helps anyway.

I need a second , just a breath. I need some water on my face.

I stand, my knees stiff from crouching by the chair. The magazines are still a mess, but I can't look at them anymore.

I head toward the bathroom, following the trail of red streaks.

That's when I see it – her hairspray can.

I blink down at it. The can lies on its side resting near the baseboard. The cap's still on. Handprints cover the canister, leaving behind fingerprints and more questions.

Why is it here? This isn't where it belongs.
This shouldn't be on the floor, not in the middle of everything.

I twist the cold tap and splash water on my face. It stings, sharp and grounding.

When I look up I see it. The door. From this angle, in the mirror's reflection, it's worse.

The dent is deep. It's chest level. Like someone hit it.

I freeze, my eyes flitting to the hairspray can's reflection on the floor.

She grabbed it. She couldn't get it open. She must've tried.

And now it's just... here. Like it failed her.

I set the hairspray on the counter like it might shatter.

And then I remember–

Abbi, standing right here, curling her hair for what we eventually found out was her engagement. Mom was in on it. She made the ring. She told Abbi to dress nice.

She had one side curled, the other still wild, and she kept squinting at the mirror like it was lying to her.

"I look like a Victorian ghost," she laughs. "A fashionable one. But still."

Kasey was perched on the edge of the tub, waving a box of red dye like it was a dare. "Just do it," she said. "You'll look like a forest goddess. Josh won't know what hit him."

I leaned against the doorframe, trying to look serious.

"Red is bold," I said. "Red is commitment. Red is meant for heartbreak or weddings. You ready for either?"

Abbi rolled her eyes, curling iron in one hand, her phone buzzing on the counter. "I'm ready for dinner and maybe a kiss. That's it."

Kasey gasped like she'd been betrayed. "You're wasting your potential."

Abbi laughed and reached for the hairspray.

I blink at the mirror, still half lost in the memory.

Abbi laughing. Kasey waving the dye box. Me teasing her.

I almost smile.

Then I hear Jared's voice beside me.

"What do you want done with the magazines?"

I flinch, then turn towards him. He's standing in the doorway, one hand resting on the frame, the other holding a few of the crumpled pages. He's not looking at them. He's looking at me.

"I don't know," I say. My voice is thin. "They're mine. But I was letting her use them."

He doesn't move.

"But they're ruined."

I glance down by our feet, the can a dark red beacon on the white carpet. *She couldn't get it open.*

I swallow the lump in my throat and nod.

I step out of the bathroom, the water still cooling my cheeks.

Jared's stacking the magazines like I might change my mind.

I don't look at the blood.

I don't look at the bed.

I don't look at either door.

I just watch Jared tuck the last torn page under the cover, gentle like it's glass.

There's still so much we don't know. Still so much missing. I hate it. But hate won't help. So for now, all we can do, is clean.

Chapter 39

Rees

The sofa is wrecked—Not just torn, not just dented. It's *covered*.

Blood stains one of the cushions in a wide patch. Another cushion's pierced clean through, stuffing spilling out like it's trying to escape and splashed with red. It's unsalvageable. No amount of patching or bleach is fixing this.

I crouch beside the frame. The glass top's shattered—fragments scattered across the carpet, some still clinging to the metal like teeth. A few pieces glint with red. Not rust. Not wine. *Blood.* Drops, streaks, smears. Like someone bled across it mid-fall.

And the metal?

The end is dipped in red. Not splattered, not brushed – *Dipped.* Dipped like it was used, like it was a weapon.

I don't touch it. I just stare.

This wasn't panic. This was impact. This was force.

I glance at the wall Don is examining with a flashlight he found in the kitchen.

"This whole thing's gonna need to be replaced." Don states sourly. "The stud behind it is snapped."

Sure, we can clean this up. But it's not just a room that needs fixing. It's a story we haven't heard yet.

I dig the shop vac from the shed and roll it into the front room. I plug it in and flip the switch.

It roars to life. Low and steady. Like a beast waking up. The hose rattles against the floor as I drag it towards the mess.

The first shard hits the nozzle with a sharp *clink*. Then another. Then a dozen more.

It sounds like hail on metal.

Like glass teeth being swallowed.

Some pieces scrape as they go–*skrrtch* against the plastic, high and thin. Others thud, heavier, like they're reluctant to leave the carpet.

The vacuum hums louder when it catches a cluster.

The motor strains, then settles.

A rhythm builds. *Clink, clink, skrrtch, thud, whirr.*

I keep going.

The blood-speckled fragments vanish one by one, pulled into the belly of the machine.

It's not satisfying.

It's surgical.

The shop vac hums behind me, steady now.

Most of the glass is gone. When I shut off the vacuum, the room feels too quiet.

Don's working on the wall, measuring the crack in the stud. He doesn't talk much. Neither do I.

But my mind won't shut up.

I crouch beside the sofa, fingers brushing the edge of the torn cushion. The stuffing's still and stained. It's like someone *landed* on it.

This wasn't random.

The front room's not extravagant.

Two couches, a bench, a table, and a dresser with winter gloves and hats stuffed in the drawers.

That's it.

There's no TV, no jewelry, no tech. – nothing worth stealing.

So why here?

This wasn't a robbery. This wasn't someone looking for valuables.

They came in. Tore through this room. And then they went upstairs to her room.

Why?

What did Abbi have that made someone climb the stairs instead of running?

I don't know how many people were here. One? Two? Three?

But I know this... They didn't come for *things*. They came for *her*.

Then what happened upstairs?

Because there's blood on the sofa. Blood on the glass. Blood on the metal. Blood on the carpet.

If this isn't the worst of it–if this is just the entry point–

Then whatever happened in her room wasn't just worse.

It was the reason.

I let my curiosity get the better of me.

I reach the first landing and stop.

The family portrait of Abbi and her parents is on the ground, face down, a hole where the corner pierced through the wall.

I pick it up and examine the photo. Abbi's bright smile framed by her long blonde hair.

Something twists in my chest.

Who could hurt her?

I hang it back where it belongs, straightening the frame. Avoiding the bloody wall and railing.

The second flight creaks louder. The air shifts–thicker, heavier.

And then I see it - her door – it's splintered and red near the handle. The wood is cracked like it took more than one hit. It's the first sign I was right.

I push it open. The room's lit by her reading lamp in the corner.

Cienna and Jared are on their knees by the bed, scrubbing hard.

The stain isn't lifting. It's spreading. Turning pink.

Cienna's crying.

The brush slips from her hand.

She grabs her hair, fists tight, and screams–raw, guttural, like it's been building for days.

Then she curls in on herself, small and shaking. Like the grief finally found its way out.

Jared doesn't speak. He just sets the brushes down and shifts closer. He doesn't touch her, but the closeness seems to soothe her.

I step farther into the room. Cienna's sobs are quieter now. The air smells like bleach and grief. That's when I notice the bed.

At first I thought there was new bedding, but it's empty. There's no sheets, no blankets, no pillows – just a red stained mattress.

Downstairs the couch was torn, the table shattered, the wall split open.

But this? This is *intentional.* Like someone didn't just hurt her. They wanted to erase her.

I glance at the floor. No comforter, no pile of laundry. No sign it was stripped for cleaning.

Just gone.

And suddenly I'm thinking about the blood on the sofa. The glass. The metal. And how this room–quiet, stripped, stained– might be worse than all of it.

Because the front room was chaos.

But this? This had to be personal.

Chapter 40
Abbi

I haven't moved in ten minutes, not since they told me. The doctor said I could go home. They smiled like it was good news. It's anything but.

A chill begins to set deep in my bones. My brain's not here. It's back at the house.

James' breath in my ear.
The sound of the table cracking.
The glass.
The hairspray.
Frantically trying to find my phone.

I blink, and the ceiling tiles blur. I blink again, and I'm on the floor.

Not here.

There.

His voice, low and sharp. It's too close.

I flinch.
Josh says something, but I don't hear it.
Dad shifts beside me, his hand brushing the edge of the blanket.
I grip the blanket tighter.
I don't know what's happened to the house while I've been gone, but I remember the sound of the door. The way it cracked. The way he looked at me like I was something to break.
I press my fingers to my temple.
Breathe.
But the flashes keep coming.

The shove.
My screams.
The silence.

Josh shifts in the corner. Dad's eyes meet mine, calm but strained.
I grab the blanket tighter and stare at the door and the images continue.

Broken and splintered wood.
The smell of alcohol.
Him pressing on my thighs.

How am I going to do this?

"I come baring gifts," Connie steps through the door, my vision sharpening back to my hospital room.

Connie lays out the clothes on the bed. Soft green pajama pants, Josh's loose grey hoodie, and a front clasp bra. Nothing tight. Nothing that pulls. Just enough to feel like *me* again.

Dad turns towards the window, giving me some privacy.

Josh stands nearby, hands fidgeting, waiting for permission.

"I need your help." I reassure him, even though I'm not so sure I'm ready for the contact.

Connie picks up the bra first. "Start with the left arm," she guides gently. "That's the injured one."

Josh crouches, bunches the strap, and slides it carefully over my wrist.

My shoulder protests. The gash in my side pulls. I wince, but not just from the pain.

He freezes, his eyes widening.

Connie steadies me with one hand and guides him with the other. "You're okay. Just go slow. Let her lean forward when she's ready."

I manage after some hesitation, my pain a constant protest.

Josh eases the strap over my shoulder, careful not to tug. His fingers brush the edge of the bandage. He doesn't flinch, but I see it in his eyes – the memory of how I got it.

Connie helps guide the left strap next, then fastens the clasp at the front.

I exhale.

One more thing people have to go through. It's sturdy against my body. It isn't tight, but I feel more grounded with it.

Josh smooths the hoodie down next, threading the sleeves with Connie's help. The pants follow, gentle, slow, and deliberate.

I'm dressed for the first time in seven days.

I'm not strong, or ready, but at least I'm covered. For now, that's all I can ask.

Dad checks his watch, then leans down and kisses the top of my head. "I'll pull the truck around. Take your time."

I nod, but don't speak.

He squeezes my hand once, then steps out of the room. The door clicks shut behind him.

Josh glances at Connie, who nods towards the tray. "Brush is there."

He picks it up slowly, like it might bite.

I bite the inside of my cheek hard enough to draw blood.

Because no one knows about the hair.

Not about how James yanked it – dragged me by it, twisted it, used it like a leash.

I never told them.

Josh crouches behind me, fingers brushing the ends first.

Connies beside him, guiding. "Start low. Use your fingers. She's sensitive."

He's so gentle and careful, like he's learning a language I forgot how to speak. The brush follows–soft strokes, no pulling. I flinch, causing him to pause .

He pauses, looking up at Connie.

"You're doing fine, love. Just keep it loose."

I bite the inside of my cheek again, the taste of blood the only thing keeping me here.

Because it hurts. But it also feels... good. Like something kind. Like something mine.

Connie hands him a tie. "She likes it braided."

Josh hesitates. "I've never–"

"I'll show you."

She guides his hands. Three section. Left over middle. Right over center. Repeat.

He fumbles. She resets. He tries again.

The braid forms—soft, uneven, imperfect.

But it doesn't hurt.

Josh helps me to my feet.

It's slow. Everything is slow. My ribs protest. My shoulder pulls. The gash near my side burns beneath the bandage.

But I'm standing.

Connie helps me sit in the wheelchair, adjusting my braid so it doesn't catch.

I grip the armrests. Not for balance. Just for *something*.

The hallway blurs past—white walls, soft shoes, polite nods. I don't look at anyone. I don't wave.

I'm not ready. I don't know what I'm going home to.

We reach the doors. Sunlight spills in. The truck's parked at the curb. Dad's already out, door open, seat pushed back, pillow at the ready.

Josh crouches beside me.

Connies voice is calm. "We'll help you in. Slow and steady."

I nod.

My rib spikes with pressure as I shift. My shoulder refuses full movement. The gash pulls like it's stitched to gravity.

Josh helps me stand. Connie supports my other side. Dad steps forward, lifts the bag from Connie's hands without a word.

I climb in—inch by inch, breath by breath.

Josh eases the seatbelt across me, adjusting it so it doesn't press too hard on the bandage. His fingers linger for half a second, then retreat.

The truck hums beneath us.

Dad's hands are steady on the wheel, his eyes are forward, his jaw tight.

He hasn't said much. He just turned the music low and the air up.

My seat's pushed all the way back.

The pillow helps, but every bump still finds my ribs.

Josh climbs into the back, smack in the middle.

It's close enough to be near me, but far enough not to crowd.

He settles in, knees angled, hands resting on his thighs. He doesn't speak. I feel him there – quiet and solid.

Outside the world blurs – trees, signs, sky. It's all too bright – too fast.

I press my fingers to the seatbelt. It's loose enough not to press the bandage, but tight enough to feel like something's holding me together.

Dad doesn't look at me. He can't, not from here. Maybe that's better. Because if he saw my face right now, he'd ask... And I'm not ready to answer.

We turn onto our street. The turn is gentle. But my stomach flips.

Dad doesn't speak. He just drives like it's any other day. Like we're coming back from groceries, not the hospital.

Josh shifts behind me, his knee brushing the back of my seat.

We pass the first house. White shutters against grey stone. Children play on the front yard swing set.

Then we pass the second. A dented mailbox being opened by our elderly neighbor. She waves as we pass, slowing to turn into our driveway.

My body goes cold. Everything looks as it should but feels...wrong. Like a bandage over a broken bone. It isn't healed, but you can't see it from here.

Dad parks the car, and my breathing stops.

I don't think I can get out.

I don't want to.

We sit in silence, the only sound is the car settling after being shut off. No one moves.

Chapter 41

Don

I flip the burgers, pretending I'm not counting the seconds. The backyard smells like charcoal and fresh paint – like effort and distraction. Like we *aren't* trying to convince ourselves everything is normal. Rees is pacing near the gate. Jared is lining up cups like the space between each cup will keep us whole. Cienna is folding napkins again, just to keep her hands busy. Alec watches the back door like it's going to swing open on its own.

We can't see the driveway from back here. The fence and garage block it. But we know they're here. We can feel it. Like the wind shifted. Like the light went flat for a second. No one says anything, but Ryan straightens up, Dad turns down the music, even Jared's hands slow down.

The house looks good. Better than good, considering. Front room's clean. Walls are smooth. Fresh paint covering the hole like it was never there. The couch is gone. We replaced it with two thrifted armchairs, blue and grey. They're surprisingly solid. We moved the grey ottoman from the den to replace the table. No sharp edges. We didn't want anything that could hurt, even by accident. We had no choice but to replace the carpet in the front room, the stairs, and Abbi's room. It seeped in too deep. Now there's dark chocolate oak in the front room and on the stairs.

Her room's quiet. Cienna picked purple florals for her new bedding. Rees helped lay the light purple rug. Big enough for around her bed. The flooring we replaced with light pine to keep it light for her. She was never one for dark rooms. Her mattress we hauled to the dump and Josh ordered a soft new one in its place. No one talked while we cleaned and cleared. Alec replaced the doors himself. He didn't ask questions, he didn't need to.

We fixed what we could. Not everything though. Not the stuff that sits behind her eyes. But the house? The house is ready.

I flip another burger. The sizzles seem too loud now. The music's too soft. I'm trying not to look at the back door, trying not to be the first one to move. But someone has to. Someone needs to be the first thing she sees that still keeps her here with us, and not in her mind.

So I wipe my hands, take a breath, and head to the doors. No fanfare. No speech. Just showing up. Because that's what today is. It's showing up, even when you don't know how.

I slip through the back door, through the den, up into the kitchen, and through to the front room.

It's quiet inside. The kind of quiet that makes you notice every little thing. The way the fridge hum, or the faint scent of lemon cleaner. The way the light hits the new paint.

Abbi's standing just inside the threshold. She's wearing a hoodie that's loose around her frame, a braid trailing over her shoulder. Josh is behind her, close but not crowding. John's a few steps back, hand still on the knob of the front door. Like he's not sure if he's coming in or staying out.

But it's Abbi I'm watching.

Her face is slightly puffy and bruised - one eye the green and yellow color of healing. She looks at me and forces a smile. It's small, tight, like she's afraid to open the stitches on her lip if she smiles any wider. But it doesn't reach her eyes. There's something in them. Not surprise, but something deeper – something colder. *Fear.* Not the kind that makes you jump or scream. The kind that settles in your chest and makes everything feel too loud, too close.

My blood runs cold. The way she's standing like she's bracing for impact. She's *waiting* for something to go wrong. Like she's already halfway out of her body.

We fixed the house. We patched the walls, painted over the cracks, replaced furniture. We made it look like home again. But none of that matters if she walks in and still feels like she's in danger. If the room still feels like it remembers what happened.

"Everyone's outside." It's all I can manage to say.

She walks slow and careful – like she's measuring each step before she takes it. Josh stays close, just behind her. John trails a few feet back, quiet and unreadable as he takes in the room. And me? I'm trying not to stare. Trying not to let it show. But it's hard. Because this isn't the Abbi I remember.

I think about the water tower on the edge of town—

In ninth grade, Rees dared her to climb it. He was half-joking, half-serious. We all thought she'd laugh it off. But she didn't. She looked up at that rusted ladder, tied her hair back in a braid, and started climbing like it was nothing. No hesitation. No drama. Just grit.

She made it to the top. Stood there with her arms out, wind in her hoodie, yelling down, "You owe me ten for style!" And I remember standing there, looking up at her, and feeling something shift. I'd known her since we were little kids. But that day? That day I had a crush so fast it made my head spin.

It didn't last long. I never said anything. But it was real, and it was because she was fearless.

Now?

She's walking like she's afraid the ground might give out. Like her own body's a threat. I don't know the full story. None of us do. But watching her move like this – slow, cautious, fragile–it makes something burn in my chest.

Whoever made her afraid of herself. Whoever took that girl on the water tower and left this quiet, careful version behind, they better sleep with one eye open.

I clench my jaw but keep my hands loose. I try to breathe. Because this isn't about me. It's about her. And right now, she needs all of us. She doesn't need the anger, or the loud. So I match her pace, and I remind myself that showing up means being what she needs–even if what I feel is fire.

Chapter 42
Abbi

I step out into the backyard, slow and careful. Josh's hand wrapped in mine. The air is warm. The grass is soft. Everything looks...normal. Why wouldn't it? The flowers are bright and the smell is soothing. The tables and umbrellas are set up, but everyone is standing.

There's food on the table, drinks, cups, the works. Lance's speaker hums low with country music. Cienna moves forward, holding something out to me. When she gets close enough I see it. It's green case is cracked in the corner.

My phone.

It's clean. It's charged. It's mine. I reach out and take it, ignoring the protest in my shoulder.

The thing I needed most that night. It had disappeared. The magazines had hidden it from me.

I remember my fingers scrambling across the paper.

276

The chair.
The floor.
The panic.
The way everything blurred.

Josh squeezes my hand.

Not hard. Just enough for me to come back.

The back yard. The music. Cienna's face, soft and open. My phone in my hand. Josh beside me.

"Thank you," I choke out.

Cienna's already moving towards the drinks, pretending not to hover.

The yard is too quiet. Everyone is too quiet. Like if they make a sound I'll break.

"What–no Welcome Home sign?" I joke.

That gets a few grins.

"I thought you said there was going to be a red carpet?" I turn to Josh, pleading silently he laughs.

His shoulders shake in silent laughter. The tension in the air eases slightly. Lance turns the music up. Alec is removing the burgers from the grill. Ryan and Lily even step closer, their posture not so rigid.

It worked.

The gate bursts open and Kasey comes running through it, her hair pulled back in a short ponytail. She's across the yard in seconds, her arms wrapping around me.

I yelp.

She pulls away, horror openly visible on her face. "Oh Abbi, I..."

"It's okay," I breathe a few times in through my nose, out through my mouth. "I'm fine. Just sore."

But the guilt is already there.

Please not that look.

"I'm actually a little thirsty. Do you think you could get me some of that peach lemonade?" I release Josh's hand and point towards the table where a tall sweating pitcher stands with pale yellow liquid and chunks of dark yellow peaches. "I just know Alec made that."

"Guilty," he murmurs.

"You know it's my favorite." I flash as wide a smile as I can muster without splitting my lip further. "It's not even my birthday."

"We're just glad you're back." Lily has made her way across the yard and places a gentle hand on my back. "And we're all here for you."

I choke back the tears that are dangerously close to falling. Quick, think of something else to say.

"Well, then let's eat. I'm starving. You know green Jello doesn't compare to these burgers."

Just like that, the air is clear.

Josh grabs a plate and asks me what I want. I know he knows, but I also know he's trying to give me at least some control here. I deeply appreciate that.

"Do you want ketchup?" He asks as I sit down in the folding chair at the end of the table.

"You know what? I don't think it's a good idea," I point to my lip.

"I take that as a no for pickles and tomato too?"

"Don't be silly. No burger is complete without pickles." I pretend to be horrified.

"Okay. So no to tomato, but yes to pickles?"

"And mayo."

Once it's made per my instructions, he sets the plate in front of me. How am I going to eat this? My slinged hand still clings to my phone, which leaves me with one hand.

"Josh?" I ask.

"Yes?"

"Would you cut this up for me into smaller sections? I only have one hand."

"Of course." Without another word, he slices the burger into four smaller parts.

"Thank you," I smile sweetly. That's when I see his shoulders relax.

I eat in silence, enjoying the taste of normal food for the first time in days. After finishing the first section, I reach for my lemonade. Dad had gotten a straw from the kitchen for me to use so the citrus didn't touch my lips. The taste is sweet, and it helps ease my own tension just slightly.

Listening to everyone laughing and joking was the best I could ask for. The food's good. The air's warm. No one's asking questions. No one's watching me like I might fall apart. It feels almost normal.

James steps through, root beer in hand, grinning like he's part of a joke. "Now hold the phone. We can't have a party without root beer floats."

The reaction is instant.

Lily squeals and runs straight to him, flinging her arms tightly around his shoulders. Cienna's close behind, arms already half outstretched. Ryan is grinning and patting James on the back.

"The prodigal son has returned," Ryan jokes.

Don calls out, "How did you know we'd be here?"

James laughs, easy. "Dad texted. Said I was missing all the fun."

He's surrounded in seconds. Hugs. Laughter. Questions. The kind of welcome reserved for someone who's been gone too long and missed too much.

"When did you get back?"

"About an hour ago," he checks his watch. "I got home and the place was deserted. So I texted Dad."

That's a lie.

"Where's Lisa? I thought she'd be with you." Lily asks, looking over James' shoulder like she'd be arriving any second.

"She decided Italy was her scene. She's with her new boyfriend, Antonio. She left me in Vienna. I didn't have enough money for a train ticket. Ended up working at a hostel. I cleaned rooms, did laundry, whatever they'd let me do. Took me two weeks to save enough to get back."

"Why didn't you tell us? We would have paid for you to come home?" Lily chides.

"I wanted to try to make it on my own."

"So she just left you there?"

He shrugs. "Eh, you can't win 'em all." He takes a can of root beer and opens it, the fizz flowing down the sides of the can.

Then he looks at me – just for a second.

"Dad told me what happened. Glad you're still kicking," he says, lifting his root beer like a toast, a smile playing at the corner of his mouth.

The memory of trying to kick him off flashes behind my eye.

Him pinning my legs down.
The pain in my hips as he forces my legs open.

I look anywhere but him. My hands are shaking and my chest is tight. I can't breathe.

I need out. I need...

"We don't have ice cream," my voice is barely a whisper.

"What?" Josh leans closer.

I clear my throat, trying to keep my voice steady. "We can't do root beer floats without ice cream."

"Did you want to go get some?"

I'm up and moving, ignoring every ounce of pain screaming through me just to get away. I go straight for the gate instead of the house. I can't be *there* right now. I can't be *here* right now.

"We'll be back." Josh tells the group. "Abbi wants to go get ice cream." Josh rushes to my side. "Slow down, Abbi. You don't want to tear your stitches."

But I don't feel the pain. Every nerve is awake in me right now, but they are all telling me to run. Get away. "I'm fine."

The seatbelt presses across my ribs. No pillow this time. I forgot it. I don't care.

The pain is dulled. Not gone. Just hushed. Like everything else except my heartbeat. *That* rings loud and clear in my ears.

Josh drives like he always does. One hand on the wheel, the other resting near the gearshift, available if I want to take it.

I stare out the window. Houses blur past. Trees. Street signs. I don't see any of it.

James is here, smiling, toasting - saying things only I understand.

My shoulder throbs. My lip stings. But it's the ribs that remind me I'm still breakable.

Josh glances over. "You okay?"

I nod. "Tired."

The truck hums. The road stretches. And I sit there, trying to breathe without wincing. Trying to forget the grin. Trying to remember I'm not trapped anymore.

The lot is mostly empty for a Saturday afternoon. There are a few cars scattered around, like they forgot they were supposed to leave hours ago.

Josh pulls into a spot near the front. I stare through the windshield. The automatic doors slide open, then close. No one walks through. No carts rattling. No kids begging for candy. Just stillness.

The silence feels wrong. Like the world's holding its breath. Like something's waiting.

Josh shifts into park. His hand lingers near the gear shift. I could take it. I don't.

I reach for the door handle instead. My fingers are stiff. Cold. The seat belt catches on my ribs as I move. I wince. Not loud. Not enough for him to notice.

Outside, the sun is too bright. The asphalt's cracked.

I step down and my foot catches under me.

I stumble hard. My shoulder jars. My side flares. I grab the edge of the door to steady myself.

Josh is already out his door and at my side. "Hey –"

I swat his hand away. "I'm fine," I snap.

He freezes, his eyes on mine. He waits in that quiet way Josh always does when he's worried but he's too kind to push.

"I'm sorry," I mumble. "I didn't mean to – "

"It's okay."

I straighten. I can take my time here. I allow myself to slow down. Not snail pace, but just enough to walk like I've got nowhere else to be.

Inside, it's as empty as the parking lot. An elderly couple is searching through the apples, trying to find the 'right' ones.

We walk to the back of the store where the frozen goods are. The cold is refreshing, but I'm instantly shivering, even through the hoodie.

"Vanilla bean or Classic Vanilla?" Josh asks, holding up one bucket in each hand.

"Classic Vanilla," I manage to stutter out.

"Let's get you out of the cold." He tosses the bucket in the cart and guides me towards the front of the store to check out.

While the cashier scans our singular item, Josh slips away. When he returns, he's holding a bouquet wrapped in brown paper. He has the cashier scan it then hands them to me.

"What's this?" I take the bouquet and smile. Dahlias.

They're white, but with just a hint of cream in the center. Their petals are symmetrical and perfect.

"Figured you needed something calm." I look up at him, and see he's not looking at me, but down at his shoes. I rise up on my toes and kiss his cheek. It's not much, but it's all I can handle right now.

On the way back to the truck, I cling to the dahlias like a shield. The paper crinkles in my hand, but I don't let up. The thought of going back to the house now causes me to start shaking again. This time it isn't from the cold.

Josh unlocks my door and freezes. "Abbi, you're bleeding."

"What?"

He gently grabs at my hoodie and I jerk away.

"I need to look at it, My Love."

The way he says 'My Love' brings my mind back to where we are now and I allow him to check.

"Your stitches popped. I'm taking you back to the hospital."

I don't fight him. I'm actually...relieved. It means I don't have to go home. Not yet. That's the best I could hope for.

***

"Now you make sure you take it easy." Connie reprimands. "I don't want to see you back here again."

"Yes, ma'am." I say, my stomach churning at the thought it's time to go home. It took less time than I thought. Only twenty minutes.

"Thank you again, Connie." Josh wraps her in a hug before guiding me gently towards the doors.

"I'm sorry about the ice cream." I mutter.

"I don't care about the ice cream." He opens my door and helps me into my seat. "I just want you safe."

Before climbing into his seat, he grabs the liquified tub and tosses it in the bin near the front door. "Besides," he says. "Jared found some in the freezer."

"Oh good," I fake relief.

Josh senses it. I know he does.

"If you want me to send them home, I will." He starts the car.

I don't answer.

Is that what I want? I want him gone, but do I want everyone else gone too? Once they're gone, we'll be inside. I haven't even seen my room yet, and I'm not sure I want to. Is it better than him being there?

"Is that terrible of me?"

"Of course not. They love you. They wouldn't want to do anything you aren't comfortable with." He's already pulling out his phone.

I think about his words.

Is that true?

***

I'm not ready.

I don't think I ever will be. But I don't have a choice. All my things are in there. My whole life is in there.

I take the stairs slow, fighting the memory and pain from exploding in my vision. Each creak is like a countdown to the inevitable.

"I got you." Josh doesn't touch me, but I can feel his warmth behind me, like a shield from the cold trying to settle in my bones. I make it to the top step and stare at my closed door.

It's new and green. There are panels on this one. One large one above that curves on the top and a square one below. It's strange and foreign.

In the center is a purple wooden heart. It's hollow, but a small banner along the center holds my name is gold glitter. It must be Cienna's idea. I can feel her in it as I stroke the heart, feeling how real it is under my fingers.

Slowly, I reach for the knob. I swallow, fighting my urge to flee, and turn the knob.

It's my room - but it's not. My sheets are gone. Replaced by deep purple and black flowers against a white backdrop. My carpet has been replaced with a pale wood.

I step through the threshold, my stomach in knots. The room starts spinning, and before I can catch myself, I'm on the floor, the pain in my ribs and shoulder screaming at me.

"Whoa..." Josh catches me before I can hit my head against the door frame.

This is too much.

"We don't have to do this."

But we do.

"This is *my* room. I *have* to." I choke out.

He helps me stand up, my chest tightening with each second I'm in here. But I need to keep going. If I don't, I'll never recover.

I take a tentative step towards my bed – then another.

I gaze over the rest of the room. Everything in its place. The magazines and chair are gone. Cienna probably took the magazines back.

I don't want them anyway. But why my chair?

I gaze down at my ring. I almost always forget it's there. It's part of me. Something he *can't* take from me.

I look over at Josh. His face has gone pale. He's looking at the bed.

Was he the one that found me?

I don't dare ask.

I turn my attention back to my room. My bathroom door has changed too. It has the same paneling the other door has, but this one is white. Nothing else changed.

The same books, dresser, vanity, desk, even the mirror on my closet. I walk over to Josh who's still frozen, staring at the bed. I take his hand and speak softly.

"Are you here with me?"

His eyes seem to refocus, and his body straightens.

"I'm here," he croaks.

"I can't do this alone."

He follows me over to the bed. We both slowly sit down, exhaling as we sink into the mattress. This mattress is softer, and just a little taller.

The images in my mind flash like a channel's being changed.

James is standing at the edge of the bed, taking down his pants.

He's on top of me, his weight crushing down.

I can't get the bathroom door closed.

I can't find my phone.

Everything going black.

"Abbi!" Josh is kneeling in front of me. "Abbi, breathe!"

I can't breathe.

He breathes slow and exaggerated.

I try, but still nothing.

Then he grabs something and presses it into my hands.

"Feel this," he says. "You're safe. You're here with me."

The texture of the binding grounds me. The bumps on the ribs. The smooth cover. Our scrapbook.

I gasp. Air rushes in like I've been underwater for hours.

When my breathing steadies, I look around. I'm in my room. Just me and Josh.

"I wish you would talk to me." He brushes a strand of hair from my face. I flinch, and his hand jerks back.

"I'm sorry. It's not you..." *I need to tell him something. You can do this.* "It's my hair. It... hurts."

"Why didn't you say anything this morning? Was it the way I brushed your hair?"

"No..." I try to calm him. "It was... it happened the other night."

Tears silently fall down his face. My stomach churns at knowing I upset him.

"I'm sorry." I mutter.

"You have nothing to be sorry for."

Chapter 43
Abbi

We slip into old habits like muscle memory. Cienna's sprawled across the couch in the den braiding Kasey's hair with practiced fingers. Kasey's flipping through movie options narrating each one. I'm curled on the couch, blanket tucked under my chin. Trying to keep up.

It feels like before...Almost.

They ask questions, but I miss them. They laugh, but I smile a beat too late.

Cienna nudges me with her foot. "You good?"

I nod. Because it's easier than explaining the static in my head.

The movie starts. Something we've seen a dozen times. I should know the lines. I should know the plot. But I keep zoning out, drifting into the hum of the fridge. The flicker of the candle Moira sent with Kasey. The weight of the rose quartz she "charged" for me last night, safe in my pocket.

Kasey passes me popcorn. I take it, but don't eat it.

Eventually I speak quietly. It's not dramatic, but it's truth – truth that I can say without letting them too far in. "I remember some things," I say.

"I remember the glass, the stairs, the bed – not what happened, just...how it felt. But I remember... I remember being raped. "

Cienna shifts closer.

Kasey doesn't speak.

"I remember being cold, and loud, and quiet all at once."

I don't cry. They don't ask for more. Cienna reaches for my hand. Kasey leans her head on my shoulder.

We don't finish the movie, but the silence is peaceful.

Chapter 44

Josh

I didn't want to come. I never said it out loud, but I think Jared knew.

He gave me that look. The half apology, half-"you need this."

I don't.

But Abbi's not alone. That's the only reason I agreed.

We're at Jared's place. The basement smells like old pizza.

Quint's already halfway through a 2-liter of Pepsi. Jared's setting up the game. Don's talking about some girl he met at the gym. Rees is trying to get me to laugh. I'm not laughing. I'm sitting on the edge of the couch, phone in my pocket. Screen face-up – just in case.

They're trying, I'll give them that.

Jared keeps glancing at me like he's waiting for me to crack a joke. Quint's being loud on purpose. Rees brought snacks he knows I like. Don's pretending this is normal.

It's not.

I keep thinking about her room – about the way she curled up last night.

Now I'm here. Pretending I'm okay. Pretending this isn't the longest I've been away from her in days.

Jared nudges me. "You good?"

I swallow, my head moving in a small nod. He doesn't push. He just hands me a controller and says, "We're doing teams. You and me."

I take it because it's easier than explaining why my chest feels like it's caving in.

And James? James is watching me. Not obviously. Just...listening. Too closely.

I say something about work. He asks how Abbi's doing. I say she's resting. He asks if she's been sleeping. I say she's quiet. He asks if she said anything about that night.

I blink.

He shrugs. "Just wondering. I mean, she's been through a lot. She may not be *my* girlfriend anymore, but she's still my friend too. I know I'd murder whoever put their hands on her."

I don't mean to say it. Don't plan it.

But once it starts, I can't stop.

I break. "The sick Fuck raped her."

The room goes quiet. Even the game pauses.

Jared sets down his drink. Quint leans forward. Rees shifts. Don blinks like he didn't hear right.

"She was unconscious, in her bed. The house was completely wrecked... blood, glass, everything was broken."

291

I grip the edge of the couch. My voice shakes, but I keep going.

"She didn't move when I said her name. She didn't even flinch."

No one speaks – no one except James.

"Did she say what happened? Does she remember anything at all that can help catch this guy?"

I shake my head. "She hasn't said much. Just fragments."

James nods. "She's lucky you found her."

Jared's jaw tightens, and Quint looks sick.

"I'm sorry guys. I didn't mean to get all dark and heavy." I run a hand through my hair, trying to think of what to say.

"Let's just play. It might help get your mind off it," James suggests.

"Yeah, you're right." I pick up the controller and everyone else follows suit.

Jared and Rees begin the trash talking like it's any other day. Don tosses a bag of chips towards James, and Quint is burping the alphabet, finishing on 'T'.

I pull my phone from my pocket and check for any messages – radio silence.

I don't know if that's good or bad, but my heart begins racing, worry starting to etch across my face.

Jared holds up his phone with a message on it from Cienna.

Abbi's doing ok. She's sleeping now. Let Josh know, please. I don't want him to worry.

I let my shoulders relax and allow myself to sink back into the couch.

"She's tough," James leans in and whispers. "She'll get through this."

I nod, praying he's right.

But the image of Abbi from that night replays in my head like a broken record.

Will I get through this?

Chapter 45
Abbi

Peppermint steam rises from the mug in my hands like it has every right to be here. I hold it still, careful, letting the warmth soak into my palms but keeping my nose just shy of the scent. It's too familiar. *James familiar.* That lingering sweetness on his breath after kisses I used to chase. Now it just makes my throat tighten.

I angle my face subtly, hoping Kasey won't notice, though I suspect she already has. She always does. I don't want to talk. Don't want to drink. I want the mug to vanish between my fingers.

She doesn't say anything. She just sits quiet beside me with her own tea and the kind of posture that means she's waiting but not demanding. The silence doesn't press. It holds onto the space. Like it understands what I can't say yet.

And then finally, she says. "I used to think I was broken."

Her voice is steady, but her hands aren't. She's tracing the bottom of her mug with her thumb.

I don't speak. I just listen.

"I didn't tell anyone for a long time, not even Quint, not really." She laughs, but it isn't a happy sound.

"I'd wake up and feel like I was already failing. Like the day had decided I wasn't worth showing up for."

I bite the inside of my cheek. Because I know that feeling. I've lived it. Every day this week.

"I didn't want to die," she says. "But I didn't want to be awake either."

The room feels smaller now – not suffocating – just... smaller.

"I used to count the cracks in my ceiling," She continues. "Like if I could name them all, I'd fix myself.

"I'm not saying this to try and fix you," she reaches a hand and tentatively touches my knee. "I'm saying it because I remember what it felt like to be silent. And I don't want you to feel alone it in."

I blink. Hard. Because I didn't know I needed to hear that. But I did.

Kasey's curled into the corner of the couch with her legs tucked under her. She's staring at the bookshelf like it's saying something.

"I used to think I was just dramatic." Her voice is soft. " I'd cry for no reason. Sleep too much. Sometimes not at all. More times than I care to admit. I'd cancel plans and then hate myself for it.

"I didn't know it was depression. Not until I started therapy."

I blink. She's never said that before. Not to any of us.

"I thought therapy was for people who couldn't handle life. Turns out it's for people who are handling it. Just with more tools." She laughs. It's small, but it's also real.

"I'm on meds now," she sighs adjusting her position on the couch. "It's a low dose. Took me *forever* to say yes. I started them several months ago. But they help. Not in a magic way. Just enough to keep me from drowning."

Her eyes are clear now. Her voice is quiet. "If you ever want to talk to someone... I'll help you find them. No pressure. Just...*if.*"

I don't say anything at first. Just let the words echo.

Therapy.

Meds.

Tools.

She's not trying to convince me. She's just opening the door – one I didn't know was there.

I stare at the steam rising off my mug. It's barely warm now, but I wrap my hands around it a little tighter.

"I've always been afraid of that," I say. My voice is small, but honest – the most honest I've been all week. "Afraid of saying something out loud and not getting better."

Kasey doesn't interrupt. She just watches me, her eyes gentle and focused.

"What if I'm too much?" I ask. "Or not enough? What if I get there and I can't even speak?"

She reaches over and takes my hand.

"Then you're there," she squeezes. "And that's really brave."

Her hand stays around mine. She doesn't try to hold eye contact, or coax or coach. She just stays. Her thumb moves slightly, like she's thinking about comfort but doesn't want to

296

overstep. The air between us has changed. It's less like glass, more like fabric. Still delicate, still a little tense, but soft enough to breathe through.

I stare at the tea. The surface has stopped steaming. Cooling into something lukewarm and unwelcoming. I think about how Kasey said "brave" like it didn't need fixing.

The quiet stretches, but it doesn't scrape. It settles. My mouth doesn't want to move, but my tongue feels coated in memory and something sour in the back of my throat. It needs to come out. Not everything. Just something small. Something ugly and *real*.

I set the mug gently on the side table. "It tastes like alcohol and blood."

Chapter 46

Abbi

The office smells like lavender and printer ink. The couch is soft – too soft – like it's trying to trick me into relaxing.

The therapist, Marla, has kind eyes.

She doesn't push. She just waits.

"I don't know what I'm supposed to say," I start. My voice sounds wrong in here. Too loud. Too small.

"You don't have to say anything you're not ready for," she says.

"I've been having nightmares," I finally say. "And I don't sleep much. And I feel like I'm not in my body half the time."

She writes something down. Not fast. Not like she's cataloging me. Then she just waits. Like she's used to silence.

"I remember the room," I say. My voice is thin. Like it's been stretched too far. "The way the light looked. The way the air felt. I remember the sound of the door. I remember the smell."

She nods but doesn't write anything down. Just listens.

"I remember being held down." My hands are shaking. I tuck them under my thighs.

"I remember what he said. Not all of it. Just pieces. Just enough."

I stop, and she waits.

"I can't say his name," I whisper. Like a failure.

"You don't have to," she says.

But I still feel it, like it's stitched into my skin. Like no matter what I say, he's still there, hiding between my words.

***

August 18th

I don't know what I'm supposed to write. Marla said I could start with how it feels. Not what happened. Just the shape of it.

So here it goes:

It feels like static in my chest. Like I'm turned to the wrong frequency and everything hurts. I don't feel like I'm in my body most of the time. It's like I'm watching someone else live my life. I'm scared that I'll break. Like glass. Like the table. I don't say his name. I can't. My throat gets all tight and itchy and I feel like I'll throw up.

***

"You here with me?" Josh squeezes my hand.

"Yeah, just... thinking." I slowly walk over to the kitchen sink and dump the tea down the drain.

"Do you not like mint anymore?" Josh asks carefully.

I shake my head. "It tastes like blood."

Josh stands up from the bar stool and walks over to the pantry. He takes the mint tea box from the shelf and drops it into the trash. He doesn't say anything more but grabs for the apple cider instead.

After adding an extra dash of cinnamon, he passes me the new mug. "Thanks," I sip it, enjoying the taste of the cinnamon and nutmeg.

Josh faces the sink, his fingers curled tight around the counter edge. His shoulders are rigid. The silence between us isn't tense. It's thick.

I cross the kitchen slowly. I reach for his hand and wrap mine around it. His knuckles are pale.

He turns slowly. His eyes flick to mine and then away. He's trying to soften his face, but the strain shows.

So I rise onto my toes. It pulls at my side, but with the stitches gone now, all that's left is a scab. I'm grateful for my lip being healed and no longer worried I'll pop a stitch from moving my mouth. I press my lips to his. He doesn't pull away.

I pull back just far enough to whisper, "I want this."

His hands come up slowly, cupping my cheeks like he's afraid the bruises are still blooming. When he kisses me back, it's gentler than the ache in my ribs. Softer than the fear in my gut. It's not rescue, or redemption. It's choosing something warm, even while the broken parts still echo.

And I choose it.

***

August 23rd,

     I kissed Josh. He smelled like cypress and leather. I didn't freeze. My chest didn't tighten. I felt like myself for a second. It was nice. I saw his smile. It was real. I could tell he was worried, but he let me. Maybe we can get past this.

I close my journal and hand it to Josh. He places it inside my nightstand so I don't have to twist. He never opens it or even asks to.

I curl as best I can into his side, avoiding too much so my ribs don't protest. Most of my injuries are healing. My ribs aren't like they were before. Deep breaths still hurt, but the ache isn't consistent. The bruising on my face is gone aside from a slight yellow hue around my forehead and cheek.

I've avoided mirrors as best I could, but I can't avoid them forever. I've pushed myself to look at them in passing throughout each day. That way I know I'm getting better on the outside, even if the inside still feels broken.

Chapter 47
Abbi

I've been dreading this day for weeks. August 29th. James' birthday. I told Josh I didn't want to go. I came up with the excuse I wasn't ready to be away from home just yet. Cienna took that and turned it into having the party *here*.

I don't know how I'm going to get through it. I've been able to successfully avoid him since the Welcome Home barbecue.

I can hear the others downstairs shouting and laughing while they set up the decorations. Josh is still upstairs with me. I'm curled up against the headboard, my knees as close to my chest as my ribs will allow. Josh is sitting next to me, scrolling through his phone.

There's a knock on my door, and it startles me from my thoughts.

The blood leaves my face. "Hey," James peeks into the room. His eyes scan the room, a smile playing at the edge of his lips. "They won't let me downstairs. The decorations aren't done, and they won't let me see until they are." He shrugs opening the door fully. "I figure I'd come up and hang with Abbi."

I bite my tongue hard. The taste of blood trickles down my throat, and I have to fight a gag.

"Maybe I should go help hurry things along." Josh tucks his phone in his back pocket and shoots me a worried look. "You okay up here?"

No. I am not okay up here. Don't leave me. Please!

I force a small smile, in response.

"Besides," James flashes a wide smile at Josh and steps into the room. "I'm still waiting on that story."

"What story?" Josh asks.

"Your engagement."

Josh blushes and turns to me with a soft laugh.

"Well now I *really* need to hear it." James struts over to my desk chair and pulls it over to the bed. He plops himself down and doesn't take his gaze off me. "She always did leave the best parts out."

"She's private," Josh is still grinning.

I watch as Josh leaves the room, closing the door softly behind him.

Please leave it open.

"Not to me," James whispers.

I haven't moved since he stepped through the door. My tongue feels heavy in my mouth. Every nerve is screaming at me, my ribs reminding me of what happened last time he was in here with me.

"Please," I croak.

"Is that any way to talk to me on my birthday?" James stands up from the chair and moves to beside me on the bed where Josh had been moments ago.

I shake my head, and stare at my knees.

He leans close, and whispers in my ear, "You smell intoxicating."

I dig my fingernails into my sleeve and curl myself as tightly as I can, ignoring the protest of my aching ribs.

"You're smaller than I remember." He brushes my hair back from my face. "Looks good on you."

Josh will be back any moment. Don't worry. Nothing is going to happen to you. He's just trying to scare you.

"You've always been so good at staying quiet." He stands up and walks around to my side of the bed. The side furthest from the door. He pulls me by my ankles and lifts me from the bed, forcing me to stand.

He kisses me, his hands preventing me from pulling away. I wouldn't even if I could. I'm too scared.

When he pulls away, he's smiling that crooked smile. His finger trails from my lips down my chest, to the drawstring of my sweat pants. "Maybe this time you'll stay awake."

He flips me around and pushes my face into the bed. I feel him yank down my pants and underwear.

Any minute someone will come in.

Pain shoots through me when he enters. I gasp, but I keep my eyes closed. My breath is sharp.

Please someone. Anyone.

With each thrust and grunt, I realize no one is coming. I can hear them all downstairs laughing and joking. But up here, the room is heavy and cold.

After one final thrust, he leans over and kisses my neck.

"That's the perfect birthday present. Thank you."

I hear his zipper as he zips his pants up. Then he pulls up my underwear and pants.

Shaking, I curl myself back up against my headboard.

James walks over to my desk and starts flipping through the papers. "You kept my letters." He holds up the pile of papers I never put away from when I emptied my locker at school. "I knew you loved me."

I don't speak.

"Maybe you should freshen up." He gestures to my body. "Wouldn't want anyone to know you're a slut."

Dread fills me.

He steps closer. Not fast, but enough. The letters drop back to the desk. "Unless you want me to rinse you off myself."

I uncurl. I slide my feet off the bed. The floor is cold. My limbs don't feel like mine. I keep my head low, shoulders pulled in. Each step towards the bathroom feels like permission I don't want to ask for.

The door is open. I step through it, gripping the knob.

He watches but doesn't stop me. Inch by inch I close the door until it clicks closed. I lock it quickly.

The bathroom feels too bright. My sweatpants hang loose. The fabric is no longer soft. My long-sleeved grey shirt clings to my arms where sweat dried in patches. I wore it to feel safe and invisible. Now it feels like camouflage he saw right through.

My hair is a tangled mess. It's matted and twisted at the crown where his hand shoved my head down. Strands coiled in knots I didn't feel forming.

I reach up and touch the tangle. My fingers catch. There's no pain. Just horror of knowing why.

My face is pale. My eyes are too wide, like I forgot how to blink. I have no new cuts or bruises.

I pull the shirt off carefully, even though I don't feel the pain in my ribs right now. Then I remove my sweatpants.

The water is hot enough to sting. I don't flinch. I let it scald.

My skin still doesn't feel like mine yet.

I reach for the scrubbing brush hanging from the caddy. It has a cheap plastic handle, and stiff bristles. I've used it on my heels before, maybe once on my elbows, but never like this.

I press it to my collarbone and sweep it downwards, hard.

Chest, arms, stomach, then back to my neck. The spot where his mouth landed - where he whispered. Where I stopped breathing and prayed someone would come rescue me.

The brush scratches. I know my skin is red, but still I scrub.

I drop the brush. It clatters, plastic on tile, but I barely hear it.

I reach for the washcloth next. I press it beneath the stream and let the heat soak in.

Then I crouch. No angles or mirrors. I move the cloth over my skin in rough, deliberate strokes.

I don't linger. I scrub until the water feels cleaner. Until my body doesn't flinch when I press the cloth there.

Once I don't feel like I'm borrowing someone else's skin, I rinse the washcloth and hang it up like it's just laundry. Like it's any regular Saturday.

I flip my head forward under the spray, bracing one hand against the wall.

The shampoo lathers fast. My fingers slip over my scalp, knuckling through knots I hadn't felt until now.

306

I scrub harder. It's not the careful circles I learned from Mom, or the gentle massage the bottle suggests. I claw the suds. The sting reminding me I'm here.

The water slicks through strands like it's trying to erase what happened. I let it try.

I twist my hair into a rope and rinse again. My arms ache from scrubbing. Still, I don't step back. The bottle slips slightly in my grip.

Then I wash it again, making sure I don't miss anything.

When I feel somewhat livable, I step out of the shower, my skin and scalp stinging.

I wrap my towel high and tuck the edge against my chest. The tile feels colder now. Sharper. My legs ache from crouching. I glance towards the door. It's still locked. Thankfully.

There's a knock, and my heart jumps into my throat.

"It's me." Josh calls out. "I brought you some clothes."

I hesitate.

I don't want to see James. Is he even still there? What do I do?

"James is downstairs now. The decorations are done. It's just us."

I tighten the towel around me and twist the lock. Josh is holding out the clothes for me, and once I take them he steps back. I glance past him and see that we are in fact alone.

Josh doesn't wait for me to respond once I take the clothes. He leaves the room, closing the door behind him.

I rush across the room and lock the door, the clothes still in my arms. I take a few deep breaths and dress myself quickly.

The shirt is a soft dark-green long sleeve. It's Josh's shirt, but I'm grateful it is. It smells faintly of detergent and Josh's house. The black leggings slide on easier than I expected, muting the stinging of the inside of my thighs.

While sliding on my fuzzy blue socks, I flinch. There's a tenderness there that wasn't there before. When I glance down, there's a bruise blooming. A sickly purple and yellow on my left ankle. I lift my right foot to examine that ankle and see a matching bruise on that side.

The memory comes sharp. His hands on my ankles. How he yanked and dragged me from the bed. I don't touch them. Instead, I finish pulling them up, pretending the bruises aren't there.

I take a lighter, grab the pile of letters, and rush back to the bathroom, locking the door behind me. I open my window and kneel beside the tub. One at a time, I set the corners of the pages ablaze. I watch as each note, each word, blackens and disappears, like it was never there.

***

It's 6:03 p.m. when I glance at the clock, half-expecting that knowing the time will anchor me. It doesn't.

Outside, the light is soft and stretched. If it weren't for my reason being here, I'd say it was *almost* pretty. The blinds catch it in beams across the carpet.

I shift on the couch, not sure how I can stay present. There's no scent in the room, no tea, or candles. Just the whir of the A/C and the quiet throb of my bruises under my socks.

Marla doesn't press me to speak, but I know she deserves more than my silence after setting up this emergency session.

"I saw him today."

"You're safe here."

308

"They were decorating downstairs for his birthday." I swallow but continue. "I didn't help."

"So you stayed in your room?"

"They wanted the decorations to be a surprise. He said he'd hang out until they finished."

"Did you want him there?" Marla hasn't written anything down since I got here.

I shake my head. "I thought he'd leave. He said I looked better... *smaller*. He said I smelt intoxicating." I dig my fingernails into my sleeve.

Marla doesn't interrupt.

"I couldn't move. I wanted to, but my body... it... it just went quiet. Like everything turned off. I thought maybe someone would come up and stop it. That if I didn't move, maybe nothing would happen, and he wouldn't do anything worse."

"Freezing is protection. Your body was trying to keep you safe. That response *isn't* weakness."

"He held me against the bed. I wanted to scream. I kept hoping someone would come in."

"What did you notice first when it was over?"

"The laughing downstairs. They had no idea what was happening. I *let* it happen."

"Do you feel angry at Josh and the others for not coming up? For not seeing?"

I shake my head.

Marla folds her hands, voice low. "You've been carrying this like silence was a decision. Like you had control over what your body did, or what it didn't."

My breath hitches. I tug a little more at my sleeves.

"You froze," Marla continues. "Your body made the safest choice it could. That is *not* consent. That is *survival*."

Josh is driving slow, like he knows my body hasn't caught up with the rest of the day. The bench seat's warm against my side. My hand's in his, and that's enough for now.

I stare out the window at nothing. My stomach keeps folding in on itself. The sheets are still there. I left them.

I can't say it – not to him, not out loud.

"Hey," I keep my voice light. "Do you want to swing by a store that has bedding?"

Josh glances over. "Sure."

"I just... I think I want sheets that feel like both of us. After all, it *is our* bed."

It comes out smooth, soft, and believable.

But what I mean is, *I want sheets that haven't been desecrated. I want sheets that don't know what happened.*

Josh squeezes my hand, "I like the sound of that."

I nod like that was the point. Like this trip is about thread count and shared taste. But I'm already picturing the old sheets shoved into a garbage bag. Maybe I'll toss them myself. Maybe I won't.

But they aren't staying.

***

The room is quiet aside from Josh's breathing. I watch him for a minute, just long enough to memorize the way his fingers curl near his shoulder, one foot sticking out from the comforter.

I slip out of bed.

The hallway creaks under my feet. I move slow. I don't want to wake him or Dad. Not when I can't answer what I'm doing.

The old sheets are balled in a plastic bag, tangled with my clothes and the washcloth from earlier today. I double knotted the bag, a permanence I need.

Outside, the air bites. The dumpster across from us at the park is half open. I lift the lid, and drop the bag in, listening for the thud.

There's no ceremony. There's no whispered goodbye.

I stand for a second, hands wrapped in my sleeves, heartbeat pounding like I broke the law. Then I walk back inside. Josh is still asleep. I crawl into bed and curl up into his side. The gold and blue feel loud around my skin. That's good. It's what I picked.

They scream against the lilac of the walls. Not out of anger. Out of need. The lilac was Mom's choice. It stayed through fingerpaint years, fever nights, and birthday sleepovers.

Now, it's a reminder that pain has coated every inch of this room in some way. I just hope it doesn't bury me alive.

Chapter 48
Abbi

September 27th

    Breathing's not the war it used to be.
That's new. I noticed it this morning. There
wasn't any tightness in my chest. Just ordinary
air. It scared me more than the pain. I'd gotten
used to the sharpness. The bracing myself. Now
that it's not there, I don't know what to do with
the space it left. But I'm here. I didn't think I'd
be here.

Being around him is still hard. Some days I can do
it. It's easier outside when there's noise or people.
It's worse when it's quiet. When there's nowhere
to move if I freeze. I think he knows I stay

away. I think he likes pretending nothing's changed.

We lock our door at night now. Me and Josh. Or when I'm alone. No one comes in unless it's Cienna or Kasey. I said it's a "no guys allowed" thing. Everyone accepted that. It's not a lie... exactly. It just makes things feel a little safer.

***

I'm curled into the corner of the couch. I'm not hiding. It's just comfortable. Marla's chair is angled slightly towards me. She asks how I'm feeling today. I tell her, "Better. Mostly."

She smiles, softly. "Mostly is progress."

I nod. I look at the bookshelf behind her, then back. My thoughts come quieter than usual, but I let them surface.

"I didn't panic," I say.

She doesn't interrupt. She knows I'll fill in the space myself.

"Last night, Josh and I...we got close. Not all the way, but almost. I let him. I didn't freeze."

Marla tilts her head, the way she does when she's listening past the words. "How did that feel?"

I have to pause for that. Not because I don't know. It's because saying it makes it more real.

"Gentle," I tell her. "It felt like I had space inside my own skin."

Her expression shifts to something tender but proud. "You felt safe."

I nod. "I wasn't afraid. Not of him. Not of myself. Not of what it meant."

313

She leans forwards just a little. "That's *huge*, Abbi. That's trust. In your body, in him, in your choice.

I swallow. It doesn't catch in my throat like it used to.

"I didn't think I'd ever feel that again," I admit. "I didn't think I could be close to someone without unraveling."

She gives me a moment. I let it be quiet.

"I think I wanted it," I say finally. "And I *got* to want it. That felt... good."

Marla smiles. "That sounds like freedom."

***

October 29th,

    I don't feel like I'm drowning anymore. Maybe that's all I can ask for.

    I'm not dressing up for Halloween this year. I'd rather stay inside.

    I've been feeling really sick lately. Especially in the evenings. The smell of oranges and pumpkins makes me hurl. The doctor told me it could be a side effect of the trauma I've dealt with. Even my depression meds. I'm not sure.

***

The air is crisp, and the trees dance in the breeze. I'm enjoying the feel of the wind on my face, Josh's hand in mine. We've adorned Mom's headstone in Halloween decorations. Her favorite movie was *Scream*, so we have a *Ghostface* mask propped up against the marble.

"It's getting easier, Mom." I swallow and stroke her photo. "Josh and I have finally set a date. June 1st. We wish you could be there with us."

We sit quietly, listening to the rustle of the leaves for just a few minutes more.

Then we stand, brush off our clothes, and stroll back to the truck. "Are you in the mood for some pumpkin pie?" He opens my door and helps me step up into the cab.

I wrinkle my nose. The thought of food has me on the verge of vomiting.

Josh laughs. "I'll take that as a no."

***

November 3rd,

       Marla thinks I should take a pregnancy test. I laughed. Not really. Just that weird thing people do when they don't want to cry. I told her no. Then I said maybe. I keep thinking about what it could be.

I gagged while brushing my teeth yesterday. The taste is off. The smell of oranges still makes me sick. I keep smelling the candle in my room even when it isn't lit. Everyone says trauma messes with your cycle. So I believed that. I wanted to. Now I don't know what to believe.

315

Chapter 49
Abbi

Two pink lines.

My breath catches in my throat, bile and tears trying to claw their way out.

I don't cry, I don't scream – I just sit.

The test is perched on the edge of the tub like it's trying not to fall. Like it's giving me time.

I curl up on the floor, cold tile pressing into my spine, knees drawn so tight I can feel my pulse behind them. The throb in my shoulder is back. Doctors told me that could happen. The pain isn't strong enough to distract from this, though. I wish it was.

Josh is waiting. He knows. Not everything though. Just enough. I told him there's a chance. That things don't feel right. That I'm scared.

If I hide in here too long, he'll worry. I wrap the test in toilet paper and stuff it down in the trash, under receipts, tissues, and wrappers.

When I hoist myself up, I look in the mirror. The mirror doesn't offer any clarity. It just stares back. I can't see fear in my face, but I can feel it threading through my ribs.

It has to be his. I know that. And if James ever finds out, he'll come back. Not for me. For control.

I grip the sink tighter. My fingers ache.

Josh wouldn't understand. He'd say all the right things, do everything soft and careful. But he'd look at me differently. He'd look at *it* differently.

I open the door before I talk myself out of it.

Josh is on the edge of the bed, his elbows on his knees. When he sees me, he jumps up. He doesn't step closer, but his eyes are full of the questions he isn't asking.

"Negative."

His shoulders drop just a little. He nods but he doesn't smile.

"Okay," he says quietly. Just that.

I climb into bed and curl towards the wall. His warmth shifts beside me, slow and steady. He places his hand lightly on my side like a question. I grab his hand and pull it tighter around me.

I don't flinch, not even a little, and that feels almost like grace.

His breath evens out eventually, soft and warm against the back of my neck. I keep my eyes open. The dark doesn't feel threatening tonight—just thick.

My phone is under the pillow. I slide it out slowly, careful not to shift too much. He doesn't stir.

I open the thread with Kasey.
My fingers hover.
Then I type:

**I need help. Can you come by tomorrow?
Please don't ask yet.**

I stare at it longer than I should.
Then I hit send.

***

I shut the door too hard. It sounds final.

The seatbelt slides across my right shoulder, smooth and indifferent. But when I sit back and shift, the pain shoots through the left. It's a deep, hot, wrong. I press my palm into it, hard, trying to ground myself. It doesn't help.

Kasey doesn't ask where we're going. I tell her anyway. "The Grove abortion clinic on Main."

She nods once and backs out of the driveway.

I stare at the dashboard, counting the bumps in the road like they're personal. Each one sparks the pain again. My left side lights up like a warning.

"I didn't sleep," I say quietly at first. "Kept thinking about the trash. The lines. Josh believed me, I think."

The words tumble fast. I don't know what I'm trying to say. I just need noise.

"My stomach's wrong. It isn't cramps. I'm not sick. Just...*off*. Like my body wants me to admit it but I don't want to hear it."

I pick at the hem of my t-shirt.

318

"I need it not to be real. I need Josh to stay close. Doing this is the only thing I can do because–"

My breath stumbles.

"It's *his*."

The car keeps moving and I keep talking.

"I can't have this baby. If I do, I'll be stuck with James forever. I can't keep doing this."

The brakes slam.

I jolt forward, the belt catching across my right side, causing the left shoulder to hit back harder, like punishment from the inside out.

Kasey's hands stay frozen on the wheel. She doesn't look at me. But I feel it. Every part of her attention is locked in place. "Did you say *James*?"

"What?" I can feel the color drain from my face. The cold creeps in, deep and permanent, like a season that won't leave.

"Abbi," she turns slowly to me. "Did James rape you?"

I feel it hit my stomach. Before I can stop it, I break. I don't cry pretty. I don't cry loud. The breath leaves my body in fragments. My chest caves. My jaw locks and I bury my face in my hands and try not to fall apart completely, but it's too late. The sob rises through me, quiet and deep.

Chapter 50

Josh

The sun's warm on the concrete, especially rare for the first week of November. Rees is unfolding chairs beneath a canopy next to the driveway, arguing with Don about three-point range. Jared's bouncing the ball off the garage wall, rhythmically while laughing with Cienna. Dad has the cooler open and is talking to John who is doing more listening than talking. Quint's calling dibs on corner shots while fiddling with the Bluetooth speaker.

It looks normal.

But my phone's still hot in my hand.

Come to the abortion clinic on Main Street. Now. The test was positive. It was James. He attacked her.

Kasey's message doesn't feel like a text. It feels like a trigger.

I haven't told anyone yet. I haven't moved.

The ball bounces once. Twice.

Then a car pulls up, tires biting the edge of the curb like it's a joke.

James.

He jumps out like he owns the day - hoodie loose, sunglasses half-on – *Arrogant*.

"Ready to lose?" He shouts.

A few guys laugh. Jared flicks the ball toward him casually.

James catches it with one hand, easy, like it was always his. He dribbles twice, spins it off his hip, then smirks like the hoop belongs to him.

I haven't said a word.

John stands slowly. His eyes lock onto mine. He knows something's wrong. Dad's looking now too, reading my silence like a warning.

James glances my way but doesn't clock the shift. He doesn't know.

Or maybe he does.

Something in me snaps. I step forward.

It's not fast. Just deliberate. Just enough that chairs scrape. Dad stands up, and John turns fully towards me, already bracing.

James spins the ball in his palm, smirking. "You want first drive or–"

"You touched her?" My words cut through everything. They are clear, cold, and impossible to dodge.

James blinks. The spin slows. "What?"

"You put your hands on her. You didn't ask. You didn't care. Is that how it went?"

His grin flickers. Rees squints. Don freezes. Jared has Cienna half way behind him, silently bracing.

Quint mutters, "What the hell..." but nobody moves.

James steps back half a foot, eyes darting. "I don't know what Abbi told you, but–"

"You don't speak her name." I'm right in front of him now. Close enough to see every twitch.

John's already halfway towards us, quiet but carved like iron. Dad stands, silent. Nobody stops me.

James twirls the ball once, smirking again.

"Josh," he says, like we're still friends. "You're acting wild, man. I don't know what she told you, but–"

"She doesn't lie," I say. In my mind though, every flinch, every sob, every moment I could see fear and anger, it was always around James. But like an idiot, I brushed it off.

"She's confused. You know that. She was upset. She said things she didn't mean."

He's trying hard to keep the smile - to stay chill - to let the guys hear laughter and not truth.

"She was upset," he repeats. "I was just trying to help. She let me in. It wasn't like what you're saying."

"You *raped* her."

Everything stops.

James doesn't blink. But his face tightens around the edges. Like the word hit deeper than he planned for.

Rees goes still. Don's mouth opens but no sound comes. Jared is still covering Cienna.

John's eyes are locked on James now. Dad stands straighter, watching my hands.

When James speaks, it's a forced laugh. "That's a heavy word, Bro."

"Good," I say. "It should be."

He swallows. His smirk is now gone, but there's no fear – no worry. "That's not how it was," he defends. "She was *mine*. We had a thing. You know that. She wouldn't have pulled back if you had stayed out of it."

He looks around, waiting for someone to nod.

No one does.

James lifts his chin. "I didn't force her."

The silence that follows is different now. There's no confusion or hesitation. It's just heavy. Everyone remembers.

Quint lowers his eyes. Rees goes pale. Don mutters, "We had to fix the damn wall," like he only understands what that meant.

Dad stops breathing for a second. "She was unconscious, " he says, voice thin. "When you left her there."

James blinks fast. That catches him. For a flicker.

"She passed out," he says. "She was just... she does that."

"She was bleeding," I snap. "I found her *alone*. Unconscious. The paramedics had to lift her body from the bed because she couldn't move."

James opens his mouth. Then he closes it.

John steps in now, steady and silent. "She's my daughter," he says. "I sat beside her bed while she couldn't look anyone in the eye. And you thought walking in here with a grin would rewrite that? I let you into my home. I let you near her."

James backs up slightly.

Before I can charge forward, Cienna's voice cuts through the silence.

"You still think she's yours?" Cienna's voice doesn't rise, but it hits like a bullet. "Then tell me what part of her you get to keep." She doesn't wait for him to speak. "The blood on the carpet? The sheets soaked straight through? How about the door ripped off the hinge like she tried to run and couldn't?"

Her voice wavers but doesn't break. "You weren't there. *I* was. I had to clean it. Had to touch what *you* left behind." She moves past Jared now.

"So when you say she's yours," she says stepping closer to James, "you better tell me what that means. Because if it means you get to erase her, use her, ruin her... then no. No, James. She's *not* yours. She's not anyone's."

She turns away now, tears breaking free, but somehow she keeps her voice steady. "And if you think this ends with Josh hitting you– "

She pauses, letting the driveway hold still.

" –then you have another thing coming."

I'm done waiting.

James flinches too late. I'm already chest forward, fists curled, heart pounding in my throat. I don't want words anymore. I want him to feel something that doesn't belong to her.

My phone slips from my hand and skids across the concrete.

James backs up, arm half-raised.

But Don grabs my elbow. Dad's hand clamps around my chest. They pull me back.

"Josh!" Dad snaps. His voice cuts through the heat in my ears. "Stop!"

I don't stop. I strain forward. I want blood.

Then Dad stoops and picks up the phone. He reads the screen and his breath catches – his grip tightening.

"Don't waste yourself on him," his voice is low and cold like stone. "Go to her, son."

Everything in me crashes sideways. The rage doesn't vanish, but instead it redirects.

I turn and Dad lets me go.

Suddenly, I'm running. To my truck. To her.

Every road is familiar, but today they feel sharper – colder – like the town learned how to echo.

The turn onto Main Street hits too hard. I fishtail slightly, correct myself, and keep going. The clinic's at the end, past the bank and the old thrift shop. I know exactly where it is. I hate that I do.

She's pregnant. She's at *that* clinic. Because of *him*.

I grip the steering wheel so tight my palms ache. My breath's shallow, chest locked. I run a red light, but I don't care. I swerve around a pickup truck creeping past an empty church lot. The driver honks once, but I barely hear it.

Grove Clinic comes into view. It's a small building with blue trim, frosted windows, and a clean gravel lot that looks too ordinary for the decisions made inside.

I barely get the car stopped before I'm out. It's crooked in the lot, half over the painted line, door left open, engine humming like it might stall from guilt. I can't care about it.

She's outside. Not inside with a clipboard. Not curled up in some sterile chair under flickering lights. She's on the side of the building, walking tight circles like she's trying to stay whole.

She's wearing a T-shirt. Her short sleeves are too thin for November, even if it's unseasonably warm. Her arms are clamped around herself like it's the only way to stay upright.

Her steps are rigid, looping back and forth over the gravel. I watch the way her shoulder moves. Her left one is slower, uneven. It's still not right. The shirt rides up slightly when she turns, and I see the edge of the scar. She probably doesn't even know.

She's not crying. Her face isn't blank. It's hollow, like something left and didn't come back.

Her eyes flick past everything without landing on it. She's lost.

Then I see Kasey. She's standing off to the side, near her car, watching. She catches my stare and gives me one small nod.

I walk faster. Then I run. My boots crack against gravel and she hears me. Abbi turns, eyes wide, her shoulders locking. For a second she almost steps back. I know it isn't because of me, but because she's afraid.

Afraid I'll look at her and leave. Afraid I'll know and retreat. *How did I not see?*

I stop just short, hands open, breath visible between us.

"I got Kasey's message," I say. "I came because I needed to be here."

Her lips part, but no words come out. Her arms tighten again.

"I don't care if this baby isn't mine. I will love it in every way that matters. I will protect it, and you, without asking for a reason."

Her eyes fly past me. Her skin loses its color. She's shaking now. Not visibly. Just enough for me to feel it.

Then I hear a voice behind me. It's smooth, calculated, smiling.

"You're pregnant?"

I turn.

James is standing five feet away, hands in his pockets, a smirk curling on his lips.

I shift immediately, angling my body between them, my shoulders tight, shielding her.

Abbi doesn't move, but her breathing changes. It's fast, tight, and shallow. Not because she's afraid I won't protect her. It's because she's afraid it won't matter.

James steps forward, still smiling, voice just loud enough to hit her like a bruise. "Guess I got deeper than I thought."

It's quiet around us. The kind that happens right before something breaks. Like the eye before the storm.

Abbi doesn't speak. Her jaw tightens, her body folding tighter.

"You don't get to speak to her that way."

James doesn't even look at her. Just grins, smooth as ever.

"She was quiet at my birthday too," he says, like its proof of something. Like pain was the gift she gave him. "Didn't even touch the cake."

Abbi flinches – not visibly, not enough to call out. But I see it in her fingers, curling into her jeans like she's gripping memory.

Suddenly, the puzzle shifts. It all makes sense - the shower, the bedding, the emergency therapy session – it was all him.

James is still grinning.

He thinks he's still the one writing the story.

His lips curl, but there's no humor in it. There's just certainty. "Doesn't matter what you think. I've already been inside every version of her she's been trying to leave behind."

That's when everything inside me shifts. The blood drains cold, and my breath shortens to a pinpoint. The words hit like a cold hand on the back of my neck. It's revolting and precise.

Not shouted. Not screamed. Just planted. And Abbi's silence behind me tells me everything. She heard it. She felt it.

I don't think or plan, I just move.

Gravel cracks beneath my boots, sharp and deliberate. James doesn't even flinch at first. Like he's too confident in his performance, too sure no one will touch him. I slam into him mid-sentence, shoulder first, sending him stumbling back towards my truck, the impact ringing through metal.

He scrambles for balance, but I'm already there. My fist catches his ribs. He doubles over gasping. He grabs at my shirt like it will give him leverage, but it doesn't.

The others have arrived now, leaping from their trucks and cars. Kasey's shouting. Rees is moving. Dad is trying to circle wide. Don is yelling something, but I don't hear it. Not through the blood rushing past my ears.

James tries to speak again, but I cut him off with a shove that sends him back against the truck.

"You don't get to speak to her like that," I spit. "You don't get to narrate her pain like it belongs to you." Jared and Rees are on either side of me, preventing me from getting any closer to him.

James is still laughing. It isn't loud or cruel. Just that smug, quiet kind.

I strain against Rees' grip, my fists clenched. Jared's holding harder now, telling me to breathe, to stop, but it's not about me anymore. It's about her. It's about Abbi standing behind me, absorbing every word, every implication, every theft of her name. Because I'm watching him watch her. Like he still owns something. Like she'll shatter if he waits long enough.

Then I hear her.

"Josh."

Her voice is soft – nearly weightless – the kind of sound you only catch if you're listening from the center of your chest. I twist in Rees' grip and turn towards her. She's swaying, her arms are limp now. She's looking down. I follow her gaze to the gravel at her feet.

Blood.

It's trailing down her leg in a dark jagged line, pooling at her feet, catching in her shoes.

The world stops around me. All sound fades.

My heart misfires. Her knees buckle just as I reach her, arms out and catching–barely–before her head hits the pavement. I'm on the ground with her, one hand under her shoulder, one cradling her skull.

The blood is pooling fast. I don't know what it means. I don't know how much is too much. I don't know if it's her or the baby, or both. I just know she's not responding. Her body crumpled, and now she's limp in my arms, breathing shallow, skin losing color by the second.

I'm crouching on the pavement, gravel digging into my knees, her weight pressed against me like she's already half gone. I grab her hand. It's cold.

"Abbi." My voice cracks. "Look at me. Come on."

Nothing.

I press my palm to her cheek, gently patting, hoping something in her eyes flickers. Hoping she's still behind them.

"You're okay," I whisper, then louder. "You're okay, please– just wake up."

John kneels beside us. His voice is in the background, tight with urgency. He's asking someone for towels, calling for pressure, stabilizing. I don't hear the words – not really.

She's still not moving.

I shift, holding her closer, her head tucked against my shoulder.

"I've got you," I say. "You hear me? I'm right here."

Cienna's next to us now. Her hand brushes Abbi's hair back, her voice shaking. Jared's pacing, swearing in the phone. Rees runs up with something clutched in his hands–blankets, maybe–but my focus narrows down to just one thing.

Her breath.

It's still faint. It's still there, but it's slipping.

I kiss her temple.

"Don't leave me. Not like this. Not here."

Behind me, I hear movement. Kasey's yelling towards the clinic and doors fly open. People rush out in scrubs and sneakers, one calling for pressure, another yelling for a stretcher.

She doesn't respond to her name. She doesn't flinch when I say it louder.

"Abbi, please. You gotta stay. You hear me? You have to stay."

Her eyelids flutter once, but it's weak. Barely there then gone.

One of the nurses kneels beside me, checks her pulse, calls something toward the clinic doors. I don't let go of her. Not for a second.

Even as they position the stretcher, even as John helps steady her legs, her hand stays in mine.

"She's unconscious," someone says. "Possible hemorrhage."

They've got her loaded.

The nurses move fast, one stabilizing her head, the other adjusting the blanket over her legs. Her skin's ashen, like the color left without warning. Her lips are parted but still. I'm walking beside the stretcher, hand wrapped around hers, refusing to let go.

Then I hear it. Sirens.

Not distant. Not approaching. *Here.*

The ambulance pulls up hard, tires skidding slightly on the gravel. Doors fly open. EMTs jump out, already gloved, already scanning. One of them calls her name, checks her vitals, asks for a rundown. The clinic nurse rattles off stats to the EMTs–pulse, blood loss, time unconscious.

I don't speak. I just hold her hand tighter.

Then–another set of lights.

Police.

Two cruisers. One marked, one unmarked. Officers step out, scanning the scene. One heads towards James, who's still standing off to the side, arms crossed, face unreadable. Another approaches Dad and Don, asking what happened.

I don't care what they say.

I care about her.

The EMTs lift the stretcher into the rig. I climb in without asking. One of them starts to protest, but the other sees my grip on her hand and nods.

"She's not alone," I say. "She's not going without me."

John's outside, talking to paramedics, giving them what he knows. Kasey's near the clinic doors, arms folded, eyes wet. Rees is pacing. Jared's talking to the cops now, voice sharp.

And James?

He's watching the ambulance – silently. He's not grinning anymore.

He knows he's not the story.

She is – and I'm not letting go.

The inside of the ambulance feels too small. It's not tight – just compressed. Like the walls are moving in while times stretches out.

They lay her flat on the stretcher, legs slightly elevated. One EMT hooks up a blood pressure cuff. The other's already working a saline IV into her arm. The needle goes in clean, but her skin's so pale it looks translucent under the lights.

"BP's tanking," one of them says. "Still no response."

I don't know what the numbers mean. I just see the urgency in their faces and hear the clipped edge in their voices.

I'm still holding her hand.

She's unconscious, her head turned slightly towards me, mouth slack, lips colorless. The oxygen mask covers most of her face now. The monitor starts to beep softly behind us, each sound like a verdict.

"Eighteen-year-old female estimated ten weeks pregnant. Found unconscious outside clinic. BP 72/40, HR 132, shallow respirations. Active vaginal bleeding, suspected intra-abdominal hemorrhage – possible ruptured ectopic. Two large-bore IVs running normal saline wide open. Oxygen via non-rebreather. No known allergies. ETA three minutes."

I watch the bag swing with every pothole and hear the flush of saline rushing down the line. It looks like help. It doesn't feel like enough.

"Wh-what does that mean? Ruptured ectopic?"

He doesn't look away from her. Just keeps checking the IV line, adjusting the oxygen.

"It means the pregnancy implanted outside the uterus," he says, like he's reading a pamphlet. "Probably in the fallopian tube. It tore."

"Tore?" I echo.

"Yeah. It ruptured. That's why she's bleeding. Internally."

I feel my stomach drop. "Can you fix it?"

"We're doing everything we can," he says. "But she needs surgery, fast."

I brush my knuckles against her jaw, then pat her cheek with the gentlest rhythm I can manage.

"Stay," I whisper. "You're strong. You always have been."

Her fingers don't twitch. Her chest rises, but barely.

The ambulance hits a turn hard. One EMT grips the rail to steady himself while adjusting her blanket. I try not to shake. I try not to cry.

The ambulance jerks to a stop. Doors burst open. They wheel her out, and I follow – blood still slick on my hands, feet stumbling after, the monitors behind us shrieking.

Inside the ER, it's blinding and too loud. They cut her clothes—quick and clinical. Someone shouts for more blood. I try to stay close. I just need to see her, need to be near enough to believe she's still here.

John sees her first. And something in his face breaks so fast it steals the air from my chest.

Then he and Dad shove through the doors, their presence sudden and solid. One of them tries to push me back, but I don't move. All I see is her—pale. Still. Too still.

The monitor flatlines. Her heart stops.

I grip the edge of the wall. I think I scream. Maybe I don't. My voice is gone or buried somewhere beneath everything they're shouting.

John's beside me, silent – rigid.

Dad's hand lands on my shoulder.

But I'm not here.

I'm back on the porch last fall, when she sat knees-up in her hoodie, sleeves swallowing her fingers. She didn't speak. Just looked at me. Like the world was beautiful.

I'm in the truck when she traced the glass without saying a word and held my hand like it was enough to keep her from unraveling.

"Clear," someone calls.

Her body jumps.

Nothing.

They start compressions. A nurse climbs onto a stool, arms locked, hammering rhythm into her chest. Her body rocks. The room folds inward.

"Clear."

Still no pulse.

I see her in the grove. The lights dancing like starlight in the breeze. Her eyes bright and open. Agreeing to marry me, her smile wide.

"Clear."

The monitor twitches. Then silence.

They keep pushing. Chest rising only from the force. Breaths stolen from machines. Meds pouring into the line.

Then –

"Clear."

Her body jumps.

A blip.

Then another.

Then a rhythm.

"She's back," someone says.

I don't move. I don't speak. I just stare at her chest, waiting for it to rise on its own.

It does – barely – but it does.

John's hand grabs the edge of the rail like he's bracing against collapse. Dad exhales behind me, quiet and broken, his hand still on my shoulder.

The room is still spinning, but her chest is rising. The monitor rhythm is fragile, erratic – but it's there.

They're prepping her for surgery. I hear someone call for OB. Another nurse is pushing meds. Someone else is checking the blood units. The urgency hasn't faded, but there's a shift. Almost like they *bought* seconds instead of losing them.

I step closer. No one stops me.

She's pale. Oxygen mask fogging with each breath. Her lashes barely twitch. But she's here.

I lean in and brush her hair back from her forehead. My hands are shaking.

"You don't get to leave me like that," my voice is low, cracked from every emotion trying to claw its way out of me. "Not like that. Not ever."

Epilogue

Abbi

Iris by Tommee Profitt and Ruelle spill softly across the grove. Our song. The one we danced to when the world wasn't so large. It doesn't play loud – it doesn't need to. It's the kind of quiet that remembers everything and forgives.

The grove wears its colors like old truth, beautiful for early June. White, yellow, gold, and green all fill the space as if to say, *'you made it.'*

White chairs line either side of the matching white cloth aisle Kasey laid out this morning. Yarrow is scattered along its edges. Some petals are torn, some are pressed, some still whole, almost like a thread of hope and healing beneath each step.

Dad walks beside me, arms steady beneath mine. He doesn't speak, but I feel everything in the way he exhales slowly, and in the way his fingers tighten gently around mine.

As I walk, the grove watches in a gentle hush. The lace of my gown rippling with each step.

Kasey glances over her shoulder from the altar, her braid woven with yarrow and sunlight. No more dipped edges, just buttery soft strands woven with flowers. She wears a simple slim navy gown with gold tulle. Her smile splits wide and it stays. The light finally reaches her eyes, letting the world know how strong she is.

To our left, Connie leans into Lance, their fingers intertwined. She whispers something we don't hear, but his mouth quirks into a mischievous grin. Right now they look like two people falling in love all over again.

To the right, Ryan rests his arm behind Lily's chair, thumbs brushing lightly against her shoulder. Between them sits Cienna, her arms folded, trying to make herself smaller. She refused the title of Maid of Honor. She doesn't do wedding anymore. But she came. When our eyes meet, hers soften just slightly, just enough.

All three of them have cut off James. Lily was the most devastated when she found out what happened.

Because I refused charges, James fled back to Vienna. They feel guilty for what happened, but I don't hold it over them. It wasn't *their* fault. It was *his*.

After a lot of convincing, we got them to come today. They didn't feel welcome, but I assured them that it wouldn't be complete without them. I needed them here. They're still my family.

Don and Rees sit side by side giving Josh a thumbs up, and me a wink. Moira watches me like I'm something revered. She was always one for the wow factor. Blake smiles like he always does, on the corner of his mouth and in the lines around his eyes.

Alec leans forward, hand on Quint's back. A father watching his sons watch the love of their life walk toward everything they nearly lost.

Jared, the best man, stands next to Josh. His expression is a storm trying to hold itself still. He and Cienna eloped in January after she finally conceded on a simple gold band for her ring. We got the announcement in the mail, and a blubbering Jared on a video chat from the courthouse.

Josh stands beneath the arch, his suit crooked, but eyes that never leave mine. I walk slow.

The trees seem to lean in. The sunlight flickers through like it wants to join the music. Every heartbeat echoes in my chest. There's no fear, just proof. Proof that I'm still here. That I stayed.

Josh wipes at his eyes. The moment I reach him, he exhales like it's the first breath he's taken all day. Dad releases my hand and steps back. His silence becomes air, sacred and warm.

And the music, our music, keeps playing.

We don't speak. Not yet.

We just hold each other's gaze like the world never got so large after all.

www.ingramcontent.com/pod-product-compliance
Lightning Source LLC
Chambersburg PA
CBHW030640260626
47157CB00007B/2421